OLIVIA ELLIOTT

A Dangerous Man to Trust?

Book One in The Pemberton Series

Copyright © 2024 by Olivia Elliott

All rights reserved. No part of this publication may be reproduced, stored or transmitted in any form or by any means, electronic, mechanical, photocopying, recording, scanning, or otherwise without written permission from the publisher. It is illegal to copy this book, post it to a website, or distribute it by any other means without permission.

This novel is entirely a work of fiction. The names, characters and incidents portrayed in it are the work of the author's imagination. Any resemblance to actual persons, living or dead, events or localities is entirely coincidental.

Olivia Elliott asserts the moral right to be identified as the author of this work.

First edition

This book was professionally typeset on Reedsy. Find out more at reedsy.com

Contents

Prologue   vi
1. Pride and a Fall   1
2. When All the World's Asleep   16
3. Theatre of Manners   30
4. King of Hearts   48
5. Fantastic and Unlikely   60
6. Corsets and Compromise   80
7. Intentions   93
8. Before and After   109
9. The Devil Himself   119
10. A Real Choice   132
11. The Ship of Theseus   147
12. London Gossip   162
13. Nip it in the Bud   176
14. Our Own Rules   189
15. The Key to her Heart   201
16. Lady of the House   212
17. Raspberry Jam   226
18. Chemistry   242
19. Cinderella   255
20. The Truth   268
21. Take Flight   282

Epilogue   288
Thank You!   294

Also by Olivia Elliott

Receive a free subscribers-only steamy novella called *The Bull of Bow Street Meets his Match* when you sign up for my mailing list at oliviaelliottromance.com. This is Book 3.5 in *The Pemberton Series*.

Prologue

No one would call Miss Serafina Edgemont pretty. 'Pretty' is a word people toss out without any care where it might fall because it has no weight. Flowers are pretty. A dress might be pretty or a little girl. But Serafina? No. Serafina was not pretty. But she was striking in an odd and inexplicable way. If you saw her in a crowd at a ball, you may find yourself unable to look away. A mass of dark brown hair worn up in twists and braids pinned neatly to her head. A round face and bright brown eyes that always seemed to be searching for something lost. It might have been her posture or maybe her bone structure that gave her the appearance of someone important, even regal. And it was this intangible aspect of her person that made men angry—angry and eager. They hid their anger behind masks of pure etiquette and good manners. Smiles and bows and polite requests to dance. Pretty girls were ten-a-penny, but Miss Serafina Edgemont was something else: Serafina was a challenge and to one lucky man a conquest, for she would by necessity have to defer to her new husband. And whether the gentlemen were consciously aware of it or not, submission was the prize that they sought.

Perhaps there were some men with noble intentions, but how to tell them apart? Serafina had seen what had happened to her mother within the contract of marriage, and she would not allow herself to suffer the same fate. Madeline Edgemont, née Robertson, had once attracted a whole host of suitors. She had been the jewel of the London season once upon a time. No less than seven proposals of marriage within the space of a few months! She was often prone to reminiscing about her life before she had been married, so Serafina had heard it all a thousand times. Madeline had eventually chosen Mr. Walter Edgemont, Serafina's father.

"He had such a charming way about him," she would say leaning in close as if to share a secret. "Eyes like emeralds—so handsome in his black jacket. And so considerate as well. He had the most beautiful (and expensive) bouquets of flowers delivered to my parents' home every three days like clockwork. There was always some small note attached which was intended for me, but my mother would read it out loud and pass it around to her friends when they came to call."

On one occasion, seated in the drawing room with their needlework, Serafina's mother had lifted her head with a faraway look and stated quite out of the blue, "He once wrote me a poem, your father. He was no Byron, that is for certain, but it was exceedingly heartfelt, and I decided to marry him."

Serafina could only nod. Her mother was not well. She suffered from a kind of melancholia that often forced her to retreat to her bed. By the age of sixteen, it had fallen to Serafina to organise the household and to see that their day-to-day lives ran smoothly. Mr. Edgemont, for his part, no longer troubled himself much with his family. He was often away in London where it was rumoured he kept a mistress.

When he was at home at their country house, they ate their meals in silence, and he made a conspicuous effort to avoid eye-contact with his wife.

It was excruciating for Serafina when her father was home. The unspoken resentment and her mother's broken heart made all the more tender by his presence—these things were like a blanket that smothered the spark of each new day. So Serafina threw herself into caring for her mother, cajoling her out for walks, reading to her in the evenings. She ordered her days as if they were tiny soldiers lined up for battle. She discussed cleaning schedules with the housekeeper, gave directions to the gardener, and kept a careful account of the household bills. She made a note of all the servants' birthdays so as to give them the day off along with a small token of appreciation. And when she was alone. Truly alone. In her bedchamber at night. She unpinned her hair and untied her stay. She peeled off her stockings and walked barefoot across the cold floor savouring each chilling step. She undid everything that kept her bound up during the day, including her mind. She cast it open, and throwing herself upon the bed with a book in hand, she would lose herself in some piece of philosophy or argument of science until she fell asleep in the flickering candlelight.

One

Pride and a Fall

John had been travelling for days, and he was tired and impatient to reach his destination. The plan had been to leave the little town early that morning by carriage. But the carriage had broken a wheel on uneven ground, and so the inn-keeper had lent him a horse in order to ride on ahead to Bosworth Manor. It was early, and the air was a damp bluish fog. As he made his way along the road that cut through the woods, his vision was obscured save for the dark silhouettes of trees that loomed into view, their ill-defined edges giving them the appearance of existing in some in-between place, as if they were not even trees at all but merely thoughts taking the form of trees, evaporating into the fog as he passed them by. The soft sound of hooves on the damp earth, a snuffle from the horse, and his own raspy breath—all sounds that were quickly absorbed by the heavy atmosphere.

The black mask he wore over half his face to conceal his

deformity had become increasingly uncomfortable in the damp, close air, and he had thought nothing of removing it. There was, after all, no one around. The better part of his forehead and one side of his face was unnaturally puckered and scarred. It looked as if a bear had shredded half his face with its claws, and the wounds had frozen in time, crimson ripples of flesh. An eyebrow was missing, and one eye looked alarmingly large and wide, a consequence of his partially missing eyelid. Part of his upper lip had been damaged on one side giving it the look of a permanent snarl.

John let out a breath he had been holding for some time. It felt good to feel the outside air on his face. He turned off the main road and down a small path he knew as a shortcut to the house, but no sooner had he done so, then a dark spectre appeared suddenly from the fog alarming his horse who reared up onto its hind legs flinging him to the ground.

"Sir!" came a lady's voice. He could hear her quick approach.

"Stay back!" he growled reaching his palm forward to halt her. He attempted to stand, but he was surprised to find he could bear no weight on his right ankle, and he collapsed once more to the ground.

"Let me help," came the voice, closer now. Too close. He did not look up. He did not want her to see his face, and he certainly did not want to see her face as it took in the horror of his mutilated form.

"I SAID STAY BACK!" he growled once more, arm raised in warning and head bowed.

But she had approached nonetheless.

"A gentleman must not allow pride to get in the way of accepting help when it is needed." She said it as if she might be scolding a child. "Allow me to help you to your horse."

Pride and a Fall

She took his outstretched arm (the one intended to keep her back) and bent down so that he might place it upon her shoulder. As she did so, he looked up, and their eyes met. She saw his face. Uncharacteristically for a lady, she wore no hat or bonnet, and her dark brown hair although carefully twisted and pinned was starting to frizz in the damp. A long lock of hair had broken free of its pin and had tumbled down over one shoulder. John took all this in as he waited with resignation for a scream. But it did not come. The lady did look somewhat surprised, but she caught herself and forced a smile, not once averting her gaze.

Oh God. Pity. John could not tolerate being the object of pity. Fear? Sure. Disgust? Fine. But pity? It was too undignified. He gritted his teeth.

"Come now," she said. "Your horse will not wait all day." Again, he felt he were being spoken to as if he were a child, and his irritation grew.

Reluctantly, he supported himself to standing with the help of her shoulder, and the two of them stumbled their way towards the horse. John's teeth were pressed firmly together. He could not wait to be rid of this lady and her pity. *This lady? It was strange that she was out at all at this hour, but without an escort? Who was she?*

"Where is your lady's maid?" he asked in a tone of accusation, arm still across her shoulder. He winced inwardly. It was a weak attempt to gain the upper hand, but the question had already been asked.

She did not answer, but she turned her pale round face up to his once more. Her pink lips parted, and she laughed. He smiled quizzically—he couldn't help it. The situation was so odd and unlikely. He had not been this close to a woman, let

A Dangerous Man to Trust?

alone unmasked in six years. His irritation melted away under her breath which smelled of raspberry jam and fresh baked bread.

Still fixing her eyes to his, still smiling (a genuine smile this time), she said, "I am no longer in need of a lady's maid, for I am no longer a lady. How is that for an answer? I will bid you good day."

She shrugged her shoulder to encourage him off, and he took hold of the horse's mane with one hand, releasing her with his other. He mounted his horse and called out after her as she continued along the path towards town, "What's your name?" He was for some reason desperate to know, but his voice was gruff, and he barked the question as if it were a command to an inferior. He still needed to put her in her place. He would have none of her pity.

She called out through the fog, her voice fading as she walked away, "It's of no use to you." And she was gone. As if she had been, like the trees, only a thought, just a fleeting impression disappearing back into the ether. John gripped his horse with his thighs and pressed it forward.

He proceeded on his way through the trees, grimly anticipating the tasks that awaited him at his ancestral home. Ledgers and accounts to be settled, tenants to be seen, and a household full of servants to manage. Not to mention the little girl. His half-sister whom he had never met. While his mind muttered to itself of this and that, he found himself returning to that place where he had left the road, to the woman who had turned her face up to his, who didn't even flinch, who had laughed at her own misfortune and helped him on his way as if he had been a small child fallen in the path.

Pride and a Fall

Serafina had not thought to wear a bonnet when she left the house that morning. It was early, and there was such a fog. There would be no one about. She absolutely hated wearing a bonnet. It was hot on her head, and she could not stand tying it beneath her chin. If she did not tie it, there was always a gust of wind waiting to lift her bonnet away, forcing her to give chase . . . as if she even liked the thing, as if she even wanted to keep it. So she had set out on her walk with a scandalously bare head, and if she was being honest with herself, a bare heart as well, quite open to the elements.

The death of her employer, Mr. Thornton, two weeks prior had been an emotional blow. When her parents had passed on two years earlier, she had been left with nothing. Serafina had watched as her mother slowly faded away, succumbing to the melancholia of a broken heart. Her father had died suddenly some months later. The physician had called it apoplexy, and Serafina suspected this meant he did not actually know the cause of her father's death. She had to pay his bill nonetheless.

In retrospect, the physician was lucky to have been paid at all. Her father had made some extraordinarily poor investment decisions, and his creditors soon descended upon the property like a murder of crows. There was no inheritance to speak of, no siblings, and no relations save one distant dowager aunt—Aunt Edwina—who simply could not be bothered.

My dear Serafina, she had written, *Such is the world and a woman's place in it. You should not have been so callous with those many gentlemen who might have secured your future and position. I'm sure you have regrets.*

For the first time in her life, Serafina had actually been afraid. The parents of her good friend Patience Pemberton had invited her to stay with their family for an indefinite period

A Dangerous Man to Trust?

of time. Patience's mother, Lady Agnes Pemberton, thought to host her for a season in order to secure her some sort of emergency marriage, but Serafina had been down that road before, and while she appreciated the thought, the effort, and certainly the expense, she simply would not allow herself to be married off to a polite stranger in a tailcoat. This frightened her even more than her current circumstance. Men, she knew, were not to be trusted. They had their courting face—all politeness, and bows, and compliments, and "May I have this dance?" And then they had the face they wore to stare down at their peas as they avoided the gaze of their wife across the dinner table. Worse still, she knew, *she knew*, that there were some very respectable, dignified, and exceedingly polite gentlemen who wore quite another face entirely behind closed doors. This was a cruel face of power wielded over another—a horse, a servant, even a wife.

No. She would not marry. It was quite unthinkable. So when she heard that Mr. Thornton was seeking a governess for his six-year-old daughter, she wrote to him and was hired sight unseen based on a recommendation from Lady Pemberton. (This recommendation had been written most reluctantly, as Lady Pemberton was of the opinion that marriage would be a much more suitable solution to 'employment' – a word she pronounced distastefully, lowering her voice as she would when she did not want the servants to hear.)

Mr. Thornton had hired Serafina, had given her a new life in his home, had entrusted her with his most exceptional daughter Molly, and now he was gone. He had been a friendly, jolly man, but always suffering from some mysterious illness or other.

"Phlegmatic," he used to say by way of explanation if he was feeling under the weather. "But never mind this old man. Tell me about Molly. What did she do today? What did you teach her?"

And Serafina would say, "She can tell you herself, Mr. Thornton."

To which he would respond with a twinkle in his eye, "Yes, yes I know, but I want to hear your version first!"

Mr. Thornton absolutely doted on his daughter, and he was kind to Serafina, welcoming her into his household and treating her with respect and good humour. Now he was gone. Like her parents. She stepped out into the early morning fog and inhaled the wet air, letting out a deep sigh. A tear ran down her cheek and dripped from her chin. A brisk walk would do her good. Burn up these feelings with movement so that she could clear her head and be able to support Molly as they went about their day. She would need to hold her close. Molly appeared to be taking the circumstance in her stride, but Serafina knew better. The death of a parent (both parents) especially for one so young was simply unthinkable. It marked you forever.

But then there was the horse and that man! Serafina had never seen anyone's face so disfigured. And such a grump! She supposed that she might be grumpy too if she had to live with a face like that. But the look in his eyes—pale blue like chips of ice under a clear sky. What was that look? Asking her about her lady's maid! It made her smile just thinking about it. She looked down at her brown coat. Certainly not the stylish coat of a lady. *I was not even wearing a bonnet! How could he think me a lady? Nevermind.* She shook her head as if shaking off the memory.

Arriving back at the house, she thought to herself, *Molly*

might enjoy some puzzles today. Math puzzles. And perhaps I will indulge her in one of her experiments. To lift her spirits. No cursive or needlework—both activities Molly despised. *I will ask cook to make those buns she likes for tea, and we can sneak into the kitchen and steal them hot from the oven. Cook will yell and scold us, and Molly will flee laughing up the stairs with a bun in each hand and the dog at her heels. That is how I hope the day will go. At least, I will try.*

She sighed and entered the house through the back door to be greeted by Rupert, Mr. Thornton's enormous English mastiff, and Miss Browning the elderly housekeeper.

"Miss Edgemont, where have you been?! I have been looking everywhere for you!" said Miss Browning as she gained hold of Rupert's collar and made him sit.

"Out for a walk—it's early," replied Serafina bending down to pet the dog. She knew he would be upset with her for going out without him, but she had needed some time on her own.

"Well, Mr. Thornton is asking for you, and just look at you! What has happened to your hair?" Miss Browning cast her glance down to the hem of Serafina's dress peeking out from under her coat. "And you are spattered in mud."

"What do you mean, Mr. Thornton?"

"Mr. Thornton! The son! He has returned this morning."

"Oh!" Serafina had it in the back of her mind that he might come, but he had never visited before, and for some reason, the servants were of the opinion that he would continue to keep his distance from the manor despite his inheritance. "I shall go and change first, fix my hair."

"No, no," said Miss Browning firmly. "He has already been waiting." Serafina looked at her curiously. She seemed quite agitated. "Go now! He's in the small drawing room."

Pride and a Fall

The 'small' drawing room was no such thing. It was merely smaller than the other very large drawing rooms. It was decorated in red and cream with gold accents and cherry wood furniture. Serafina knocked. When she heard no response, she opened the door and walked briskly into the room. She recognised his voice first.

"You!" He spoke as if there were gravel in his throat. A deep rumbling sound. "You are the governess? Miss Edgemont?"

She barely recognised him by sight. He wore a black mask over his brow and one side of his face, stopping just short of the mouth. And he had an unruly shock of dark brown hair. Most noticeable now that he was wearing a mask was how incredibly handsome he was with his blue eyes, high cheekbone and strong jawline. He was sitting in a chair, leaning his strong frame back with his feet planted wide. He had removed his coat and jacket, and his white linen shirt fell open at the throat where he had loosened his cravat. This was not the way a gentleman sat. It was too casual, too unaffected.

Serafina approached him, stopping a few feet away.

"I would stand," he said, "but there is the matter of my ankle." He looked at her carefully, "And as you have said, you are not a lady, so in any event, there is no need for me to stand."

The sheer rudeness of his statement caught her off-guard. Instinctively, she knew he was looking for some sort of reaction from her.

"Quite."

"Quite? Is that all you have to say for yourself after this morning? 'Sorry' might be a better start."

This man was not like his father.

"What might I be sorry for?" she asked, immediately regretting her decision to talk back but feeling committed to the action nonetheless.

"Causing my injury for one thing," he responded, his pale blue eyes never leaving hers.

"You caused your own injury by choosing to go riding in the fog." Serafina kept her eyes on his. She would not look away first, but she was starting to feel a little weak in the legs.

"Are all my father's servants so insolent?" Serafina knew very well that a governess was no servant, but she did not correct him.

"We're *your* servants now, Sir. I should think you would like to ask me about your sister."

"She's on her way."

Oh no. He will upset Molly. He is a complete stranger and certainly no gentleman.

"And you," said Mr. Thornton rising gingerly to his feet, supported by the arm of the chair, "must be Molly."

Serafina turned to see Molly being ushered in by Miss Browning who took in the scene with one concerned glance before disappearing down the hall. Molly entered hesitantly at first, then ran to Serafina's side and took her hand.

"Are you my brother John?"

"Half-brother," he said.

"Does it matter?" Molly asked.

"You're quick, aren't you?" he said with the soft beginnings of a smile. "Do you mind if I sit. I've injured my ankle."

"I don't mind."

As he took his seat, there was silence. A breath in the room that took some of the weight out of the situation.

"Why do you wear a mask?" asked Molly.

"Molly!" scolded Serafina. "It's not polite to ask such things."

Molly turned to Serafina. "But he's my brother. If I have to be polite with my brother, the world is a horrible place."

"You are quite right!" said Mr. Thornton with surprise in his voice. "No need to be polite with me." Serafina had felt she'd taken the measure of him, but this turn in the conversation caused her brow to furrow.

"I wear a mask because my face is quite hideous," he said matter-of-factly. "It is all scarred and mangled and certainly no sight for a lady." At this, he directed a pointed look towards Serafina.

"Can I see?" asked Molly.

"No."

"Oh." Molly's disappointment was audible.

"But I will let you see my arm. It's almost as gruesome."

"Really?" said Molly as she dashed excitedly forward.

Mr. Thornton sat down in his chair and undoing the cuff of his left arm, he rolled his sleeve up to the elbow.

"Ugh," was the sound Molly made, but her voice was full of admiration. "Can I touch it?"

"Yes, but I cannot feel anything between here and here," he said pointing with his finger to his elbow and then his wrist.

"What if I pinched you?"

"Go ahead!"

Molly looked at Serafina who shrugged. She really could not anticipate how this was going to play out. Mr. Thornton's arm appeared just as his face, raised red rivulets of flesh. Serafina wondered how far the scarring stretched. She glanced at his neck and followed the scarring down to a small patch of exposed chest where his collar fell open. *As far as his chest*, she thought. *And further. Shoulder? Down the arm. His belly?* She was starting to feel a bit hot. That she was still wearing her coat certainly wasn't helping.

"He can't feel it!" exclaimed Molly. "I really, really pinched him, and he can't even feel it!"

"Do you have a pin?" asked Mr. Thornton with amusement.

Molly rushed to open a drawer at the back of the room, returning with a large pin held high and the widest smile imaginable. Mr. Thornton took the pin from her and proceeded to pierce his arm with it, letting go so that the pin stood upright in his flesh.

"Ooooh! Look Serafina! He can't feel it!" She turned to her brother. "Or are you faking?"

"Not at all. You could stick twenty pins in my arm, and I might sit here all day with not a thought for it."

"Molly, I'm sure Mr. Thornton would like to remove the pin now," said Serafina feeling a little queasy.

As he lifted the pin from his arm a bead of blood appeared. Grimacing, Serafina stepped quickly forward to hand him her handkerchief. He accepted it with a slightly bemused look and held it to his arm.

"Can you stick pins in your face?" Molly was lifting herself excitedly up onto her toes and then lowering herself back down. "What about your neck?" she asked peering under Mr. Thornton's chin.

"Molly!" warned Serafina.

"No, no. She may ask. She is my sister after all," he said. "To answer your question, no, I cannot put pins in my face. It's just this portion of my arm that has no feeling."

"Father never said you were so interesting," said Molly quietly. "He made you sound quite dull."

"Oh really?"

"He said you only liked the company of trees and flowers."

"Is that so?"

Pride and a Fall

Mr. Thornton's voice remained level, but Serafina noticed a shift in his countenance. A kind of closing up, like curtains drawn across a window.

"Molly, I have enjoyed meeting you, but I wish a word with Miss Edgemont. Alone," he added when Molly made no move towards the door.

"Oh." She looked a bit crestfallen, then quickly brightened, dashing towards him and making an awkward but enthusiastic attempt at a hug. "I'm glad you're here," she said. The man, Serafina noticed, looked absolutely terrified. When Molly didn't let go, he hesitantly drew one arm around her and placed his hand on her back. Molly lifted her head to look into his face. "Later, it will be my turn to show *you* something interesting."

Molly slowly extricated herself from his lacklustre embrace and reluctantly left the room. Mr. Thornton appeared lost somewhere inside himself. He remained quite still, gazing at the door for a considerable time. Serafina waited patiently. And then it was as if Mr. Thornton having been lost, found his path once more and reemerged with her in the small drawing room. He met her eyes.

"What kind of a house has my father been keeping here?" he asked.

What on odd question. Serafina struggled to come up with a response. Given the events of the morning, she thought that perhaps the most direct answer would be best.

"A happy one, Sir," she said.

"He loved Molly." Not a question this time.

"Of course."

"Not of course!" he said fixing her in place with an icy glare. "There is no requirement for a father to love his child."

It dawned on Serafina then that Mr. Thornton's childhood had been quite different.

"I'm sorry." The words came unbidden to her lips.

"For what?"

She couldn't answer truthfully. It wasn't her place.

"For your ankle," she offered changing tack. His face softened ever so slightly.

"As you said, it was my own fault." In that one sentence, he conceded everything to her. He paused. "You look warm. You should go and remove your coat, return to the rest of your day."

"Yes. Thank you. It's been a pleasure to make your acquaintance." *Ugh*. Serafina immediately hated herself for saying that. It was the kind of thing you said to someone when it had not at all been a pleasure to make their acquaintance.

"When?" His tone was sharp now. The softness gone. He sounded almost angry for some reason.

"Excuse me?"

"When was it a pleasure to make my acquaintance? In the woods or here in the drawing room?"

He knew! He knew it was a disingenuous statement and suspected she meant nothing of the sort. How could a man be so sensitive?

"Both," she answered with some defiance.

"Why was it a pleasure in the woods then?" *He pressed on!*

Serafina was so startled by his line of questioning, she could only think to answer truthfully.

"If you must know, it was a pleasure in the woods because you made me laugh." She willed her legs to keep steady. This was a bit too much. "Sir," she added quickly, "I'm feeling unwell. I must take my leave."

Without waiting for a response, she turned and strode out

of the room, stopping in the hallway to lean with her back pressed up against a wall. *What had just happened?* She felt somewhat ill, as if she had lost all sense of balance. He was quite the most insulting man she had ever met—it felt as if every word he spoke was a blunt instrument with which to beat someone over the head.

As she recovered her balance and headed carefully down the hall, Serafina reviewed the events of the morning. They had been a lot to take in. What disturbed her most was that she did not know where to place Mr. Thornton in the schematics of her mind. *Long lost brother? Rude stranger? Dashing gentleman? No, certainly not 'dashing gentleman'—why had that come to mind?* Regardless of how Serafina felt about her new employer, Molly had loved him! He had truly seen his sister for who she was—right away. And he'd known exactly how to win her over. No one did that. Not with Molly. She was not the kind of little girl anyone expected to encounter, and people were woefully unprepared for her questions and her intelligence.

Serafina decided that Mr. Thornton, despite his . . . irregularities of manner, would be good for Molly. She'd lost a father but somehow, magically, gained a brother. This thought gave Serafina some semblance of relief. Molly's welfare was first and foremost in her mind. She loved that little girl more than she'd ever loved anyone and would do anything for her. A brother! How one's world can shift in a morning. *Math puzzles*, she thought, recovering her composure. *Then morning tea, and I'll ask her about her latest experiment.*

Two

When All the World's Asleep

John had suspected he was still a terrible person, but now he knew it to be true. He had acted atrociously with Miss Edgemont. There was something about her that pricked at him like a thorn in one's boot.

Was it her appearance? The way she stood tall and did not look away? Her demeanour? It felt as if she condescended to engage with him. So what? None of this was any excuse. What had he hoped to achieve with his boorish and offensive manner?

A lesser man would not even ask the question of himself let alone answer it, but over the last six years, John had learned to value a certain degree of honesty, even with himself. The answer came to him: *I had hoped to unnerve her, intimidate her; I had hoped to dissolve her pity and replace it with hate or revulsion.*

But Miss Edgemont had not reacted as expected. She met every insulting remark with grace and dignity, even defiance. There was something to be said for that, especially for someone in as tenuous a position as she was. He had clearly upset her, but she had left him in the worst possible way. She had left him with words of truth and kindness. Since his accident, he had developed a sixth sense for insincerity, and it was clear that Miss Edgemont was anything but insincere. He thought again of her face turned up to his in the woods. He knew it would be better if he kept his distance. He was, after all, a terrible person.

And so it was decided all at once in the moment—John would simply have to avoid Miss Edgemont as best he could. It was not the honest course of action, true, but John was capable of only so much soul-searching. He had spent the last six years relatively alone, and he was not ready to disappoint himself the way he had done repeatedly in the past.

For the next week, he spent most of his time in his study looking over the accounts or out in the garden taking a survey of the grounds and speaking with the gardener. He found a certain peace in contemplating the green things of the earth and over the last several years, had immersed himself in the art of horticulture. In fact, he had brought with him several of his favourite plants as seeds, bulbs, and clippings.

The doctor had been to visit and had determined that his ankle was not broken, merely a tendon strained. Rest was advised and crutches to be used for a week or so.

Molly would search John out at least once each day, and to his relief, Miss Edgemont did not accompany her. When Molly was with him, he felt as if he had stepped outside himself. It was as if he shed his skin, leaving the monster of a person he was on the floor so that he might walk—or rather, lurch on his crutches—with his sister down to the lake where she would explain in alarming detail her experiments

A Dangerous Man to Trust?

with a small model sailboat she had constructed entirely on her own. She was a marvel of a child! John could only wonder at the circumstances that had produced such a bright and charismatic creature. He surprised himself by looking forward to her visits, and he wondered at the manner in which he found himself engaging with her—asking questions, making suggestions, and recounting anecdotes related to her interests.

Molly, John soon came to realise, carried a wealth of information in her tiny head.

"A heavy object will fall at the same rate as a lighter object," she said, stepping up onto a chair and then from the chair, stepping atop a table to demonstrate.

Holding a large coin in one fist and a crumpled piece of paper in the other, she released them at the same time but not before instructing John to "Watch carefully!"

"Gracious," said John when he had witnessed both the coin and the crumpled paper hit the floor at the same time, "You are absolutely right!"

"It's not me who is right—it's Galileo," corrected Molly as she took John's hand to step down from the table. "I told you I would show you something interesting."

It eventually became apparent to John that Molly's exceptional learning was in no small part down to Miss Edgemont's exceptional teaching. As governess, she had clearly gone above and beyond. Any child of Molly's age would by rights be spending her days practising cursive letters and learning her seven times table. Miss Edgemont had seen that this would not suffice for Molly, and she had combed the libraries—the larger one downstairs and the smaller one in the upstairs east wing. While the books she had found were not appropriate for an eight-year-old, she had managed to use them to devise her own lessons for Molly in order to convey something of that brighter and larger world beyond the schoolroom walls. John's estimation of Miss Edgemont grew considerably in the days that followed as each of his encounters with Molly revealed something new about her extraordinary governess.

"Serafina says . . ." was the way Molly would often begin a sentence.

"Serafina says that there is always more than one way to solve a maths problem."

"Serafina says that the stars hide many secrets."

"Serafina says that patience and persistence are good friends that will help us find good answers."

"Serafina says that the truth is like a hidden treasure waiting to be found."

When John asked Molly why she so casually referred to her governess by her Christian name, she responded, "Well, Serafina says that as long as we know how to conduct ourselves properly in company, we can make up our own rules at home." To which she added with a wide smile, "At home, we can relax. But I dare say, Miss Browning does not particularly agree. I once called her Elizabeth, and she stared daggers at me until I thought I might bleed!"

This provoked a chuckle from John who could not help imagining his elderly housekeeper's reaction to Molly's impertinence.

"And does Miss Edgemont say that it's all right for you to climb up onto the table?" asked John.

Molly gave him a mischievous look. "No," she laughed, "Serafina would not like it one bit."

A Dangerous Man to Trust?

Occasionally, John would spy Miss Edgemont out with Molly or sometimes in the very early morning out walking with Rupert, his dog. John remembered Rupert fondly, but it seemed that Rupert did not have the same feeling towards him. He would often search out the huge mastiff only to find him at Miss Edgemont's heel or lying at her feet.

One morning as the sun rose lighting the leaves of the garden in slanted rays of pink and then gold, John came upon Miss Edgemont making for the woods with Rupert. She was at a distance and did not see him. John noticed that she was not wearing a bonnet, nor gloves, and before he was able to catch her eye, he saw her pick up her skirts (up to the knees—no stockings!) and actually run, racing the dog for a stretch over the dewy grass. She finally came to a halt, bending over her thighs to catch her breath. Rupert doubled back to lick her face, and she laughed which only appeared to encourage Rupert in his affections.

"Miss Edgemont," John called out, drawing her attention his way as he approached casually and carefully across the lawn, for it was his first day without crutches.

"Mr. Thornton," she said, her smile dropping as she straightened herself and smoothed down the front of her dress.

She brought her hands up to check her hair, which John found disarming, as if he had intruded upon her while she were still dressing. The fact that he had only a moment ago been gazing at her bare legs did nothing to dispel this feeling. She pressed one pin and then another back into place before dropping her hands to her sides.

"Is there something I can do for you, Sir?" she asked.

This question irritated John almost immediately—he didn't

know exactly why. He advanced towards her with long strides despite his still tender ankle.

"You could return my dog for a start," he said sharply.

He was peering down at Miss Edgemont now, and she was forced to tip her face up to his as she had done that morning in the woods. John realised he was standing much too close to her when she took two steps back. Rupert quickly filled the gap between them and directed a low throaty growl John's way.

"He's all yours, Mr. Thornton," she said with a tentative smile.

Why? Why, thought John, *am I behaving this way?* He stood staring at her in silence for an uncomfortable period of time. Inside, he was struggling with how he might proceed. He decided to change the subject.

"Molly," he said.

"Yes?"

"It has come to my attention that Molly has had no musical instruction whatsoever. She cannot even plunk out the most basic tune on the pianoforte. Is that not something you should be teaching her? As her governess?"

"I cannot play the pianoforte, nor any other instrument," responded Miss Edgemont.

"And why is that?"

"No time," she responded cryptically.

"What does that mean? What kind of a governess does not even know the basics of playing the pianoforte?"

Miss Edgemont looked away from him across the garden and into the past. She heaved her shoulders up and then released them with a sigh. When she turned back towards him, he was startled to see that same open face he had witnessed in the woods at their first meeting.

"I cannot play because my childhood was not . . . normal. My mother was unwell, and she took up much of my attention even as a child. It fell to me to run the household at a very young age. There certainly was no time for musical endeavours."

Hearing her answer, and knowing it to be the plain truth, John's entire body softened. He found himself saying, "Your father must have appreciated the help."

"Perhaps," responded Miss Edgemont, a subtle note of anger to her voice. "Although he spent most of his time in London visiting with his mistress."

As she said this, she took a step towards John, and he could not help but feel that this accusation was somehow being directed his way. It was not a shocking truth—many married men had mistresses—but it was shocking that she had shared it with him so openly.

"Molly should have a tutor then," said John trying to regain control of the conversation, bring it back to business.

"Your father decided against a music tutor since her interests lie elsewhere," responded Miss Edgemont.

"I have spent some time with Molly over the last several days," said John. "I see where her interests lie, and I do not doubt for a moment that she will enjoy some instruction in music for the simple reason that she loves mathematics. Music is simply mathematics in action, Miss Edgemont."

He could tell from the look on her face that he had made the right call. She actually looked pleased, and for some reason this flooded him with a feeling of considerable well-being.

"Enjoy your morning, Miss Edgemont." He gave her a nod and turned to leave.

"Don't you want your dog?" she asked as he started walking away.

He turned but continued to slowly step backwards away from her and towards the house.

"I do want my dog, but it appears that my dog does not want me. I believe Rupert has made the sensible choice."

Walking through the woods with Rupert, Serafina did not know what to make of Mr. Thornton. She had been studiously avoiding him all week. Each interaction with him left her feeling somewhat rattled but also curiously warm. While his words were often barbed, he displayed a kindness and attentiveness towards Molly that Serafina found deeply moving. With Serafina, however, Mr. Thornton seemed always to be on the offensive, but then invariably that offensive front would crack, and Serafina would get a glimpse of someone different, someone softer. And he was a clever man as well. *He was quite right: Molly would take to music because of the mathematical nature of it!* Serafina quietly berated herself for not realising this earlier.

Rupert ran on ahead of her. Serafina lifted her face up to the trees and breathed in the scent of the forest.

As the days passed, Serafina found herself in a state of permanent but subtle agitation. Her senses seemed heightened, but her mind was unable to focus on any one subject for very long. Remembered fragments of her various (but few) conversations

A Dangerous Man to Trust?

with Mr. Thornton would interrupt her thoughts, and she would attempt to shake them off the way Rupert would shake himself free of the lake's water after a dip. In the end, though, just as Rupert would remain quite damp despite his efforts, so too did Serafina's mind remain distracted by these intruding thoughts.

Such was her discomposure one evening that she could not even contemplate going to bed at the usual hour. Instead, she lit a few candles in the schoolroom and set about devising some new lessons for Molly. It must have been quite late when the door to the room creaked open to reveal the housekeeper Miss Browning carrying a lantern.

"Oh, it's you," she said. "What are you doing up so late?"

"I couldn't sleep," replied Serafina.

"Well, just be sure you don't leave those candles burning in here."

"Of course not, Miss Browning. Is it not late for you as well?"

"There is always something to do for a housekeeper—especially one who is on her own without the help usually provided by a lady of the house. It was so much easier when Mrs. Thornton was with us, God rest her soul. And she was such good company as well."

Miss Browning's eyes seemed to mist over as she thought back to happier days.

"You mean Molly's mother?"

"Yes. She was a wonderful lady."

Serafina couldn't help herself. She knew she shouldn't pry, but . . .

"And what about Mr. Thornton's first wife? Do you have fond memories of her as well?"

When All the World's Asleep

Miss Browning's face took on a rather pinched expression. "Those were more difficult times, but nevermind."

"Were they difficult times for Mr. Thornton—the current Mr. Thornton?"

Miss Browning arranged her features into a neutral mask to give nothing away.

"It is not proper for me to gossip, Miss Edgemont. Neither is it proper for you to ask such questions."

"Oh. I only mean to gain some understanding. Our past informs our present—would you not agree, Miss Browning?"

Miss Browning smiled then, a rare occurrence.

"Indeed it does, Miss Edgemont. But you must remember your place here. The former Mr. Thornton was of great good humour, at least in his later days. The present Mr. Thornton is a good deal less predictable. We must tread lightly." She raised her eyebrows in a friendly manner to show that this was advice rather than a scolding. As she closed the door to leave, she said, "The candles, Miss Edgemont. Don't forget to put out the candles."

"I will make certain," Serafina assured her. "Goodnight, Miss Browning."

Left alone once more, Serafina closed her notebook and pushed herself back in her chair. The pins in her hair were causing her head to ache. They always did so by the end of the day, but she had stayed up quite late, and the pain in her head was now fairly intolerable. Reaching up to remove each pin one-by-one, she let down her hair with a sigh of relief. Time for bed. Serafina snuffed out all candles but one which she carried with her out into the darkened hall.

The servants' quarters were located on the lower level of the house, but as governess, Serafina was set apart. There was a chamber for a governess located up a flight of stairs by the schoolroom, but it had fallen into a state of disrepair, and Mr. Thornton—the old Mr. Thornton—insisted on providing her with more suitable accommodation. To Miss Browning's clear opposition on the grounds of 'propriety', Mr. Thornton had given Serafina one of the larger guestrooms in the east wing.

"It's not as if we host many guests these days," he had said to Miss Browning whose face looked as if she had been sucking on lemons.

Serafina gingerly picked her way along the hall, up a flight of stairs, and then along another wider, carpeted hallway. The candle cast a glow about her, illuminating her immediate surroundings, but she could not see more than a couple of feet ahead. So when Mr. Thornton's unmasked face loomed unexpectedly into view like a ghoul in the night, it seemed to appear out of nowhere. Serafina screamed.

John never slept well, but he found himself feeling exceptionally restless that night and had decided to distract himself with a book in the upstairs library. He had taken a candle with him, but he would not light it until he was seated by a table. He knew every inch of the house by heart, so there was no need, and in any case, he would not see a candle lit unless it was quite necessary. Fire was nothing to trifle with in his experience.

John had seen Miss Edgemont floating towards him in her orb of light, and forgetting that he was not similarly visible, he had simply walked right up to her. When she screamed, he remembered that he was not wearing his mask.

"That is exactly the sort of reaction I usually provoke," he said, pleased to have caught her out. *Perhaps she is like everyone else*, he thought, and his body relaxed. Maybe he would be able to sleep after all.

"You gave me a shock," said Miss Edgemont. "It was nothing more."

As she said these words, he took her in properly for the first time. Her hair was down! A dark waterfall. It cascaded over her shoulders and fell in ripples all the way to her waist. She looked quite otherworldly.

"Good God," he said, not realising he spoke out loud.

"Excuse me?"

"What keeps you up so late, Miss Edgemont?"

"Nothing," she said quickly. "I couldn't sleep earlier, but I am quite tired now." She stifled a yawn with the back of her hand as if to prove her point. Then she lifted the candle, he noticed, to better see his face. His white shirt was untucked and open at the top exposing his neck and a portion of his chest. Her eyes darted to his chest then back to his face.

"And you, Sir, you could not sleep?"

He shook his head. They gazed at each other for a few moments.

"It's treacherous on these carpets in the dark. I shall escort you to your room," said John.

It was the gentlemanly thing to do.

"Oh." A pause as she appeared to consider this. "I should be fine."

"Nonsense. I will blame myself should you trip or, God forbid, drop that candle."

He reached for her hand and lifting it, placed it in the crook of his arm. She did not rest her hand there lightly as other ladies tended to do. Instead, she gripped his arm quite firmly through his loose shirt.

"Well, thank you," she said, turning her face up to his.

It felt for all the world to him as if they had been here before. She had held his arm before in this same fierce manner, and there was nothing more natural than walking with her down the hall in the candlelight. When they reached the door to her room, she turned to him and lifted the candle once more, peering up into his face.

"You have no mask this evening," she said.

"And you have no pins in your hair," he said with a snarl of a smile.

"Oh, I'd forgotten. They hurt my head by the end of the day," she replied. "Do you find your mask uncomfortable?"

He hadn't expected the question.

"I, ah, yes. Sometimes I could do without it."

"It's a shame we have to wait until all the world's asleep to simply be ourselves," said Miss Edgemont, her dark shining eyes never leaving his.

John was struck. It was possibly the most intimate thought someone had ever shared with him. Miss Edgemont was still holding his arm, and for the life of him, he did not want her to let him go. They stood there, breathing into the darkness.

Finally, she said, "Well, I really should be getting to bed." She released his arm and opened the door to her room, stepped inside. But before she closed the door, she turned around.

"You don't have to wear it for me," she said. "Your mask," she added.

He could see her blushing in the candlelight with the sudden realisation of how forward this might sound. *Of course she would not mean it that way.*

"I didn't m-mean . . ." she stammered, "It's just that I prefer to be able to see the person I am speaking with. Don't you?"

John felt himself coming untethered under her gaze. He nodded very carefully, willing himself to take control over his entire body, willing himself to move away from her door, away from her.

"Goodnight, Miss Edgemont."

"Sleep well, Mr. Thornton."

Needless to say, John did not sleep well at all that night, and he woke in the morning with one thought: he must put some distance between himself and Miss Edgemont.

Three

Theatre of Manners

John would have to leave Bosworth Manor. At least for a little while in order to clear his head and gain some measure of control over himself. Miss Edgemont deserved to feel safe in his house and free of any unwanted attention. If he could guarantee this by leaving, then he would. He did so immediately, ordering his cases packed and a carriage readied first thing that morning. He had to meet with his father's solicitor anyway. Now was as good a time as any.

By the time he arrived at the solicitor's office in London, he was feeling significantly more composed. He would attend to his business and reconnect with various persons of standing to reassert his family's presence on the London social scene. A recognised and reputable family with connections in London would be of benefit to Molly in the future. Molly. Yes. He would focus his attention there.

The solicitor, one Robert Cavendish, was a portly man with wispy hair, all smiles and big teeth as he ushered John into his office. Once John was seated opposite him, his smile fell abruptly from his face.

"My condolences, my condolences," he said bowing his head slightly but looking up curiously into John's masked face. "Your father was a wonderful man."

"I'm sure," said John wishing to get on with the business of the will.

Mr. Cavendish was diligent in his reading, his explanations of this and that.

"Basically, everything has been left to yourself, Mr. Thornton. Your father expected you would be Miss Thornton's guardian in the event of his death. Standard stuff. Standard stuff. There is only one other matter, not so standard." He paused, John thought, somewhat dramatically. "Your father has left a rather large amount—a dowry actually."

"For Molly."

"No, no. I believe he expected you to take care of that when the time came. No. It's a dowry for a Miss Serafina Edgemont. I believe she is Miss Thornton's governess." Mr. Cavendish looked to the exposed half of John's face to judge his reaction. "The sum is rather outlandish," he added, sliding a piece of paper across the table. When John read the paper but made no reply or comment, Mr. Cavendish added, "It will be subtracted from your inheritance." He paused, waiting for something from John.

"I see," said John giving nothing away. "Shall I inform Miss Edgemont, or should you?"

"I can send the papers with you. Please tell her to reply by letter to my office."

A Dangerous Man to Trust?

"Fine." John stood, sliding his chair roughly backwards.

He supposed this was a good thing. Miss Edgemont would certainly be able to marry someone of standing—a much better situation for her than governess. With this size of dowry she would, in fact, be spoilt for choice. His father must have held her in very high regard. This was the kind of dowry a father bestowed on a daughter. Someone loved. *Why did he feel so disheartened?*

John found himself standing outside the solicitor's building in a daze. *How had his father managed to cultivate so much love when before he had so little to spare?* He thought back to his childhood, his parents' strained marriage—one that had been arranged between families with financial concerns outweighing any consideration for the two people whose lives would be upended. John's early years were spent with a nurse, and his parents seemed as strangers living in the same house. Strangers who despised each other with a tenacity that only those who are under contractual obligation to love each other can employ. Occasionally, he would see them together, but inevitably such events were marred by an argument or a tense exchange and a slammed door. Then there were the silences that sometimes lasted weeks. Somehow, he was a part of it— their hatred. He was the product of something that should not have been.

At the age of six, John was sent away to school, and he could not have been happier for it. He traded the unpredictable situation at home for the predictable hierarchy of a boys' school. At school, the teachers taught him good manners, mathematics, and Latin, and the other boys taught him to show no weakness, to take what he could, and to always be ready for a fight. He had survived the ordeal of school, but it had taken a toll on his soul. He had become like so many of those other young gentlemen he had grown up with—a perfectly presentable outer shell of politeness and insincerity hiding a world of selfish motivations beneath. A terrible person.

That was why his fiancée Eleanor had left him after his accident. His presentable shell had cracked, and she could quite literally see how ugly he was underneath. When he looked in the mirror, he could not blame her. It was not that she was shallow, caring only for his appearance: his face was just the physical manifestation of a grasping and conceited soul. It had been a real shock when she had broken the engagement. He had been angry then, but now he saw things differently, more clearly. He hadn't seen it coming because he had not truly seen Eleanor at all. What he had seen was an extraordinary beauty—hair like spun gold with the delicate features of a china doll. He had seen her smiles and demure glances to the floor, and he had seen the perfect lady—pleasant, agreeable, of even temperament. What he had not seen was *her*, that unchanging centre of a person, the bit that looked out through her beautiful green eyes, the bit that saw him. And she saw him all right. At first, she'd seen his handsome face and good manners, but then she had seen deeper and was quite justifiably repulsed.

John, if he was being honest with himself, and these days he was, could easily admit that he had not loved Eleanor so much as wanted her because everyone else had wanted her. It was school all over again—take what you can, assert yourself, dominate. Everything a competition. He had won Eleanor's pretty hand with pretty words. When she had accepted his proposal, he was elated—not so much to be marrying her, but to have won. He broke the news at his London

A Dangerous Man to Trust?

club with a smirk, savouring the envy and frustration of his competitors, his boyhood companions. He was overcome with a warm feeling of smug satisfaction as he casually sipped at his whiskey, one ankle crossed over the opposite knee.

John returned to the present with a jolt and realised he was still standing outside the solicitor's building, his back to the shiny black door. He would return to Bosworth Manor, but he needed some time first—time to compose himself. In the end he stayed three weeks in London. He might have stayed longer, but at every corner he was reminded of why he had removed himself from society for the past six years. It was all a show, a theatre of manners designed to secure each person a position. And there were gossips everywhere: the gentlemen at the club, the aristocratic ladies at the functions he was obliged to attend (all eager to bend his ear and ask him the most intrusive questions), the actresses and other self-sufficient women who would glide through every public gathering like a ballet of swans, ever alert, always gathering information that might be of use at a later date.

He would have shunned them all except that he was now well aware that anything he said or did would necessarily reflect on the entire family, and by that he meant Molly. His connections were hers. His standing in society was her standing and would necessarily impact her future—her place within the wider society and her marriage prospects. He had not known Molly long, but he was already quite taken with her. So enthusiastic and genuine. So curious! That she was the product of his father's love—for his second wife and for her—grated a little, but his childhood was not her fault, and the fact that he was now her guardian weighed heavily upon him.

John ran into several old 'friends' at his club and was forced to make their reacquaintance. It was all handshakes and back pats. No mention of the six interceding years or the unhappy situation with Eleanor. He had inherited now—he had a position and a place. John could barely stand to be himself these days—Mr. Thornton of Bosworth Manor. In London, where the social wheels turn relatively predictably, he was welcome to the extent that he brought with him an air of mystery and the exotic. He looked as if he'd just stepped out of a masquerade ball, and the exposed snarl of his mangled upper lip made him appear somewhat dangerous as well. The good people of London were practically falling over themselves to say hello, to look inquisitively into his concealed face. The ladies especially went mad for him (he may only have half a face, but he did now have the entirety of a small fortune). He was polite with everyone if not verbose—a man of few words, but that just made him all the more enigmatic and appealing.

One night, he was forced to attend a particularly excruciating social engagement (a ball, no less), and while he would not ask any of the eager-eyed young ladies to dance, he felt obligated to attend since it was hosted by an old family friend—Lady Leveson-Gower—and she had been quite insistent upon his attendance. Lady Leveson-Gower would have been of an age with his father were he still living. She was a kind woman who had watched with some concern as John had frittered away his early years in a pointless pursuit of . . . what? John couldn't even say what he had been chasing back then. Pleasure? Power? His own self-destruction?

Lady Leveson-Gower was only too happy to see him again. How was he faring? Would he be in London long? How was Molly? Once John had decided that enough time had been spent at the ball to satisfy his hostess, he made his excuses, said his polite good-byes, and stepped out of the warm candlelit ballroom and into the cool starlit night. He was accosted on the way to his carriage by an elegant gentleman in a sharp blue jacket. Blonde hair carefully swept back, and dark eyes, black in the starlight.

"I say, you wouldn't happen to be Mr. John Thornton, would you?"

"Yes. Who would be asking?"

"Theodore Cross." The man reached out his hand. "Pleased to finally meet you."

"I'm sorry," said John eyeing his carriage, "should I know you?"

The man laughed revealing a red mouth full of perfect teeth.

"No, no. It's just that I am well-acquainted with your sister's governess—Serafina Edgemont."

John noticed the absence of a "Miss" in his reference. John also noticed the presence of her Christian name, Serafina. John's heart picked up its pace. He felt a swell of anger rising within him.

"You know Miss Edgemont?" he asked, his voice steely.

"Yes," said Theodore with a mysterious smile. "Serafina and I were quite close. We courted, you see."

"I see. But clearly, you are no longer courting."

Theodore ignored the comment.

"She is not well," he said. "Up here." He placed a finger to his temple. "I dare say she is not the best influence on your sister."

"I beg your pardon?"

"Her manner. She has no sense of propriety. No sense and no actual manners. I probably shouldn't say this, but it is the truth. Sometimes, she is even prone to fits of nervous excitement. Your father indulged her as governess to your sister, but . . ."

"But what?" John felt a flush of hot blood reach his face. He was containing himself, but only just.

"But it's your sister who will suffer—raised by someone like that." He caught John's gaze. "Oh, I'm not saying it's Serafina's fault. She is a true innocent. It's just that she is unwell."

Theodore paused to arrange his features in a 'how unfortunate' kind of way.

"If you ever feel the need to find a new governess, one more suitable, you can be assured that Serafina will not be without options. I have some affection for her despite her unhappy mental affliction. I would offer to take care of her."

John could not believe what he was hearing.

"You mean marry her?"

"Yes, I would offer to marry her, poor thing."

John's hands were clenched by his side, fists so tight his knuckles had turned white.

"I must be going," he said through his teeth, and he climbed into the waiting carriage.

I must be going home, he thought as the carriage rocked forward over the cobbles. John had immediately recognised Theodore Cross for what he was—a terrible person. Someone who sought to win at all costs.

God protect Miss Edgemont from men like that, he thought. *Men like me*, he added.

Serafina had written three furious letters to Mr. Thornton, and she had ripped each one of them up. She was absolutely livid. He had left the following morning without so much as a goodbye to Molly. No explanation, no indication of when he might be back. Molly had cried! She hadn't cried when her father had passed on, but she had cried the day her brother left. And again the next day. And the next!

"He doesn't like me." Molly had spoken the words gasping between sobs.

"Don't be silly. Of course he likes you," said Serafina as she held the little girl against her body. "He probably just had some urgent business to attend."

"So urgent he couldn't say goodbye?" Molly had lifted her red-eyed face to look at Serafina.

"You know what some gentlemen can be like."

"No, I don't!" Another round of sobs, soaking Serafina's dress through to her skin.

Serafina had not felt this kind of anger before. *How dare he! How dare he hurt this precious little girl!*

When Mr. Thornton arrived home in the evening, she carefully avoided crossing his path, too afraid of what she might say. The following day, he summoned her to his study. As she entered the room, he was seated behind his desk, writing. When he saw her, he quickly stood and walked around the desk to meet her. Serafina had rehearsed some calm and even words. She would draw his attention to how he had affected Molly, but she would do it carefully. She had imagined her emotions were under control, but her proximity to Mr. Thornton made her feel like a kettle on the stove, shuddering with the expansion of hot water within. When she opened her mouth, she practically yelled at him.

"Where have you been for the last three weeks?!"

He responded with a confused look.

"I don't see how that concerns you."

Theatre of Manners

"You don't see?! You don't see?! It concerns me because it concerns your sister. She is beyond devastated. She has been crying a lake of tears all over me."

Serafina pulled (a little madly) at the front of her dress which was still damp from that morning's weeping.

"I'm soaked in your sister's tears," she said, her voice softer now, her eyes welling up.

"Miss Edgemont," he said with some concern, stepping closer, lifting an arm out towards her, then dropping it down by his side. "I don't understand."

Serafina wiped at her eyes with the back of her hand, angry with herself for her lack of restraint.

"You left, and you didn't say goodbye. And she did not know when or if you would ever come back. You're her brother."

"Molly's been crying?"

"Yes."

"About me leaving?" He sounded genuinely surprised, but also somewhat alarmed.

"Yes." Serafina took a deep breath, letting it out in one long rush.

"I see."

"I'm not sure you do see because if you did see you would not have left like that." Serafina had lost all control over her mouth.

Mr. Thornton will dismiss me, she thought. *Why am I speaking this way?*

There was a long silence then as Mr. Thornton held Serafina's gaze in his. Serafina waited to receive the consequences of her impulsive behaviour. Finally, Mr. Thornton spoke, and there was wonder in his tone.

"You love Molly too, don't you?"

A Dangerous Man to Trust?

"Of course."

"Not of course," he countered. Then, "I'm sorry."

"Excuse me?"

"I'm sorry," he said again. "I apologise unreservedly. And I will offer my apologies to Molly as well."

Serafina was taken aback. "I don't . . . yes . . . well . . . thank you."

Mr. Thornton continued, "I thought it would be better if I left. I have been on my own for a very long time, and although that is no excuse, I'm sure you would agree that I am not always the most pleasant company."

"Oh." Serafina wasn't sure what to say to that.

He opened his mouth to speak again and then paused. A marked hesitation as if he were rethinking what he was about to say. He shook his head slightly.

"I have something for you," he said, "from my father."

He turned to rummage through the papers scattered over his desk, and Serafina let her gaze slide up to the collar of his jacket where she lingered over the exposed top of his neck, his ear. Mr. Thornton turned back and handed her a cream envelope.

"From my father's solicitor. He has left you a dowry—a tidy sum. It will secure your future."

Serafina's mind struggled to take in this information and all that it entailed with growing discomfort. She pressed the envelope back into his hand.

"Thank you, but no." When he looked at her questioningly, she said, "I do not wish to marry."

"You do not wish to marry, or there is no one you wish to marry?" When she did not answer, "Governess is not the best situation for a lady," he said.

"I'm a lady now, am I? Now that I have a dowry?" Serafina's mouth was at it again. She couldn't help it. The whole marriage idea made her feel irritated and petulant.

"You know very well that you have always been a lady. I apologise for intimating otherwise."

What had happened to Mr. Thornton? He was all apologies and genteel manners today.

He stepped forward and handed her the envelope once more.

"My father wanted you to have this."

"Sir," she said looking down at the envelope in her hand, "I don't want to sound ungrateful, but this money is not for me. It's for my future husband." She reached around him to place the envelope on his desk. "Please talk to Molly," she said entreatingly.

Serafina left Mr. Thornton's study and strode briskly down the hall with the air of someone who knew where she was going. But her face was flushed, and she felt as if she were spinning wildly through empty space not knowing at all where she might land.

A dowry?! It was very generous. But marriage? No. She had made that decision two years ago. It was not for her. She had Molly now, and Mr. Thornton . . . Mr. Thornton was turning out to be a lot more pleasant than he thought himself to be. That he had not dismissed her on the spot! In her heart, Serafina knew that she would not have spoken to anyone else like that. After all her careful planning of what and how to speak with him, her outburst had been a spur-of-the-moment impulse triggered by the simple sight of him. There was something about Mr. Thornton. She had instinctively felt that speaking anything less than the truth would make him think less of her. And for some reason, she wanted his good opinion. He was, of course, her employer. One always sought the good opinion of one's employer.

And that is the very reasonable reason for why I had to yell at him, thought Serafina.

She took a deep shuddering breath. Mr. Thornton would speak to Molly. He had promised, and she did not doubt his promise for an instant. She thought of this, and she smiled (just a little) to herself. Things were going to be all right.

Left alone in his study, John leaned his weight back against his desk and let out a breath. His body was flooded with an unaccountable sensation—relief. Miss Edgemont would not marry. And certainly would not marry Theodore Cross. She would not leave him alone . . . with Molly. To turn down such a sum was quite unthinkable! He conjured her indignant face before him. Who else in her position would have done the same? The words of Mr. Cross came back to him: "She is unwell." *Perhaps she has her reasons*, thought John. *She seems perfectly well to me.*

John was deeply moved by Miss Edgemont's honesty in dealing with him. She had hidden nothing, including her own emotions. No theatre of manners with her! *No one would speak that way with someone they did not trust*, thought John. He thought this, and he was touched to his core in a manner he had not experienced before. *I will not betray that trust*, he thought. He had never been in a position like this: he was actually needed (or at least wanted) here. With Molly. *And*, he thought, *with Miss Edgemont.* The weight of his new responsibility settled over him once more, but he was buoyed up by the thought that Molly's care need not be a mere obligation. It could be, as it was for Miss Edgemont, an act of love. Could he do this? He would try.

Everything else in his life had been a complete failure up to this point. His accident—the fire— came to him now during the day as it always did at night in his dreams or rather nightmares. How had he survived when Eleanor's brother William had not? He could see William now, trapped at the back of the room, surrounded by fire. *Everything made of bloody wood*, he thought, *and a thatched roof.* The inn was consumed by flames, and as he struggled back through the debris towards William, a roof beam crackled and collapsed from above. He could feel the crushing weight of the burning timber even now. It hit his head, pushing him back and down as it pressed into his face, pinning the left side of his body to the floor. *My God, the heat!* He had thought he would die there, cooking in the flames with the smell of the innkeeper's specially brewed ale steaming up around him, but instead a huge man, a local farm hand, had risked himself to pull John clear. William, however, was lost. The next time Eleanor had looked at John, he could see it in her face. She knew. She knew as well as he did that if it had to be a choice, William was the one who deserved to live—not him. The least John could do now was to make some use of his life. And with Molly, he had been given that chance.

A Dangerous Man to Trust?

Serafina found that Mr. Thornton was a man true to his word. It was not an hour before he found her and Molly pouring over a logic problem together, brows furrowed.

"We need to make a chart, a grid," Molly said, "and then we can work it out through a process of elimination."

"That's a clever idea," said Serafina as her gaze lifted to see Mr. Thornton standing quite still in the doorway. He tugged nervously at his cravat, an incongruous movement for someone who looked so confident.

"Molly," he said hoarsely.

Molly looked up at him, but she did not respond.

"Molly," he said again, stepping into the room and coming to rest on one knee beside her chair, at eye level. "Molly, I must apologise for my terrible behaviour. I left without saying goodbye, and that was a thoughtless thing to do."

"It was," said Molly, dry-eyed now, arms crossed as if to protect herself from the apology.

"I will never do so again."

"Never?"

"Never."

"What if you have important business in London?"

"There is no more important business than being your brother," said Mr. Thornton. "I would take you with me."

"You would?!" asked Molly, wide-eyed.

"Of course." Mr. Thornton pulled at his cravat once more and succeeded in loosening it so that his scarred neck was exposed. "Can you find it in your heart to forgive me."

"I'll think about it," said Molly.

Serafina smiled to herself—that was as good as Mr. Thornton was going to get today, but it would do. Mr. Thornton glanced over at Serafina.

Theatre of Manners

"I hope you will be able to forgive me as well, Miss Edgemont."

He was kneeling between the two of them at the table. Serafina thought it the oddest arrangement of persons—her employer on his knee begging forgiveness! At first she was lost for words, but she soon found the right ones.

"I'll think about it as well." She looked over at Molly and gave her a wink which made Molly laugh. It was the first time she'd laughed in weeks.

Mr. Thornton stood up to his full height, smiling now, that snarl of a smile.

"I gather, Molly, that you are a lady of science. Am I right?"

"I like working things out," said Molly noncommittally.

"Last year, I was in Dorset for a brief spell, and I encountered another young lady of science. She was perhaps only a few years older than you. You will never guess at the project with which she was engaged."

"What was it?" asked Molly sitting up a little straighter.

"She had found a kind of monster in the rock by the seaside."

"Monsters aren't real," said Molly, but she looked like she wasn't so sure.

"I saw it with my own eyes. This one looked like an enormous crocodile turned to stone. Its head was four foot from end to end. The young lady's name was Mary, and she was chipping away at the rock to reveal the entire length of the creature, its ribs and spine, its claws and tail."

"Really? Is this true?" asked Molly suspiciously. "Or is it just a story? Because I don't like stories."

"It's true. I swear it." Mr. Thornton pressed his hand to his heart. "There are all sorts of creatures to be found in the rock by the seashore. I cannot show you anything quite so enthralling as an enormous crocodile, but I did pick up a few small curiosities while I was there. Would you like to see them?"

"Yes!" Molly was out of her chair.

Mr. Thornton looked to Serafina. "I hope you don't mind if I steal her for a little while."

"Not at all. She's your sister," said Serafina with a slight bow of the head.

When she looked up, he was still gazing at her. Serafina had felt eyes on her before when she had been out in society, and she had never appreciated the feeling. She always felt like a piece of mutton hanging in a shop window, the gentlemen peering through the glass, sizing her up, imagining how she might taste compared to some other piece of meat on offer that day. This was not that feeling. He was not looking at her dress or her hair. (He had never slid his gaze up and down her body as some men had done). She couldn't explain it, but in that moment, she felt that Mr. Thornton was actually looking at *her*, that eternal essence that was Serafina. It gave her a warm fizzy feeling in her belly that radiated out through each of her limbs.

Serafina stood from her chair and mouthed the words "Thank you." Mr. Thornton nodded, then took Molly by the hand and left the room. Serafina could hear Molly chatting animatedly with him all the way down the hall.

Finding herself with a bit of free time, Serafina went in search of Rupert. She found the mastiff under a large table in the kitchen licking his chops and looking decidedly guilty. He got up to greet her, to lick her wrist.

"He's been thieving pork pies," said the cook.

"Rupert!" scolded Serafina. "How could you?"

Theatre of Manners

Rupert lowered his head looking suitably ashamed. Out of the corner of her eye, Serafina caught a look between the two kitchen maids who were slicing apples at the table. They tittered softly to themselves. Serafina had the feeling that it was one of them who had passed Rupert a pie under the table.

"And why not?" she said to Rupert once they were out in the garden. "You deserve a little treat now and then, don't you?"

Rupert barked happily and ran on ahead, anticipating their usual route down to the lake. He would chase the ducks, and Serafina would remove her shoes (she didn't bother with stockings in summer). She waded into the cool shallows savouring the squishy silken feel of the silt between her toes, but her mind soon travelled back to the school room, to Mr. Thornton on his knee beside her.

"Mr. Thornton." She said his name out loud to herself. "Mr. John Thornton."

Rupert ran towards her in the shallows, and Serafina laughed, bending down to hold the dog's face, to kiss his nose.

"Your master is full of surprises, is he not?" she said looking into Rupert's adoring eyes.

Rupert answered her with a sloppy lick of her chin.

Four

King of Hearts

Dear Serafina,

    I hope you are well and that Molly continues to bear the loss of her father with courage. I am sure that your presence is a comfort to her. Much has transpired here in London since your last letter. George has seemed at a loss since he was spurned by that Katherine woman. He has left for the seaside and taken little Grace with him for an adventure! They will be visiting friends in Cornwall. I (having spurned no one, and more's the pity) have been taking portraiture lessons, and my technique is coming along nicely. There is something about capturing the essence of a person, the set of their features, even the thoughts behind their eyes—it is quite magical!

    As for social news, the entire town has been buzzing with Mr. John Thornton's arrival upon the scene. He has been mobbed at every function by a gaggle of young ladies (yours truly not included) keen for his attentions. I dare say it is the mask that really draws them in—so mysterious. Of course, his inheritance is likely the more practical consideration, and we ladies must be practical, mustn't we?

What I write next is at Mother's direction (she is standing over me now). Mother has seen Mr. Thornton at a number of gatherings, and she does not have a good feeling about him. She thinks he looks dangerous! And she is concerned for your welfare, bound up as you are in his employment . . . in his house . . . (and Mother insists that I add) without a chaperone. Mother would like to extend an open invitation for you to come and stay with us whenever you like for as long as you like. I, especially, would be happy for your company. Even a short stay with us would be something to look forward to, would it not?

(Mother has finally left the room). I would like to add that in all fairness, Father (unlike Mother) has actually met Mr. Thornton at his club, and he thought Mr. Thornton to be "a sensible fellow with a good handshake". How is that for a character assessment? I am sure you are in the best position to make a judgment about all this. Although Mother says that it is not what is true so much as what people believe to be true that matters. And she believes that people believe what she believes—that Mr. Thornton is an altogether rake-ish sort of man and that you are not safe in his home.

To be honest, Serafina, I am a little concerned for you myself. Mother, as you know, can be quite convincing. Please write to let us know how you are keeping and to put our minds to rest over this mysterious Mr. Thornton. You are always welcome in our home.

Your friend,
Patience

Serafina re-folded the letter and slid it back into its envelope.

A Dangerous Man to Trust?

Well! She stood up, walked over to her bedroom window to look down into the bright garden where Mr. Thornton and Molly were walking together towards the lake. Rupert was in tow this time. It looked like he may be warming to Mr. Thornton after all. Serafina turned from the window and came back to her writing desk, picked up the envelope once more, and removed the letter for the second time. She read it again. *Well, indeed! Dangerous?!*

Serafina, despite Mr. Thornton's somewhat prickly demeanour, had never once felt unsafe in his presence. Annoyed? Yes. Rattled? Sometimes. But lately, even these upsets were few and far between. It was as if Molly had been slowly wearing down Mr. Thornton's sharp edges. He had certainly never been inappropriate . . . apart from his general rudeness . . . but not inappropriate in the way that Lady Pemberton was imagining. Serafina thought back to that night in the darkened hallway. She could still feel his hand—hot and dry—as it lifted hers to his arm. She could see in her mind's eye the way he had nodded and started backing away when she had made that (inadvertently forward) remark about his mask. She thought of the way he was with Molly, his "unreserved" apology. No. Mr. Thornton, if anything, made her feel quite safe. Lady Pemberton had him all wrong.

Dearest Patience,

Thank you for your and your dear mother's concern. I am truly blessed to have such thoughtful friends. I am glad to hear you are expanding your artistic talents—what a joy it sounds! And I hope your brother George will find some solace entertaining little Grace by the seaside. Grace is so lucky to have a brother who would invite her along for a holiday. On a similar note, Molly for her part is blossoming in the company of her new-found brother. Mr. Thornton, despite his dangerous appearance, clearly has a way with children! He is most attentive towards his sister and spends considerable time with her each day.

I believe your father is correct in his assessment of Mr. Thornton as a "sensible fellow". However, I cannot speak to his handshake. While Mr. Thornton does at times display an irregular manner, he has never behaved inappropriately or made me feel in any way unsafe. Patience, I know your dear mother will not consider a housekeeper as chaperone, but I have felt Miss Browning's stern but caring presence to be a comfort ever since my arrival at Bosworth Manor two years ago.

You can rest assured that I am well, and I am also heartened to see Molly so happy. As for your invitation, thank you. I would very much like to come for a short visit sometime soon. <u>Not</u> because I need the respite or feel unsafe but simply because I would love to see you. Molly has her brother now, so she will not miss me quite so much. Let me discuss the matter with Mr. Thornton, and I will let you know.

Lovingly yours,
Serafina

"Serafina! Serafina!"

Molly came charging across the lawn in her bright white dress under a dismal grey sky. Serafina was making her way towards the house, Rupert at her heel.

"John has been teaching me to play cards," said Molly, stopping short, face flushed.

"Has he?"

A Dangerous Man to Trust?

Of course he has, thought Serafina.

"It is ever so much fun! There is the matter of remembering which suit is trump and which cards have already been played, and then since the entire deck—John has a French deck with 52 cards—since the entire deck is not in use, one must calculate the odds of certain cards being present. I mean, well, you don't *have* to calculate the odds, but I do! So far, John has won four games, and I've won five. It's not really a proper game with only two people. Three would be better. Four would be best, but we only have you, and I would not even dream of asking Miss Browning to play."

Molly took a breath, her smile as wide as the ocean.

"Molly, are you asking me to join your card game?"

"Well, yes, but not now. John must attend to some business this afternoon. He said we could play in the evening after dinner."

Molly's look turned a little sheepish.

"John said not to bother you. He said you would probably prefer to rest in the evening. But please, Serafina! Please! It will be so much fun if you play."

Serafina, for her part, was not entirely sure she should. But she could not bring herself to deny the sheer glee with which Molly had approached her. She certainly had to hand it to Mr. Thornton—he knew exactly what would engage his sister.

That evening, Serafina found Molly and John in the large drawing room after supper. They were both sat at a card table, heads together, cards spread out in front of them. John was explaining something in the low rumble of his voice, and Molly was nodding seriously. Serafina stood very still in the doorway watching them together. *Now this would make a portrait,* she thought. It started as a warm sensation in the centre of her chest, and then it was as if her heart were blooming, expanding underneath a bright sun. She had never seen Molly so content. By the time Mr. Thornton lifted his head and caught Serafina's eye, she was smiling—not at him, just to herself.

"Miss Edgemont," he said standing. "Molly tells me you will be joining us for a game of Whist. I hope this does not inconvenience your evening."

He gave Molly a sharpish look, but Molly just shrugged her shoulders as if the matter was nothing to do with her.

"Not at all," replied Serafina. "But is three enough? Don't we need partners for Whist?"

"So you know how to play!" said Mr. Thornton looking pleased. "Yes, partners are usually the way it's done, but we'll be playing a different version—one I learned from a friend at university. The mechanics are the same, but . . . you'll see." He looked to Molly. "Deal her in."

"Right," said Molly trying to contain her delight as she began to shuffle the deck.

Mr. Thornton stepped quickly to the chair opposite his at the table in order to pull it out for Serafina. She hesitated, looking to his face in surprise. A governess pulled out her own chair, but of course, a governess also did not play cards in the drawing room with her employer. As Serafina took her seat, she couldn't help but feel the heat of Mr. Thornton's presence behind her as he helped slide her chair forward.

The evening passed in a haze of laughter and good cheer. It could not be helped—playing cards with Molly and Mr. Thornton was most diverting. Molly would go out of her way to knowingly play a card that was sure to frustrate Mr. Thornton's efforts.

A Dangerous Man to Trust?

"I don't suppose this king will take your jack," she'd say, eyeing him mischievously. And Mr. Thornton would stare Molly down with a ferocious look that would set Molly off in a fit of giggles.

There was something about focusing on the game of cards that allowed one to relax and feel less inhibited. After all, it's quite difficult to concentrate on two sets of rules at once—the rules of the game and the rules of decorum. In the end, it was all they could do to focus on the rules of the game, and even Serafina found herself shrieking in surprise at an unlikely play or slamming a hand to the table with a "Hah!" when she took a trick. Mr. Thornton was prone to table talk which was the height of bad manners when it came to playing cards.

"A low diamond would suit me nicely," he'd say as Molly was deciding which card to play.

"Mr. Thornton, you cannot make suggestions," scolded Serafina. "It's against the rules."

"Mm," said Mr. Thornton lifting an eyebrow. "But at home we can make up our own rules. Isn't that right, Molly?"

"I'm trying to think!" was Molly's reply. "Shhhhh!"

Serafina went to bed that night feeling as light as a feather floating on the lake. She could not have felt more content as she sank her head into her pillow and drifted off into a deep and dreamless sleep.

The evening card games became a fairly regular affair. Miss Browning would occasionally be drawn to the door of the drawing room by the boisterousness of those within. She would shake her head and make disapproving sounds, but it was difficult even for her not to crack the occasional smile. Joy, after all, is contagious.

King of Hearts

John was rather pleased with the way events were playing out. Molly was happy, and this warmed his heart. It did not hurt that Molly's happiness was catching—Miss Edgemont, he noticed (and he always noticed), seemed more relaxed, a soft smile lighting up her face whenever she looked to his. This was what he could do. He could love Molly. He could keep a happy home. He could share Miss Edgemont's responsibility for Molly's welfare.

Miss Edgemont.

John could still not believe that she had rejected the offer of a dowry. He felt ashamed with the way he had behaved with her at the start, and he thanked the Good Lord every day that she remained in his household. He could not do without her, and he would see to it that she felt safe and appreciated in his home.

Occasionally, John would glimpse her in his mind's eye . . . in the candlelight . . . with her hair down . . . clinging to his arm . . . and he would feel as he felt that night . . . as if that were the moment for which he had been born. It had happened. It had passed. He would try to let it go. He did not deserve her, and she certainly would not want him anyway. Regardless, she was here. In his house. Sipping tea from his cup. Stroking his dog. Shuffling his cards. It would have to be enough.

Their card games gave John the time and the opportunity to study Molly's governess—her mannerisms, her patterns, her tells. He did not do so consciously, but his senses were so heightened in her presence that he simply could not help it. John soon came to know her every expression, and he became quite adept at predicting her hand or even her next move based solely on the slight fluctuations of the face we so often

A Dangerous Man to Trust?

believe give nothing away.

After a few weeks, John was sensitive enough to notice that Miss Edgemont was on to him and his powers of prediction. She would go out of her way to frown when she had a good hand or lift her eyebrows delightedly when in fact the cards she held were quite atrocious. Occasionally, she would dart John a sly look to see if indeed he was watching. This amused John no end. And his skills of observation were put to the test once more as he eventually came to determine which of her expressions were honest reflections and which were intended deceits. It was a game within a game that they played—just the two of them—and it was by far the more fascinating.

One night, Miss Edgemont had shooed Molly off to bed, and it was just the two of them left in the drawing room to gather up the cards and slide the chairs beneath the table. Miss Edgemont crouched down on hands and knees to fetch a couple of hearts that had fallen beneath the table. Her mood was still lifted up on that evening's tide of laughter.

"I will never win another hand if you do not stop," she said, breaking the silence. John could not see her face. She was still reaching under the table.

"Stop what?" he asked, all innocence.

"You know very well of what I speak, Mr. Thornton," said Miss Edgemont rising to her feet and handing him the errant cards. She sounded as if she were scolding him, but John could see that she was holding back a smile.

"I'm afraid I have no idea, Miss Edgemont. Perhaps it is simply that your card skills are lacking. Perhaps a little more practice is what you need."

Miss Edgemont pressed her lips together to stifle a laugh, but did not truly succeed. Then her face fell in a way that John knew to mean she was hesitating over her next move. She looked down, then back up at John, opened her mouth as if to say something, then closed it again. She was gripping the skirt of her dress with one hand, slowly twisting it nervously.

"Mr. Thornton, while I have you here, I would ask you a favour."

While she has me here.

"Anything."

"Oh." She looked down at her hand gripping her dress, let it go. "I was wondering if I might take a short absence. Perhaps a fortnight. I have been invited to stay with friends, and I would dearly love to see them. It has been such a long time."

John's heart sank into his belly. *A fortnight?*

"Of course," he said, "Think nothing of it. Molly has much to occupy her while you are gone. She has her own projects, and her tutors, and I can step in occasionally. We could repurpose one of the maids as a temporary nurse. I will talk with Miss Browning about that."

"Really? It will be all right?"

"Of course." John managed a smile. "May I ask where it is you are going, whom it is you are visiting?"

"Yes. It is Lord and Lady Pemberton. Their daughter Patience is a childhood friend of mine."

"The baron? Lord Pemberton?" John had not imagined the governess would have such lofty connections. "I do believe I made His Lordship's acquaintance in London."

"Yes," said Miss Edgemont. "He was impressed with your handshake."

John could see from her face that she regretted this last statement. He did not like to think people spoke of him, but clearly they did.

"The Pembertons are at their country house now. It is not too far. Patience writes that they will send a carriage for me once a date has been arranged."

"Send a carriage?" asked John, feeling for some reason as if the whole world were dropping away from him, and he standing at the edge of a cliff gazing out into a vast expanse of nothing. "Nonsense. You shall take one of our carriages. That way I will know you have arrived safely."

Miss Edgemont looked down at her shoes so that John was unable to read the look on her face.

"Thank you, Sir. Goodnight."

John listened to her skirts swish and swoosh as she made a brisk dash for the door.

"Miss Edgemont."

"Yes." She stopped and turned, but she was still looking at her shoes. John cocked his head to one side to better see her expression, but it was no use.

"Goodnight," he said.

"Goodnight, Sir. Thank you."

Once she had left, John sat down alone at the card table. He could do without her calling him 'Sir'. He could do without her 'Thank you'. But he could not do without her. How would they survive for two whole weeks? If someone had told John that the sun would not rise for the next two weeks, he would have felt less gloomy. *Lord and Lady Pemberton indeed.* That they would invite a governess to stay said a lot for the character of their family as far as John was concerned. *Surely if Miss Edgemont was so close with their daughter, surely they would have seen to it that she was not forced into employment at all.* John thought of Miss Edgemont's vehement refusal of his father's offer of a dowry, the stubborn set of her mouth. *She is not like everyone else*, he thought.

Serafina closed the door to her bed chamber and let out a breath. That was close. It had not occurred to her until tonight that Mr. Thornton's powers of observation might prove troublesome. *That he would send her in his own carriage! To make sure she had arrived safely!* His thoughtfulness touched her in a way she felt might be too apparent on her face. She was embarrassed at the wealth of emotion he had elicited and certainly did not want him to notice how she felt. *Mr. Thornton was simply being kind. He is a gracious employer . . . who does not dismiss an employee who yells at him . . . who apologises for his mistakes . . . who offers up his own carriage to the governess . . . Oh dear.* Serafina could feel the wave of emotion building again within her. *Some time away will do me good,* she thought as she sat down at her writing desk to pen a letter to Patience.

Five

Fantastic and Unlikely

By the time Serafina arrived at the Pembertons' country home, George and little Grace had returned from their "Cornish hiatus" as Lady Pemberton had taken to calling it. The entire family was together except for Lord Pemberton who had to remain reluctantly in London on political business. Patience was practically bubbling over with joy to see her old friend, and Serafina was absorbed into the family dynamic as if no time at all had passed. Knowing that Molly's brother was with her set Serafina's mind at ease so that she could truly enjoy her time with the Pembertons.

Patience herself had not changed one bit. Her dusty blonde hair was arranged more stylishly these days, but her huge delphinium blue eyes were the same, shining with a permanent enthusiasm. She was full-figured and curvaceous in a way that Serafina was not, and she moved her body with a confidence that Serafina admired. Patience had never been a shrinking violet.

"This is what I've been working on," said Patience, excitedly pulling Serafina through a doorway and into her artist's studio. "Mother was terribly impatient sitting for me at first, but now that she's seen how complimentary the portrait is, she is quite happy to set aside an hour or so here and there."

Serafina stepped up to the canvas perched upon its wooden easel.

"Oh Patience, this is marvellous!"

Patience grinned. "Yes, it is, isn't it?"

Serafina's eyes grew wide at her friend's naked pride. She couldn't help swatting gently at Patience's arm to chide her, at least mockingly.

"Patience, you must remember that pride precedes a fall," she said smiling.

"Does it?" asked Patience, feigning ignorance. "But what if it's an accurate assessment of one's accomplishments? I should rather think that it's foolishness that precedes a fall . . . or perhaps a lack of agility."

Serafina laughed. "I've missed you," she said.

"I've missed you too."

"And this," said Serafina stepping closer to peer at Lady Pemberton's portrait, "is a magic I can barely comprehend."

"Mother has never had much to say about art," said Patience, "but now she fancies herself a—what is the French word?"

"Connoisseur?" suggested Serafina.

"Yes, a connoisseur. Mother now has opinions about art. She has reacquainted herself with the other portraits in the house and has many critiques to offer the absent artists. 'Why such a flaccid use of light?' she'll say."

"Flaccid?" repeated Serafina.

"Yes, flaccid." The two friends stifled a giggle.

"Or the other day, she said that the portrait of Great Uncle George makes him look like he has a mouth full of unchewed biscuits. Father replied that that is what Great Uncle George looked like. His mouth always seemed that way on account of him having too many teeth all crammed in together at odd angles."

"But your mother must love *this*," said Serafina gesturing at the canvas.

"Indeed," replied Patience holding in any further compliments she had for herself.

"Can I ask why you have placed a book in her hand? Your mother is a clever lady, but she is not exactly an avid reader. I would have thought flowers or a letter might be more suitable—she loves to decorate and to socialise."

"But the book is her favourite part of the whole painting," countered Patience. "She loves how learned she appears."

Serafina could see in Patience's look a certain impish mischievousness she recognised from childhood.

Patience continued. "I haven't put any writing into the book yet . . . but I was thinking . . . wouldn't it be funny—" She leaned in towards Serafina and lowered her voice, "—to put it in upside-down." Patience pulled back to gauge Serafina's reaction. Serafina was horrified and amused all at once.

"You mustn't, Patience! People will notice."

"Not if it's in Greek."

When Serafina fixed Patience with a scolding gaze, she backed down.

"Of course I won't actually do it," she conceded. "I will turn it into a book of prayers. Right side up," she added, "so that all of our descendants can know how devout the Lady Pemberton was."

"That's more like it," said Serafina smiling. "A picture of patience."

"You're too clever, do you know that?" asked Patience.

"If I did know it," said Serafina, "I would be too proud."

Her joke, Serafina was pleased to see, landed. The morning could not have been brighter.

John was miserable in a way he had not fully anticipated. He had many tasks to attend to, and his days were full, but he felt as if he were some kind of machine cranking its gears through their repetitive motions. He was doing his best to engage with Molly in his usual manner, but even she had noticed his muted demeanour.

It was a gorgeous afternoon, and John had walked with Molly and Rupert down to the lake. Rupert was splashing towards some unconcerned-looking ducks, and Molly was crouching patiently by a bucket of water and sediment she had scooped from the lake.

"It just takes a while to settle," she said. "Then we'll see what we can find." She pulled a magnifying glass from her pocket. "You will not believe how many strange tiny creatures live here in this lake. I see something new each time!"

Molly looked up at John for some sort of response, but he was staring out into the middle of the lake with a blank expression.

"I miss her too," said Molly.

When John did not respond, lost as he was in his own thoughts, she said a bit more loudly, "John!" He looked down at his sister. "I said I miss her too."

John was startled to have his thoughts spoken out loud. He felt like a turtle who has just realised he has no shell. *Was he as obvious as all that? That an eight-year-old should be able to read his heart?*

"Miss Edgemont will be back soon," he said forcing a smile.

"Ten more days," said Molly. "Plus one more evening and a night," she added to make a more accurate account.

Ten more excruciatingly tedious days, thought John. *What is wrong with me?*

John decided there and then to snap out of his misery. Or at least to put it in his pocket for the day. He could pull it out at night and dwell, but the day was for living. There was much to be done. His tenant farmers needed him to resolve their farming issues, their disputes. There were accounts to be balanced. *And Molly was here. She needed him.*

"What have we got?" he asked his sister as he crouched down next to her.

She lowered her magnifying glass and looked across at him, delight lighting up her face like a ray of sunshine.

"You have to see it to believe it," she said handing him the magnifying glass. "I'm going to make some drawings of these creatures to keep a catalogue of all the fantastic life in the lake."

"*Life in the Lake*," said John. "That can be the title of your catalogue."

"Yes!" said Molly. "*Life in the Lake: A Catalogue of the Fantastic and Unlikely* by Miss Molly Thornton."

"With a title like that, everyone will be after a copy of your book."

John looked at his sister then. He looked at her and he saw her as she was—a fantastic and unlikely creature herself hiding a virtual powder keg of potential just beneath the surface. It hurt him to consider the curbs that would be placed upon her reason and talent by a group of blustery men in top hats who would not be able to humble themselves in her presence. It was up to him now to give her the resources she needed to learn and grow so that she would be able to stand strong in the coming storm. He prayed he would be up to the task.

Serafina and Patience were seated with Grace in Lady Pemberton's very yellow drawing room, a tea set laid out in front of them. Grace was of an age with Molly, and Serafina could not help wondering what her young charge was up to at that very moment.

They will be at the lake, she thought. *Molly and Mr. Thornton and Rupert.* Serafina brought herself back to the drawing room.

"This room has been redecorated," said Serafina looking around. "It's quite cheerful—the yellow is so bright."

"Cheerful or ghastly?" asked Patience.

"Cheerful," insisted Serafina elbowing her friend playfully. "Grace, wouldn't you agree?"

"I prefer blue myself," said Grace. "Like the sea."

"How was your holiday in Cornwall?" asked Serafina.

As she spoke, George entered the room.

"Ah, tea," he said sitting beside Grace and opposite Serafina and Patience.

"I was just asking Grace about your trip."

"And I hadn't responded yet," said Grace. "What do you think I will say?" She gave her brother an accusing look.

A Dangerous Man to Trust?

George pulled his hand back through a shock of sandy hair, sending it into a tousled mess atop his handsome head. George was the eldest of the Pemberton children—a fully grown man of twenty-seven years. He was a man who chose his words carefully, and Serafina could not remember the last time he had laughed. He had not yet inherited, but he carried himself as if the entire weight of the barony, perhaps even the world, rested upon him. That, and the charge of his sisters. He took their welfare extremely seriously—perhaps too seriously.

"Not this again," he replied.

"Yes, this again," said Grace.

"It was a perfectly adequate holiday. You benefitted from the sea air and took in some exercise. What more could you ask for?"

"A bit of fun, George," said Grace peevishly. "It was like a business trip. All schedules and never-ending marches along the cliffs." Grace turned to Serafina. "It was ever-so-windy. I thought I might be carried away like a handkerchief."

"Drowning yourself in the sea would not have been fun," said George pouring his own tea when he saw that Patience would not.

"Uhh!" grunted Grace, throwing up her hands and rolling her eyes to the ceiling. "I just wanted to paddle, to look for shells and rocks."

"You can't swim," replied George with finality. "I could never have forgiven myself if something had happened."

"But I wanted to talk to the fishermen. They have stories to tell," said Grace.

"You would not have understood them," said George sipping his tea. "They're Cornish."

"That would be part of the fun, George—don't you see?"

Fantastic and Unlikely

George looked out over the rim of his cup towards Serafina as if noticing her for the first time. She had known him since childhood, and they were all familiar enough to use each other's Christian names.

"Serafina, you look different," said George.

"I do?"

"Mm."

Patience looked quizzically from George to Serafina and back to George again as she screwed up her brow. George continued to sip his tea in silence darting sideways glances at his little sister who was now sitting with her arms crossed in what could only be described as a huff.

Lady Pemberton entered the room in a rush with a maid following close behind.

"Patience and Serafina, fetch your bonnets and gloves. I need you to accompany me to the dressmaker's."

Serafina shot a questioning look at her friend who shrugged her shoulders.

"We'd better fetch our bonnets," said Patience when Lady Pemberton had left.

Serafina followed Patience out the door and down the hall, scurrying to catch up with her as her friend charged on ahead. When she finally did catch up with Patience, she reached for her arm.

"What's going on? Why do we need to go to the dressmaker's?"

Patience let out a heavy sigh.

"Please don't be upset, Serafina. I told her you wouldn't like it, but you know how Mother is." Serafina waited for Patience to continue. "She's only gone and arranged to host a ball while you're here."

A Dangerous Man to Trust?

"What?"

"She asked me not to mention it. She thought you might not come if you knew. And I desperately wanted you to come."

"Well she was right!" said Serafina.

"But you're here now," said Patience unnecessarily.

"Yes I am."

"So you'll be needing a dress."

"There can't possibly be enough time to have a dress completed."

"But this is Mother we're talking about," said Patience apologetically. "She has already had some dresses sewn—you just need to come for a fitting so that alterations can be made."

"Dresses!? Plural?"

"Bonnets!" said Patience brightly, giving Serafina a kiss on the cheek. "Come now." She turned and took off once more down the hallway.

"But I'm a governess, Patience. I can't come to the baroness's ball. It would not be seemly," pleaded Serafina as she resumed her chase after Patience.

"Mother says that while you are staying with us, you are not a governess, simply a lady fallen on hard times. You are in our care, she says. And anyway, you know very well that governesses attend balls all the time. How else are they to instruct their charges about what to expect and how to comport themselves?"

Serafina looked down at the dress she was wearing. It was one of her best, but certainly a bit dour. She did not have anything remotely appropriate to wear to a ball. Now that she was here, she certainly could not be so rude as to refuse to attend. Lady Agnes Pemberton was a vexing and meddlesome woman. *Dresses, indeed!* Serafina wanted to be angry, but when she arrived at the waiting carriage with her bonnet tied uncomfortably under her chin, Lady Pemberton glided up to her side and took her hand giving it a gentle squeeze the way a mother does when she wants to show you she is there for you.

"It will be fun, Serafina."

"You are too kind, Lady Pemberton," said Serafina, and she meant it.

Despite Lady Pemberton's machinations with the ball and the dresses, Serafina had to admit that her first week at the Pembertons' was absolutely lovely. She did miss Molly, and certainly had the occasional thought for Mr. Thornton (how could she not?), but she was quite happy to take the time to be with her friends and to sit still in the midst of their loving and lively home. Mealtimes were especially amusing as both George and Grace who were usually otherwise engaged during the day would join Lady Pemberton, Patience, and Serafina for food and conversation and the occasional argument (Grace was still smarting from the "abuse" she'd suffered on holiday with George).

Serafina spent at least part of each morning with Patience in her art studio which was a south-facing room on the second floor. Sunlight streamed in to highlight tiny motes of dust that hung suspended in the air like little stars. Serafina grew to like the smell of turpentine and linseed oil that permeated the room. Patience said it smelled to her like promises and potential: "There's always something surprising just waiting to appear upon the canvas!"

A Dangerous Man to Trust?

Patience had insisted on sketching Serafina for a portrait.

"I don't think I need a portrait," said Serafina. "It seems a bit too grand."

"But *I* need a portrait of you," said Patience, "to talk to when you're not here." This made Serafina smile. She could absolutely imagine Patience speaking quite animatedly to her portrait, pausing to listen for a response, then striking up some sort of argument with the silent canvas.

Each morning, once Serafina had finished sitting for Patience, she would leave her friend to continue her work while she took a turn around the grounds or settled into a book in the library. She was starting to feel as if she'd struck up a comfortable routine. This morning was exceptionally beautiful—a crisp blue sky and a warm breeze invited Serafina out into the garden. She stepped onto the grass, turned her face up to the sky, and inhaled deeply.

"Care for some company?"

George had appeared behind her, standing just outside the door.

"I don't usually see you at this time of day," said Serafina.

"I have a free morning," said George. "It rarely happens."

"You're most welcome to join me," said Serafina.

George trotted down the steps from the door and out onto the lawn: "I need to escape Mother," he said. "Her mind has turned to thoughts of marriage, and she will not let the subject drop."

Serafina nodded knowingly.

"Well, now you know how we ladies feel as we approach a certain age. It seems sometimes it is the only topic of conversation to which we must be subjected."

"It's different for you," said George as he placed her hand

comfortably in the crook of his arm and led her down a hedgerow of vibrant blue and pink hydrangeas.

"In what way?" asked Serafina turning to look up into his grey eyes.

George ran a hand through his hair leaving it quite disheveled.

"Because for you it is necessary—it is security and safety."

"There are plenty of ladies who are unsafe within their marriages," countered Serafina.

George winced but held his ground: "And that is why you must be careful in your choice."

He dropped to one knee and plucked a bright white daisy at Serafina's feet. Rising, he handed it to her.

"You used to bring me daisies when we were small," said Serafina. "Patience would be quite upset when you had none for her."

"Patience was always upset about something," said George.

"But seriously, George," said Serafina bringing the conversation back to marriage. She hated the subject, so she did not really understand why she was pursuing it. "I might be very careful in my choice of husband but still find that once we are married, he is a different person. Gentlemen wear many masks, and their courting mask I believe to be their most deceptive."

George appeared to ponder this.

"You're quite wise, Serafina." He stopped walking, turned to her. "I will not press you further. Just know that whatever happens, you will always have a place here with us."

"I am truly grateful for that, George. But Patience will marry. So will Grace. It would just be you and me. And your future wife"—Serafina laughed. "I doubt she would like the arrangement very much!"

"The invitation stands," said George giving nothing away in his expression.

"Well, thank you," said Serafina trying to match George's lack of amusement, "But I hope to make my own way."

They walked on for a time commenting on the flowers, the garden's new arrangement at Lady Pemberton's instruction.

"You have not yet spoken to us of your new employer Mr. Thornton," said George casually. "He treats you well?"

"He is very"—Serafina searched for the word—"forthright and expects the same of others. Which is nice because I do not have to worry about saying or doing the wrong thing. And he is very good with Molly." Her face lit up. "Mr. Thornton actually taught her to play cards! Can you believe it? She was over the moon. Now we play most evenings after supper—it's most enjoyable."

"The three of you?" asked George, casual as ever.

"Yes," she said smiling to herself.

Then, "What do you know about this Mr. Thornton, Serafina?"

"Enough," she said.

"What is enough?" asked George.

"He is attentive and gentle with Molly. He is also a man who can admit when he is wrong."

"Really?"

"Perhaps you will not believe this, but Mr. Thornton actually got down on one knee and apologised to Molly and myself after I had scolded him for taking off to London without so much as a goodbye. Molly had been absolutely devastated."

George continued to lead Serafina about the garden. A bee nuzzled its way into an orange honeysuckle trumpet. There was a faint scent of roses in the air.

"You scolded Mr. Thornton?" asked George evenly.

"Only a little," said Serafina. She stopped and turned to George. "Do you know something about Mr. Thornton that I don't?" she asked.

George looked at her in his serious way. "People who knew him before his disappearance from society have things to say." George paused, then said, "He's a man with a reputation, Serafina." She stared at George until he continued. "A reputation with women."

"I see," said Serafina in an emotionless tone.

"I worry that you may not be safe—that he might take liberties."

Serafina could not quite square this fear with the Mr. Thornton she knew. She resumed her amble through the garden with George.

"I have no knowledge of Mr. Thornton from before," she said. "I only know the man as he is now, and I do believe I have the measure of him."

"Is that so?" George did not sound convinced.

"A governess is not exactly chaperoned," said Serafina.

"No," said George solemnly.

"Mr. Thornton has had many opportunities to behave in an ungentlemanly manner," she added.

At this, George raised an eyebrow.

"Yet he has never, not once, made me feel in any way unsafe, George. He does not look at me like that."

George placed an arm around Serafina's shoulder and pulled her in toward him and out of the path of an unruly rose bush.

"I should still like to meet him," he said.

Serafina said nothing. She preferred to keep Mr. Thornton

to herself and was not entirely sure how he would come across in company.

They continued their stroll across the greater lawn towards the willows that drooped their lacy arms down to the ground. From a window on the second floor of the house, Patience was watching them. She stroked a dry paintbrush along one cheek and furrowed her pretty brow.

John had received what he could only surmise was a last-minute invitation to the Pemberton Ball. *A ball?! And Miss Edgemont*, he could only presume, *would be in attendance*. His heart began to pick up its pace. There would be any number of eligible suitors at a ball of this size. Miss Edgemont had said she would not marry, but perhaps she would change her mind. And leave him. And leave Molly. A permanent absence. An empty life rolled out like a carpet in front of him. He knew he deserved nothing more.

He would have to attend the ball. Etiquette demanded it. And he needed to see Miss Edgemont. Two weeks was simply too long. He would not stand in the way of her happiness should she find it, but he would see her, and it would have to be enough.

The corset Lady Pemberton had chosen for Serafina was from a bygone age! So much stiffer than the stays to which she was accustomed. And it had been pulled tighter as well!

"I daresay you're going to have to loosen this for me,

Patience," said Serafina when Lady Pemberton had left the room.

"I don't let Mother in the room when I'm getting dressed, or she'll have poor Delphi here pull my breasts all the way up to my chin!" Patience gave Delphi, the maid, a knowing look, and the girls fell to laughing.

"Oh Patience, I can't even laugh with it so tight—please release me," said Serafina turning around.

Dressing up, despite all its discomforts, was fun, thought Serafina. Lady Pemberton had been right on that count. She gazed back at herself from the looking glass. Delphi was a deft hand at styling a lady's hair in the most fashionable manner. Serafina's locks were braided and twisted about in a complicated pattern and decorated with bright pearls that looked as if they'd fallen against her hair like drops of rain. She was wearing a silver-blue evening dress and had borrowed a pair of silver slippers from Patience. The gloves she could have done without, but it was a ball after all. Serafina had told Patience to go on ahead without her, pretending that she had a few more things to do to get ready.

Once Serafina felt enough guests would have arrived so that she might go unnoticed, she slipped furtively into the noisy ballroom. A quartet was playing from the balcony, and the room spun with the elegance of Lady Pemberton's careful planning. Several couples were already dancing, and Serafina, unable to see Patience, found herself feeling quite alone and not a little as if she didn't belong. She tried to make herself inconspicuous, but that was quite impossible. Of all the ladies present, she was (while not the most beautiful) certainly the most startling to look upon. One pair of eyes fell upon her and then another. Serafina darted a searching look around the room noting all the exits. What would she say if a gentleman asked her to dance? Could she say no without seeming rude?

I do not have to dance if I do not want to dance, she told herself firmly.

"Miss Serafina Edgemont!" It was a familiar voice attached to a familiar young lady whose company Serafina could have done without. "What are *you* doing here?"

Serafina looked up to see the tall and sleek Sophia Crampton cutting her way across the room like a razor, a few of her acolytes in tow. While Sophia was a beauty, she seemed to Serafina to be composed almost entirely of sharp edges—cheekbones, eyebrows, shoulders, and not least, her tongue. Serafina remembered her well despite the two intervening years. Some people leave a mark, and Sophia was one of those people.

"I heard you had found some sort of gainful employment," offered up Sophia before Serafina had a chance to answer. "Perhaps she is here to polish the silver," she added, turning her head in order to draw her companions into the exchange. The ladies who had accompanied her let out a soft titter. Serafina smiled politely.

"You are as courteous as ever, Miss Crampton."

"But really," pressed Sophia with a sneer, "What are you doing at the baroness's ball?"

"She's here to dance with me," said a gruff voice.

All heads turned to see George Pemberton standing very tall and dapper in his formal black jacket. He did not even glance at Sophia Crampton but kept his grey eyes fixed on Serafina.

"May I have this dance, Miss Edgemont?" he asked with a slight bow, offering up his open palm.

"Of . . . of course," said Serafina stepping between the gawking ladies and sliding her gloved hand into his.

George placed her hand in the crook of his arm where she rested it lightly as he led her out onto the dance floor.

"It was very kind of you to save me from the dragon, George, but I must warn you," said Serafina leaning in towards him, "I have not danced in quite some time."

And this corset is still a pinch too tight, she thought to herself. She pressed one hand to her belly and made an effort to take a deep and deliberate breath.

"It will come back to you," George assured her in his usual serious manner. "I can count the steps if you like."

In the end, it did come back to her—a kind of memory that's kept stored in the limbs just waiting for a piece of music to set it free. George did not even need to count. As they danced, Serafina felt quite exposed. People were certainly watching the baron's son, so they were certainly watching her as well, and she didn't like the feeling at all. George himself would not take his eyes from hers. It was as if he were searching for something there.

As the tempo slowed and they pressed in closer to each other, George spoke quietly into Serafina's ear: "You look different, and I think I know why. May I ask, are you happy?"

Serafina was so startled by the question that she pulled away to look into his face, halting the dance altogether. The two of them stood still as the other dancers swirled around them in a blur of colour.

"Am I happy?"

"Yes," said George solemnly. "Are you happy?"

"I . . . I . . . haven't thought about it."

Serafina returned in her mind to Bosworth Manor, to her

A Dangerous Man to Trust?

life there with Molly . . . and now Mr. Thornton. Something had shifted within her. That ever-present sense of grief had all but dissipated. She had been carrying it for so long. In a way, she had lost both her parents to some degree long before their untimely deaths. It was a feeling of emptiness she had been holding inside herself for so many years. And now what was different? *That hollow space has been filled up*, she thought.

"George," said Serafina with a wondering smile, "it's possible you are right."

"I'm always right," said George in the same confident tone he used when they had been children and there was some disagreement over a game. "Take my hand, Serafina. People are watching. We should finish the dance."

Serafina lifted her hand to meet his, and he circled his free hand behind her waist to pull her in closer. If Serafina had been standing with Sophia Crampton and her friends, she would have heard a small collective gasp as the baron's son drew the governess tightly in.

"Do you remember when we used to play at pirates?" Serafina asked George as they stepped together in time to the music.

"How could I forget?"

"You were always so deathly serious about saving us from their clutches."

"And Patience would get impatient and decide that she was no longer a captive but a pirate after all."

It was a humorous memory, but George didn't smile. Serafina had not seen him smile in years.

"You would engage her in combat to save me from a terrible fate," added Serafina.

"I recall," said George, "that Patience's favourite weapon was a very long paintbrush wielded as a sword."

"Indeed," said Serafina. "I believe that is how she views her paintbrushes even now."

George did not smile at the joke, but his eyes softened as the music came to a sad end. He bowed, and Serafina dipped down into a slight curtsy.

Six

Corsets and Compromise

John had dithered at the last minute over whether to go to the Pemberton Ball at all, and so he had arrived late. Descending from his carriage, he strode with some haste across the gravel drive and took the steps two at a time up to the front door of the Pembertons' very large country home. Once he entered the ballroom, he scanned the crowd for Miss Edgemont, finally resting his eyes upon her familiar form.

She was dancing! In a blue dress! With Mr. Pemberton of all people!

John had not been formally introduced, but he had seen the baron's son at a function or two in London. The man was a few years younger than himself. An extraordinarily dashing fellow if a bit grim in his deportment.

John watched as Miss Edgemont cut short her dancing to look into Mr. Pemberton's face, to speak with him on some matter. She smiled, a smile of genuine happiness. John's heart

Corsets and Compromise

gave a lurch as Mr. Pemberton tugged Miss Edgemont quite firmly towards him to continue the dance. They were dancing and talking, always talking!

The son of a baron. Of course, she deserves nothing less, thought John. *What kind of man is he though?* John wondered. He would make it his business to find out.

"Mr Thornton! I'm so delighted you were able to come!" It was Lady Pemberton, followed closely by a clutch of older ladies and their daughters. "If my husband were here, he could introduce us, but as it stands, we will have to make do on our own."

"Lady Pemberton, I presume," said John in a low rumble that set the other ladies into a shimmer of sighs. John took Lady Pemberton's hand with a small bow.

"You presume correctly! It is so good to finally meet you properly. May I introduce Lady Crampton and her daughter Miss Sophia Crampton."

John looked over to see a middle-aged woman who for some reason resembled a farmer's goose pressing her surprisingly beautiful and swan-like daughter forward. The young lady curtsied. John knew he would be trapped here for some time as the other ladies pressed in. He cast his gaze out across the ballroom, but Miss Edgemont had disappeared.

"A pleasure to make your acquaintance," he said, politely but disingenuously acknowledging both goose and swan alike.

Serafina tried to tuck herself out of sight by one of the refreshment tables, but she was soon engaged in pleasantries with a number of young gentlemen who had seen her dancing with Mr. George Pemberton. The fact that the baron's son had shown such interest in her appeared to make her all the more enticing.

Oh George, you saved me from the dragon but somehow managed to throw me to the wolves, thought Serafina. *Patience, where are you?*

The gentlemen were most attentive. Would she like a drink? What did she think of the quartet? Was her dance card full? Serafina politely answered questions and fended off further dancing while darting panicked glances around the ballroom in an effort to locate Patience.

And that's when she saw him. Mr. Theodore Cross was heading in her direction.

No, she thought. *I can't.* Her breathing was shallow, and she was starting to feel more than a little overwhelmed.

"If you will excuse me, gentlemen . . ."

Serafina spun around and made a brisk dash for the nearest exit.

Theodore Cross was a man from her past—a man Serafina knew would not take no for an answer. A few years back, he had pursued her doggedly for months, taking every polite nod or concession from her to mean that she was in love with him, that they were in fact courting! Optimism was one thing, but this had been something else entirely. When Serafina had made it clear in no uncertain terms that they were not courting, that she would not consider marrying him, he had thought he might bully her into it! The mask of cordiality had dropped, and Serafina had found Mr. Cross to be not a gentleman at all but rather a viper in a jacket just waiting for a chance to strike. When her parents had died, he had even interrupted her mourning to reassert his intentions, to propose once again.

"But you have nothing!" he had yelled at her when she inevitably turned him down. "You are ruined without a husband! Don't you see? Do you think the Pembertons will put up with your nonsense for long?"

She had stared at him silently until he left, red frustration flooding his face.

Serafina, having left the ballroom, hurried down the hall, turned a corner, and sank herself back into a darkened alcove that hosted a large potted plant, a window, and a window seat. She pressed a hand to her belly. Her corset was still just a pinch too tight, and she was feeling out of breath.

I'll just rest here a minute, catch my breath, and then I will head up to my room, she thought. *I can send a maid to tell Patience where I am in case she is wondering.* Serafina sat down on the window seat with a little sigh.

"There you are!" It was Theodore Cross, his large frame blocking her exit from the alcove. "It seems you are quite the popular lady this evening, Serafina."

"Hello, Mr. Cross." Serafina stood up a little unsteadily.

"Mr. Cross is so formal," he said stepping closer. "Theodore will be fine."

"If you will please excuse me, Mr. Cross. I'm feeling unwell."

Serafina made an attempt to squeeze past him, but Mr. Cross moved his body against hers, pressing her back to the wall. She could smell spirits on his breath and tobacco on his jacket. His body was hard against hers as he shifted one thigh between her legs.

A Dangerous Man to Trust?

"Mr. Cross!" said Serafina alarmed.

"What will Mr. Pemberton think if he were to find us here together . . . alone . . . in the dark . . . standing as we are now?" asked Mr. Cross.

"Mr. Pemberton?" Serafina was quite confused.

"He would never marry you, Serafina. And those other gentlemen—they are only interested in you because Mr. Pemberton has graced you with his attention. I am the only one who truly cares for you. Can you not see that?"

"Mr. Cross, let me go!" Serafina raised a free hand to push him from her, but he caught her wrist and squeezed hard. "You're hurting me!" The smell of him and the weight as he pressed in on her was making her feel quite faint.

Just as Serafina was deciding that it might be time to start screaming, Mr. Cross let out an odd grunt as he released her wrist. He staggered back from her, and she realised that there was someone behind him. As Mr. Cross stumbled sideways, she could see that another man had twisted and pinned one of his arms behind his back. As the figure slammed Mr. Cross face first into the opposite wall of the hallway beyond the alcove, she caught sight of his mask in the flickering light. It was Mr. Thornton!

Serafina watched in stunned silence as Mr. Thornton loosened his grip on Mr. Cross, allowing him to regain his footing only to ram him once more against the wall with a sickening crunch. Mr. Thornton's voice was gravel when he spoke.

"If you so much as *touch*—no, if you so much as *look* at Miss Edgemont again, I will rip you apart."

He twisted Mr. Cross' arm up at an odd angle until the man cried out. Mr. Thornton leaned in close behind him.

"Do you hear me?"

Mr. Cross let out a sound that might have been a 'yes'.

"I said, do you hear me?"

"Yes," said Mr. Cross more audibly.

"Good."

Mr. Thornton released Mr. Cross who turned instinctively to face his attacker. His nose was slanted at an odd angle, and there was blood streaming down towards his chin. Mr. Thornton very swiftly planted a large palm in the centre of Mr. Cross's chest and forced him up against the wall once more. With his free hand, Mr. Thornton removed his mask, and pressed his face in close.

"I will rip you apart. That is a promise," he said quietly. "Leave now. I never want to see you again."

He pressed Mr. Cross into the wall until the man was gasping for breath, then released him and stood back. Mr. Cross looked from Mr. Thornton to Serafina who was staring at Mr. Thornton's bare face.

"You want her for yourself!" he said as he scrambled away along the wall of the hallway. When Mr. Thornton said nothing, Mr. Cross, now some distance from him, threw back, "Or have you already had her?"

Serafina's vision started to blur, and she felt her legs begin to give way. Mr. Thornton lunged towards Mr. Cross with a growl, but Serafina caught his hand. When Mr. Thornton turned towards her, the world seemed to fall away. Her vision went dark, and the last thing she heard was Mr. Thornton swearing gently as he caught her falling body in his arms.

A Dangerous Man to Trust?

While engaging in forced pleasantries with the ladies who had congregated about him, John caught a flash of silver-blue out of the corner of his eye. He looked over to see Miss Edgemont practically fleeing the ballroom. A look of sheer panic had spread across her face.

"Were you in Dorset long?" asked Lady Crampton.

John diverted his attention back to the tedious conversation at hand.

"I, ah, yes. I was there for eight weeks, actually."

His eyes flicked up to see a dark blue tailored jacket streak towards the door. There was something familiar about that jacket, that mop of blonde hair.

"Dorset certainly has its charms, but I never visited for quite so long," remarked Lady Crampton.

It dawned on John then: *It was Theodore Cross! Leaving after Miss Edgemont!* John's fingers curled in towards his palms. His entire body went stiff.

"Ladies, I beg your forgiveness, but I must take my leave. There is a matter to which I must attend."

By the time John had squeezed his way through the crowd and out into the hall, there was no one to be found. He stood for a moment wondering in which direction he should search. And then he heard a faint voice coming from some distance around the corner: "There you are!" John ran towards the grating sound of that voice. He had never felt so panicked in all his life. When he saw them, he slowed his step, holding his anger close and tight. Mr. Cross had Miss Edgemont up against the wall. John saw him grab her wrist as she tried to push him away.

"You're hurting me!" she cried.

That was it. John saw red. He took two strides forward and

Corsets and Compromise

grabbed Mr. Cross by the arm twisting it back at a satisfyingly unnatural angle. It wasn't enough. John had unleashed a fury of which he had not known himself capable, and he struggled to contain himself lest he actually kill the man right there in Lord Pemberton's hallway.

By the time Miss Edgemont had collapsed into his arms, John could not quite remember what he had said or even what he had done. All he knew was that Theodore Cross had left alive, and this meant that he did not have to add 'murderer' to his list of many failings. John carried Miss Edgemont to the window seat, but it was not long enough to lay her down, so he lifted her legs to the seat and then sat down himself, cradling her head and shoulders against him at an angle.

"Miss Edgemont," he whispered. Then louder, "Miss Edgemont." When she did not respond, he placed a hot hand to her cool cheek. "Serafina, wake up."

She opened her beautiful dark eyes, and John let out a breath he did not realise he had been holding.

"You fainted, Miss Edgemont. Are you all right?"

"Oh . . . my vision is . . ."

She fainted once more. When John brought her around the second time, she gave him a weak smile.

"I do believe," she said, clearly struggling to string her words together, "it's my corset . . . It's too tight . . . I can't breathe properly."

"I'll fetch a maid," said John.

"No!"

"Can you walk to your room?" he asked.

"I don't think so. The room is still spinning."

"Well then I shall fetch a maid to help you with your—"

"No, Mr. Thornton." Miss Edgemont gripped his arm

taking time to find the breath for the words she needed to speak. "How will it look? Me alone in this dark corner? And you the only person who knows where I am? What will the Pembertons think? You cannot call anyone!"

"Then what would you have me do?" he asked.

"Well, I can't reach it myself, but it is fairly simple." Miss Edgemont shifted herself out of his arms and up to seated, wobbling a little. She had to quickly place a hand down to prevent herself from falling over. John said nothing when her hand landed on his thigh. He certainly could not have anticipated that the evening would end up like this.

"Are you saying you'd like me to loosen your corset?" he asked quite astonished.

His mind was still lingering on her hand which in her state she had not realised was quite so familiarly placed. She gave him a pained expression.

"I'm already compromised. Help me to breathe," she pleaded. "I trust you will not take any liberties, Mr. Thornton. I know you well enough."

At the word 'trust' John felt his heart expand to fill his chest until he thought it might burst. It was an exquisitely painful sensation.

"Shift yourself, then. Turn around," he said matter-of-factly.

Miss Edgemont obeyed without the slightest hesitation. In her scuffle with Mr. Cross a few strands of hair had come loose at the back. John brushed them to her shoulder so that he might access the buttons at the back of her dress. As his fingers slid against the nape of her neck, she let out a soft, "Oh," and John could feel the word vibrate through her skin and into his hand. He closed his eyes to steady himself. His heart was beating fast.

Corsets and Compromise

Control, he thought. *Control yourself lest your body betray you and you betray her trust.*

"The laces tie at the top so it should be easy to reach," said Miss Edgemont, her head dropping forward as if it were too much effort to keep it aloft.

"I know how to undo a corset," said John firmly.

"Oh."

That word again. She would undo *him* if he was not careful. John worked quickly, trying his best not to make contact with her skin which was almost impossible.

"How's this? Better?" he asked.

"Much better."

John retied the laces, and buttoned up the top two buttons at the back of her dress. They were both still perched on the window seat. Miss Edgemont turned around to face him and inhaled deeply.

"Breathing is surprisingly wonderful, isn't it?" she said as if he hadn't just had his hands down the back of her dress.

She leaned down and picked up his mask from the floor, handed it to him.

"I should like to go home if that is all right with you, Mr. Thornton."

"What? Now? But you have four days left to your visit."

"It's too exhausting being away. From Molly," she added.

"I should not imagine that leaving is a wise idea at this point, Miss Edgemont. What will Mr. Pemberton think?"

"Mr. Pemberton?" She looked confused. "You mean George? What does it matter what he thinks?"

John could not believe he was about to say this, but he truly cared for her. He had her best interests at heart, and her best interests were not with someone like him.

A Dangerous Man to Trust?

"Mr. Pemberton will think you are uninterested. Miss Edgemont, I know you profess not to want to marry, but a baron's son? If you know him to be a good man, surely this would be a happy outcome for you."

Miss Edgemont said nothing. Just stared into John's unmasked face. He could tell from her expression that she was perturbed, but he pressed on. He wanted to make sure she had all her options on the table.

"You could still accept my father's gift of a dowry," John added.

Miss Edgemont's eyes went wide. She opened her mouth and then closed it again. Finally, she spoke.

"Mr. Thornton, you are mistaken. I do not wish to marry George, nor he me, dowry or no."

"You use his Christian name." John felt not a little exasperated. "Clearly you are close!"

"We are childhood friends!"

"Are you not concerned for your future?" John's voice was increasing in volume. It carried an emotional edge he wished it did not.

"Are you trying to get rid of me?" she asked, flushing hot pink across her cheeks.

"Get rid of you?!"

"Yes. Are you trying to dismiss me? Have I displeased you in some way? You would like to see me married off and out of your house, out of Molly's life?"

John was taken aback.

"Nothing would pain me more," he said quite honestly.

"Then why? Why are you saying all these things?" Miss Edgemont seemed quite agitated.

"I only thought—"

"If you wish to dismiss me, Mr. Thornton, then dismiss me."
Good God, she was a stubborn woman.

"I shall never dismiss you," said John in an unnaturally quiet voice.

Miss Edgemont had not expected his reply. "Oh. Well. I shall never willingly leave . . . Molly," she said with surprising finality.

"Fine," said John in a flippant tone that disguised the thankful prayer he was reciting internally.

"Fine," said Miss Edgemont looking a little embarrassed. She looked down at her lap, then raised her eyes back to his. Her face was an open book, and her words John could see were entirely forthright: "I should like to go home now, but George aside, the Pembertons might feel insulted. They have been so kind to me."

"You care for them."

"Very much," said Serafina.

"But you've had a shock, Miss Edgemont. It's understandable that you would want to return—"

"—home, that I would want to return home."

That she felt this way about his house was almost too much for John. The evening had been emotionally excessive.

"Perhaps instead of rushing back with me tonight, I could send a carriage for you in the morning. We could say that Molly is having a hard time without you."

"Is she?"

"It's not a lie," said John.

"I don't feel safe here anymore," she confided.

"That's understandable. If it makes you feel better, I will stay late. To the very end of the night."

"You would do that?"

"Of course."

Seven

Intentions

After taking some time to recover, Serafina and Mr. Thornton reentered the ballroom separately, making sure to remain apart.

There was Patience! She was hiding in a corner behind a large arrangement of pink and white flowers.

"Patience," said Serafina, "where have you been?"

Patience gave her a desperate look.

"You took so long to come down to the ball, Serafina. Mother had a host of suitors lined up for my dance card. After dancing with the first two, I'd had quite enough, so I snuck out. . . and did some painting," she added guiltily.

"Is something the matter, Serafina? You look very pale."

"I'm not feeling entirely well to be honest. Would your mother think it very rude of me if I retreated to my room?"

"Not at all," said Patience. "You attended the ball—what more can she ask of you? I hear that you even danced with

George."

It was a statement, but Serafina could feel the question in it.

"George was kind enough to save me from Sophia Crampton," she explained.

"It caused quite a fuss," remarked Patience with an odd look.

"There was nothing to it," Serafina assured her friend.

"Really?"

"Yes. George was merely being chivalrous."

"I had sort of hoped there might be something to it," confided Patience leaning her head towards Serafina's in a friendly manner. "We could be sisters one day."

Serafina laughed. "We're already sisters."

"Then why will you not come to live with us?" asked Patience in a petulant tone. "You're here now. So stay! Mother would be ever-so-pleased."

"You know I can't, Patience. I have to do things my way."

"With Mr. Thornton?"

"I suppose."

"Here he is," said Patience as she shifted her gaze out past Serafina.

Serafina looked behind her to see Mr. Thornton approach them. His mask was in place, and his blue eyes were cool in the warm candlelit ballroom.

"Miss Edgemont," he nodded. "And this must be your good friend."

"Miss Patience Pemberton," said Serafina introducing the two of them formally.

"Your mother was kind enough to invite me tonight," offered Mr. Thornton to Patience.

"It's our pleasure to have you here."

"May I ask, are you an artist, Miss Pemberton?"

Intentions

Patience lit up at the question. "Serafina has told you?"

"No, she hasn't," he said with a snarl of a smile. "It's just that you have some paint on your hands and a tiny spot of yellow on your ear."

"He's very observant, isn't he?" said Patience, lifting a hand to one ear and then the other.

"Miss Edgemont," said Mr. Thornton, as if to further prove Patience's point, "You look as if you need a rest."

"I thought so too," said Patience. "She was just about to head to her room. I shall escort her." She put her arm around Serafina who was looking paler by the minute.

"I'm sorry, Patience."

"Nonsense. This gives me a reason to leave early as well," said Patience with an encouraging smile.

"You'll stay with Miss Edgemont then?" asked Mr. Thornton, concern lacing the rumble of his voice. Patience looked up at him in surprise.

"I'll not leave her side," she assured him.

"I shall be here in the ballroom if you need me," said Mr. Thornton.

Patience could not tell if he was speaking to her or to Serafina. She searched the room and locked eyes with George who immediately made his way over.

"George, if mother asks, you can tell her that I've accompanied Serafina to her room. She is feeling unwell."

Serafina gave George a weak smile. He nodded.

"This is Mr. Thornton," added Patience as an afterthought. "Mr. Thornton, my brother."

The gentlemen shook hands as Patience and Serafina skirted the side of the room to the nearest exit.

Once Patience had Serafina safely in her bed chamber, she

removed her shoes, her dress, and her corset, wrapped her up in a warm robe and put her to bed. Patience lay down beside her.

"Shall I have George call a physician?"

"No, no," replied Serafina. "I'll be fine. The corset was just a bit tight."

"Is that all?" asked Patience suspiciously.

Serafina rolled over to face her friend. She could feel tears pricking at her eyes.

"There was an incident with Mr. Cross in the back hall," she said quietly.

"Who? Theodore Cross? Was he even invited? Serafina, what happened?! Are you all right?"

"Don't tell your mother."

"I won't tell a soul," said Patience placing a hand to her friend's shoulder.

Serafina related the events of her evening allowing herself to release the tension that was gripping her stomach, her heart. She permitted herself to cry for the first time that night as Patience held her. While she did mention that Mr. Thornton had seen off Mr. Cross, she did not mention quite how physical the altercation had been, nor the loosening of her corset, nor their conversation afterwards. In fact, she left out quite a few facts that she preferred to hold close to her heart. When she had finished, Patience continued to hold her as they lay together in the bed.

That night, Serafina dreamed that Mr. Thornton was drowning in the middle of the lake at Bosworth Manor. Rupert was barking madly at the shoreline, and the sky was a strange sickly orange like the glow of a distant fire. Picking up her skirts, she raced across the lawn to the lake, her heart

Intentions

flailing wildly inside the cage of her chest. She waded in and swam, reaching Mr. Thornton as he sank beneath the surface. She caught his hand just as she'd done the night before when he had lunged towards Mr. Cross. He gripped her tightly as she pulled him up. When his head broke the surface, he was not wearing his mask.

His blue eyes opened, and he said, "I shall never dismiss you, Miss Edgemont."

"And I shall never leave," she said as she pulled him towards the shore.

When Serafina awoke, Patience was already dressed in a soft sage green frock and sitting on the edge of her bed.

"You will never guess who is downstairs and eating breakfast with Mother," she said brightly. "Mr. Thornton!"

Serafina was still feeling groggy and weighed down with the events of the previous night.

"He is?"

"I spoke to George, and he told me Mr. Thornton was reluctant to leave until he was quite sure you had recovered. He remained so late that Mother invited him to stay the night." Patience leaned back to study Serafina's face in the light that was streaming in through the window. "How are you feeling this morning?"

"Much better, thank you."

"Your colour has returned."

When Serafina made no move to rise out of bed, Patience asked, "Are you not going to join us at breakfast?"

"With Mr. Thornton? I think not."

"What do you mean by that?"

"It will be too strange, Patience. I've never eaten with him before. I'm his employee."

"You are *not* a servant, Serafina."

"But I *am* in his employ."

"That's not the way he's been talking. He speaks of you as if you were a guest in his care. He and Mother are of one mind in that regard."

"I thought Lady Pemberton had declared him to be a dangerous character, not to be trusted," countered Serafina as she sent her legs over the side of the bed and sat up.

"She appears to have changed her mind," said Patience a little too gleefully. "Mr. Thornton has been charming her all morning, and they have found some common ground."

"What would that be?" asked Serafina.

Patience reached out a hand to smooth Serafina's hair down the length of her back.

"They both agree that you are possibly the most stubborn young lady in all of England," she said with a laugh.

"It sounds like you've been enjoying yourself this morning," said Serafina narrowing her eyes.

"Oh, very much! I don't know what has come over your Mr. Thornton. He was such a solemn presence in London—not rude, but certainly no conversationalist. Come, Serafina, get dressed. You must join us, if only to show Mr. Thornton and Mother that you have recovered."

"Very well."

Serafina sighed as Patience helped her into one of the new garments Lady Pemberton had acquired for her. It was a simple white muslin dress with tiny yellow embroidered daisies sprinkled across the skirt.

Intentions

"A morning dress for the morning," said Patience cheerfully. "Oh Serafina, you look dazzling in white. You should wear it more often."

"It's a beautiful dress and so kind of your mother, but white always seems to me to be asking for trouble. No one is ever carefree in a white dress. Grass or mud or ink—one has to be on guard at all times."

Patience chuckled. "It's just a dress, Serafina."

"Hm."

"Come. They've probably finished eating by now."

By the time Serafina and Patience entered the bright morning room where the family took breakfast among a virtual garden of potted plants, it looked as if Patience was right. The remnants of a rather marvellous meal lay scattered across the white tablecloth, silver gleaming in the light. Lady Pemberton was sipping tea daintily at one end of the table while George sat to her side with an open newspaper. The conversation had subsided, and Mr. Thornton was turned in his seat away from the door towards little Grace who was standing attentively in front of him.

"Is your card the King of Hearts?" asked Mr. Thornton.

"How could you know that?" shrieked Grace. "Mother, Mr. Thornton was able to guess my card."

"It wasn't a guess," said Mr. Thornton.

"Of course not," agreed Lady Pemberton placing her teacup in its saucer with a clink. "Guessing is for those who do not *know*. Mr. Thornton is a proper magician."

Serafina tried her best not to roll her eyes at this. Lady Pemberton had somehow fallen under whatever spell it was that Mr. Thornton had cast. Serafina wasn't sure why this annoyed her, but it did.

A Dangerous Man to Trust?

"Good morning, Miss Edgemont," said George, closing his paper and rising from his seat. "Please." He pulled out a chair for her beside him at the table. "I hope you are feeling better this morning."

Mr. Thornton rose to his feet and pulled out a chair for Patience. He said nothing, just watched as Serafina took her seat by George. She could feel his piercing eyes on her but refused to look his way.

"I am feeling quite well this morning, thank you. And I'm so sorry I had to leave your ball early last night, Lady Pemberton. You are a most excellent hostess."

"Nonsense, my girl. We are just so happy that you are all right. Mr. Thornton here has been such good company. I insisted he stay the night so that he could be assured of your recovery. He tells me that little Molly misses you terribly. You should know that we will not feel in the least bit slighted if you wish to curtail your visit in order to put that poor girl out of her misery. She has been through so much already. We shall be visiting you soon anyway," she said, lifting her eyebrows delightedly. "Mr. Thornton has invited us for an afternoon! Molly and Grace are of an age—they might just find a companion in each other."

Lady Pemberton was speaking to Serafina, but her gaze kept straying to Mr. Thornton. She was clearly taken with the man. He had gone some way to dissolving her first impression of him as something of a rake and a danger.

"Oh," was all Serafina could manage in response. "That is wonderful," she added stiffly. And even though she was still feeling perturbed by Mr. Thornton's machinations with the Pembertons, it was too unnatural to refuse to acknowledge him at this point. Her face was tilted down towards the place setting on the table in front of her, but she lifted her eyes and found herself caught in his blue stare.

"Thank you, Mr. Thornton. It's most gracious of you."

"Well, I wouldn't say 'gracious,'" he countered quickly.

"What would you call it then?" asked Serafina with a slight edge to her voice.

"I'd call it simply being friendly," replied Mr. Thornton.

"Hm." Serafina could not exactly respond as she wished. She wanted to say, "You're being friendly, are you?" but the Pembertons appeared to be watching the back-and-forth with some interest, and she did not like feeling as if she were the centre of attention.

Mr. Thornton reached across the table to a selection of jams in glinting crystal bowls. He selected one and slid it over to Serafina.

"If you're feeling well enough to eat, you should try the raspberry jam," he said. "It is exceptional."

In the end, Serafina gave in and ate. She was feeling rather famished, and raspberry jam was a favourite of hers—*how could he know?* The conversation among the Pembertons and Mr. Thornton carried on around her as she ate carefully, making every effort not to ruin her white dress with the bright red jam. Mr. Thornton shot subtle glances her way as she silently sipped her tea and buttered her muffin. For the life of her, she could not understand why she was feeling so irritated with him.

John had been left quite bereft in the ballroom the previous night. Miss Edgemont had been looking exceptionally pale

A Dangerous Man to Trust?

despite the loosened corset, and he could not help but feel that the events of the evening had taken their toll. That she was now out of his sight, beyond his care, left him feeling untethered and not a little bit anxious.

Miss Pemberton will stay with her. Surely, he thought, *she will let me know if Miss Edgemont takes a turn for the worse.*

At least there was Mr. Pemberton here to distract him—'George' as Miss Edgemont called him.

"Do not worry," said Mr. Pemberton as if reading his mind. "Patience will take good care of her."

"I'm sure," replied John slightly caught off his guard. Mr. Pemberton was surprisingly perceptive.

The men were a match for height and build, and John felt an immediate connection with this man who seemed so like him. It was clear to John that Mr. Pemberton was holding some secret sadness within him. John recognised the hard facade that had been constructed—an armour within which one could face the world. Mr. Pemberton, John noted, had not smiled all evening—not even when he was dancing with Miss Edgemont, and John could certainly not imagine dancing with Miss Edgemont and not smiling.

When Mr. Pemberton invited him for a brandy in his study, John was only too glad to escape the chatter and cheer of the ballroom. They spoke easily with one another in the dimly lit room, seated on brown leather, jackets thrown over a chair in the corner. They conversed all evening on a variety of safe and gentlemanly subjects—business and politics, horses and hunting.

Then quite out of the blue, Mr. Pemberton said, "She's happy. She told me so."

"Who?" asked John.

Intentions

"Serafina—Miss Edgemont," replied Mr. Pemberton.

"Did she say that?"

"Yes," said Mr. Pemberton. "I've known her a long time, Mr. Thornton. She has never appeared so content."

"I will take your word for it then," said John.

"The death of her parents nearly shattered her. They were not exactly a supportive presence in her life, but with them gone, and the financial complications that ensued, Serafina was left with nothing."

"She had your family," said John. "I . . . she must have been grateful for that."

"We were happy to have her, but she is—" (here he paused to search for a word) "—headstrong, sometimes intractable."

John smiled. "Yes, I've met her."

"She refused to entertain any suitors and insisted on going off on her own—finding employment."

"You must have been worried."

"I'm always worried," said Mr. Pemberton with resignation. "It's been my job since childhood, you see, to guard her from pirates."

"Pirates?"

For the first time all evening, the corners of Mr. Pemberton's lips twitched upwards. Not exactly a smile, but rather a hint of where a smile might like to sit.

"Yes, pirates, Mr. Thornton. I think you know what I mean." He paused here to fix John with his steely grey eyes. "My footman informed me earlier that Mr. Cross was requesting his carriage be brought around. I managed to catch sight of the man just before he left. His face did not look pleasant." Mr. Pemberton gave John a look that implied he had pieced it together.

A Dangerous Man to Trust?

"I see," said John.

"You have a spot of blood on your cravat, Mr. Thornton."

John reached for his throat.

"There are many reasons someone may want to hurt Mr. Cross," George continued, "but knowing Serafina's past with him, I can think of one that stands out above the rest. He is a pirate, you see, Mr. Thornton, and I am only grateful that she has someone to guard her from him. He should never have been invited, if indeed he was."

Mr. Pemberton placed his glass of brandy to a side table and leaned forward.

"Now, you must tell me, Mr. Thornton, what are your intentions towards Miss Edgemont."

"Intentions?"

"Yes, intentions."

"She is in my care, Mr. Pemberton. My intentions are honourable. I will keep her safe if that is what you are asking."

"I can see that you will, but that is not all I am asking," said Mr. Pemberton.

"I know what you're asking," said John. "I can assure you she deserves better. I can also assure you that if the question were asked, she would dismiss it out of hand."

"She is happy," said Mr. Pemberton leaning back in his chair. "Think on it."

Now that John was riding home in the carriage with Miss Edgemont, she certainly did not look happy to him. He could read her face, and her face was the picture of annoyance. Although she was seated directly across from him, she kept her gaze steadily out the window.

"You're upset," said John as the carriage lurched over a large bump in the road.

"No, I'm not," said Miss Edgemont keeping her eyes fixed to the scenery passing them by. Fields hemmed in by low stone walls, a scattering of starlings against the blue sky.

"Yes, you are," John insisted. "You're irritated with me for some reason. Should I not have invited the Pembertons to Bosworth Manor?"

"It was the polite thing to do," said Miss Edgemont without meeting his gaze. "And you are always so polite."

"What is that supposed to mean?"

"Nothing."

If Miss Edgemont had not practically vowed to him the night before that she would never leave, he would have been quite anxious. As it was, he was simply confused and wishing to understand.

"It can't mean nothing," said John.

Miss Edgemont turned her head to meet his eyes.

"It was awkward for me," she said. "That is all."

"What was awkward?"

"The breakfast, Mr. Thornton."

"The breakfast?! Of all the things that have happened since last night, Miss Edgemont, you found the breakfast was the awkward event?"

"Yes."

"And what about me?" he asked.

"What about you?"

"You had me unbutton your dress and adjust your corset!"

"That?" Miss Edgemont rolled her eyes in a dismissive gesture. "You know very well that I was trapped in a compromising situation. I imagine it was no trouble for you at all seeing as how you are such an expert at undoing corsets!"

"Pardon me?"

To answer his query, Miss Edgemont put on a low voice that was clearly intended to be an imitation of him: "I know how to undo a corset." She said it in the same firm tone he had taken with her the night before.

At this, John could do nothing but laugh. He laughed until he had to remove his mask to wipe the tears from his eyes.

"I'm mocking you, Mr. Thornton," said Miss Edgemont quite seriously, her bottom lip protruding in the most appealing manner.

"I know," he said placing his mask on the seat beside him.

He could see her entire countenance soften as she gazed into his bare face.

"You prefer me without my mask," he said with curiosity.

"I prefer you as you are," she said flatly. "Without your mask and without the false charm that was on display at breakfast."

"That wasn't false."

She gave him a hard stare.

"It was not *entirely* false," he conceded. "I like the Pembertons. I could come to like them more, especially Mr. Pemberton. And it is imperative that they like me, Miss Edgemont, that they feel you are in good hands."

"Your hands?" she asked, eyebrows raised.

"If you like," said John softly.

Miss Edgemont flushed a becoming shade of pink which John found quite gratifying. They fell into a companionable silence as the carriage rumbled over the rough track. After some time staring out the window, John turned to her and spoke.

Intentions

"I've been meaning to ask you, Miss Edgemont. Are you quite recovered? From the shock of last night?"

She was honest as ever in her response: "I do not know if one completely recovers from something like that, Mr. Thornton. But I *am* feeling better. I was lucky you were there."

"I wanted to apologise," said John leaning forward. He resisted the urge to reach for her hand which was resting like a little dove in her lap.

"For what?"

"For the manner with which I dealt with Mr. Cross. I let my anger get the best of me. A gentleman should be able to maintain some control."

"It *was* brutish," agreed Miss Edgemont with a furrowed brow. "His face was quite damaged, and you threatened to go even further—to rip him apart." She locked eyes with John.

"Did I?" John could not quite remember what he'd said.

She nodded.

"I was wondering," she said looking down at her hand in her lap, "how you would go about doing that."

"Doing what?" asked John.

"Ripping him apart," she answered, lifting her gaze once more. He could see the mischief in her large brown eyes, and he couldn't help but respond in kind.

"Oh that is simple," said John with a snarl. "I would do so with my teeth." He bared his into a hideous grin and made a quick feint towards her. Miss Edgemont let out a little shriek and then fell to laughing.

"Are you not afraid?" asked John. He could not imagine that he looked anything less than terrifying.

"Of you, Sir? Not at all," she said placing one hand to her belly to contain the mirth.

John felt that word 'Sir' like an arrow to the chest. His face fell.

"I'd prefer it if you did not call me 'Sir,'" he said.

Miss Edgemont looked perplexed. "What should I call you then?"

"Mr. Thornton," he said.

John, he thought.

Eight

Before and After

Serafina's mood had lifted considerably by the time they reached Bosworth Manor. As the carriage pulled up the familiar gravel drive, she could feel a loosening within her, a relief from the tension with which she had held herself while she had been away. She had left the Pembertons in bonnet and gloves but had removed both partway through their journey. There seemed no reason for them since it was just Mr. Thornton and herself.

"We're home," she said peering out the window at the house.

Mr. Thornton smiled before fixing his mask to his face and exiting the carriage. He turned and lifted his hand to help Serafina down. She slid her bare hand into his as she had done the night before and felt his warm flesh close around hers. Somehow, this time it was different. When both of her feet had landed on the gravel drive, she paused with her hand still in his. Mr. Thornton made to release her, but she could not bring herself to pull her hand from his. The feeling confused her, and she looked up into Mr. Thornton's masked face as if searching for an answer. The moment was broken by Molly's shouts of glee.

"Serafina! You're back early!" she yelled, rushing from Miss Browning's side and down the front steps of the house.

Molly practically threw herself at Serafina who was forced to pull her hand from Mr. Thornton's in order to catch the girl in a fierce embrace.

"I missed you too much," said Serafina holding Molly tight.

"Good!" said Molly.

"I trust Mr. Thornton has been good company for you."

"He has," said Molly eyeing him, "but he's been a bit glum."

Serafina darted her glance over to Mr. Thornton, but he was giving some quiet instructions to the footman regarding her luggage. Miss Browning approached in her usual business-like fashion.

"Good to see you back, Miss Edgemont. Mr. Thornton, I'm so glad everything is all right. We had expected to see you home last night."

"The ball ran late," said Mr. Thornton stepping up to the trio of ladies. "I was invited to stay the night. Safer travelling during the day anyway."

Serafina was thankful he had not mentioned that he had stayed on her account. Miss Browning was a kind woman, but she was prone to making judgments, and Serafina did not like to be the object of her disapproval.

Over the next week or so, John came to realise that something had shifted between himself and Miss Edgemont. There was before the Pemberton Ball, and there was after the Pemberton Ball. After was definitely better. Miss Edgemont seemed more relaxed in his company and not at pains to avoid him during the day, and he felt more at ease in her company as well.

What had changed?

For John, it had been the realisation that he could trust himself with Miss Edgemont. He liked to think that he had never taken advantage of a woman, but now he couldn't be so sure. Apart from his ex-fiancée Eleanor whom he had not so much as kissed, there had been plenty of young widows and bored actresses who had seemed more than eager for his superficial attentions. He was, as Miss Edgemont had suggested, an expert at undoing corsets. Now his feelings for Molly's governess were of an order he had not experienced before, and this worried him. He had imagined himself as some kind of beast who needed to be kept away from others—real people with real feelings he would have dismissed and belittled not so long ago. When he had first met Miss Edgemont, he had included her as one of those people who needed to be guarded from him. But he was understanding now that he had more control over himself and his actions than he had previously thought. Perhaps it had been the six long years tucked away in a corner of rural England with nothing but his garden and his own mangled conscience to keep him company. Yes, something had definitely shifted—then and now.

Miss Edgemont could trust him. He had unbuttoned her dress and adjusted her corset for God's sake! She had trusted him to do so with no hesitation. And he had passed the test if he wanted to think about it that way. If she did not wish to marry a baron's son, then she did not wish to marry. He would believe her on that count. And John was certainly happy for her to remain with him and Molly. He wondered if perhaps sometimes she felt trapped between marriage and employment. As much as her presence lit up his days, John did not like to think of Miss Edgemont as some sort of captive in his house. If she did not like it here, the Pembertons would always be happy to have her . . . although, having met Lady Pemberton, John suspected that she would encourage marriage by subtle and not-so-subtle means—another trap. *What it is to be a woman!*

No, John thought, *I will not have her here as some sort of captive. If she is to stay, it must be her choice—a real choice.*

He rubbed his chest where it had begun to ache at the thought of her choosing to leave. He had spent so much time managing his own pain—physical and emotional—that he found the dull ache of his heart easy to dismiss. He knew he deserved nothing.

I will do something for her, he thought. *Something to give her freedom to choose. A trip to London will be necessary.*

As Serafina settled back into life at Bosworth Manor, she could not help noticing that something had changed. Where before (with the exception of their evening card games) both she and Mr. Thornton made every effort to avoid each other during the day, now they somehow gravitated towards each other in those intervals when Molly was busy with one of her tutors. Mr. Thornton might happen upon her alone in the library and ask her about the curriculum she was planning. She was always planning something—adapting the mathematical and scientific principles she found in the boring and unnecessarily rambling treatises she found in the library to make them more succinct, to find an angle that would inspire Molly. Mr. Thornton seemed genuinely interested in what she was doing, and they would often lose track of time as they discussed how best to approach each topic with Molly. Sometimes Mr. Thornton would pull a book from the shelf—usually one on botany or natural history—and sit in a large chair opposite Serafina. They would read together in silence only to be eventually interrupted by Molly who had come searching them out.

If the weather was pleasant, Serafina might happen upon Mr. Thornton in the garden and venture to ask him about the new shrubs he had been planting. Unlike any other gentleman she had ever met, he had actually helped the gardener to plant them! She had once found him knelt over an open crate in the gardening shed. By the look on his face, one might have thought he was peering into a chest full of treasure. He looked up as her silhouette blocked some of the light coming through the doorway.

"Bulbs from Holland," he said brightly. "We shall have a riot of colour come springtime."

One day, Serafina went out in search of Rupert and found him lying in the shade of a bush waiting for Mr. Thornton to finish an animated conversation he was having with the gardener. It was an abnormally hot day on the cusp of autumn, and Mr. Thornton was not wearing a jacket. Serafina noticed it had been cast over a stone bench under a tree. And there was his cravat as well, tumbled loosely across the jacket. He looked quite comfortable in his white linen shirt which was open at

A Dangerous Man to Trust?

the collar exposing his scars to the sun. His sleeves were rolled up to reveal strong forearms, one of them disfigured. Serafina thought of how he had impressed Molly on that first day by pressing a pin into his flesh. She did not like the way he had so casually injured himself then, and the memory of it brought back that same sentiment but mixed with something else now. A fizzy, destabilizing sensation was swelling up from a place deep down at the root of her being.

As Rupert gave Serafina a slobbery hello, Mr. Thornton cut his conversation with the gardener short and strode over.

"Would you like to borrow my dog?" he asked, an amused look painted across the handsome exposed half of his face. "He seems to like you best."

Serafina looked up at him with one hand still resting comfortably on the back of Rupert's neck.

"Nonsense. Rupert follows you everywhere these days," she said as she tried her best to ignore the effervescent feeling rising up within her.

"I was going to take him down to the lake so that he might amuse himself with the ducks and cool off in the water," said Mr. Thornton. "Would you care to join us?"

"I could use a walk," said Serafina with calculated indifference.

Mr. Thornton offered her his scarred left arm so that she might take it with her right hand.

"Your jacket," she said turning to the bench.

"It's too hot," replied Mr. Thornton. "I'll fetch it on the way back."

Serafina hesitated, then took his arm, nestling her hand into the crook of his bare elbow, feeling the hard puckered scars of his body and the soft roll of his linen sleeve resting above her

Before and After

fingers. He led her across the great lawn and down to the lake as Rupert ran on ahead thrilled with the way the afternoon was playing out. Serafina was trying her best to disregard her awareness of Mr. Thornton's skin beneath her hand, but a disturbing sensation had begun to spread from her belly down into her pelvis, and it was sinking heavily into the space between her legs.

"No bonnet and no gloves, Miss Edgemont," said Mr. Thornton with some amusement. "I fear you will suffer when we are in London and you are forced to conform to the town's expectations."

"London?!" Serafina sounded put out, but the news was a welcome distraction from the strange goings-on within.

"Have I not mentioned it?"

"No, you have not."

"I must travel to London on business next month."

Serafina stopped to take this in as Rupert, noticing the delay, doubled back to encourage them on with a few barks and nips of their hands.

"I promised not to leave Molly behind again," said Mr. Thornton, "so if you are in agreement, then the two of you will be coming to stay with me in the London house for a few weeks, perhaps a month. I honestly do not know exactly how long these things take."

"Business things?" asked Serafina.

"Yes, business things," said Mr. Thornton lifting his gaze to the lake. "Come, Miss Edgemont—Rupert is quite impatient."

Serafina did not know what to make of this. She was loathe to leave Bosworth Manor again, to be out in society, to be always mindful of her dress, her speech, her manner. It was so easy here. At home. But of course, she would go with Molly.

A Dangerous Man to Trust?

. . and Mr. Thornton. She adjusted her grip on his arm and accidentally slid her hand above the crook of his elbow to hold him just beneath the bicep. Alarmed, she quickly removed her hand from his arm.

Mr. Thornton stopped. They were at the lake.

"Are you quite all right, Miss Edgemont? The sun is blazing today—perhaps you are too hot?"

"No . . . I mean, yes . . . I am rather hot," she said. "Perhaps I should head back to the house."

"That is another long walk in the sun," he responded. "Rest here awhile in the shade. It's coolest by the lake anyway. Here."

He led her to a large wooden bench beneath a willow at the edge of the water. Serafina sat down. *She was warm, but she knew she wasn't overheating, so what was her problem? Why did she feel so strange?* She watched as Mr. Thornton removed a handkerchief from his pocket and crouched down to soak it in the lake. He wrung it out and folded it into a long rectangle.

"Place it around the back of your neck. It should help."

It was unbelievably cool and wonderful against her skin.

"Oh," said Serafina, "that *is* nice. Thank you."

Mr. Thornton sat down at the other end of the bench leaving plenty of room between them.

"Would you prefer not to go to London?" he asked as they both watched Rupert splash towards the ducks.

"I'm not overly fond of the social scene," said Serafina truthfully, "but Molly will be excited to go, and I'm happy to accompany her."

"Perhaps we can find something of interest for you there," said Mr. Thornton leaning back and stretching out his legs in front of him.

"No need," replied Serafina.

Before and After

"Mm" was Mr. Thornton's response.

Serafina looked over at him then as he kept his gaze on Rupert. Mr. Thornton was so very thoughtful. He seemed so sensitive to her moods. She slid her gaze down to his bare forearms. She would go to London she realised, not so much because Molly needed her there, but because she herself could not be without Mr. Thornton. This thought both surprised and alarmed her.

Mr. Thornton sat up and removed his mask, then walked over to the lakeside where he bent down to splash his face. He looked back at her and noticed the alarm spreading across her countenance.

"Have no fear, Miss Edgemont," he said. "We shall endeavour to make our time in London as socially painless as possible."

Serafina managed a smile. Rupert, having dispersed every last duck from the lake, emerged from the water. He shook himself, trotted up to Serafina, and then turned back to the water. When he saw that she would not follow him, he set up a whine, coming over to place his wet chin in her lap.

"He seems to be asking something of you," said Mr. Thornton with curiosity.

"He wants me to go in with him," said Serafina.

"You usually go in with him?!" asked Mr. Thornton, clearly surprised.

"Not all the way in," said Serafina quickly. "I usually just take off my shoes and paddle about for a bit."

"So this is what you get up to on your own. It's actually quite a fine idea for a day like today."

Without any thought for the propriety of such behaviour, he proceeded to sit down on the bench to remove his boots and roll up his trousers. His feet, Serafina noticed, were perfect. Neither one of them disfigured or scarred. Rupert was bouncing about merrily in anticipation. Mr. Thornton stood up and directed his mangled smile her way before wading into the cool green water with Rupert at his side.

"This is lovely!" he shouted back when he had waded some way out but was still only knee deep.

Serafina could feel her dress sticking to her back in the heat. Beads of sweat were trickling down between her breasts, and she was now feeling quite desperate for the liquid cool of the lake and the soft sediment between her toes. It was not technically proper to do so with Mr. Thornton here, but didn't they make their own rules at home? It was not as if he cared to see or not see her feet. He did not feel that way about her. In fact, just a few weeks ago, he had encouraged her to pursue marriage to George!

To hell with it, thought Serafina, swearing wickedly to herself. *I'm too hot to keep thinking about this.*

She kicked off her shoes which brought Rupert galloping out of the water towards her. She shrieked as he shook what felt like the entire lake over her. She was soaked through, and she hadn't even stepped a foot into the lake. Rupert licked her hand encouragingly. Locking eyes with Mr. Thornton, she smiled, then started to laugh.

"I probably look as if I've been for a swim in my dress!" she yelled across to him.

"A swim is a marvellous idea!" he yelled back. He waded out into the water waist deep, turned to face her, and waved. Then fully clothed, he threw himself backwards with a splash into the green embrace of the water.

Nine

The Devil Himself

John had a vision of how the garden might look in the spring, but much of what needed to be done would have to wait for cooler weather. The day was an unusual blaze of heat and light, but when John caught sight of Miss Edgemont stepping briskly across the grass in her unassuming pale grey dress, it was as if the sun shone brighter still.

He had not realised how much more relaxed he was feeling in her presence until she took his bare arm with her soft little hand. Had he actually offered her his bare arm with his sleeves rolled up? No wonder she had asked about his jacket. But she was holding him now, and he thought, *Why create a fuss? It's not as if she cares one way or the other about my arms, and it will only make a potentially awkward situation even more awkward.*

When they had arrived with Rupert at the lake, John was careful to keep a good distance between Miss Edgemont and himself on the bench—a gesture to give her space, to set

A Dangerous Man to Trust?

her mind at ease. He knew she would never feel the same overwhelming feelings for him that he did for her. It didn't matter. He could survive this kind of pain, and if she stayed with him and Molly, he would be happy at the same time. He could not hope for more.

Rupert had given away her secret—Miss Edgemont liked to go for a paddle in the lake! This amused John no end. He imagined her stepping gingerly into the cool water, a thrilled little shiver rippling across her face. John had not been in the lake since he was a boy. It had been the absolute best part of his summer holidays home from school. The silent tension that seemed to hold the walls of his parents' house upright melted away down here by the lake. It was its own contained little world—the bench, the willows, the ducks.

Who had taught him to swim? He couldn't even remember now. Not his father, surely.

As a child, he had taken every opportunity to escape the confines of the manor, and he had spent a lot of time playing under bushes and catching insects. Sometimes when he had refused to return to the house with his nurse for lunch, she would wrap some food in a napkin and bring it out to him.

"Keep an eye on him, will you?" she'd say to the old gardener.

Anthony! Anthony had been the gardener's name. Yes, it had been him who had taught John to swim in the lake. It was all coming back to him now. Anthony always had a smile for him, crinkling up his already wrinkled face to make John feel welcome.

"Life is for living," he used to say, a hint of his mother tongue warming up the English accent he had cultivated over the years.

John brought himself back to the present. To the bench.

The Devil Himself

To Miss Edgemont. To the real lake, not the remembered lake. The memory of Anthony still fresh in his mind, John couldn't help himself. He pulled off his boots and stepped in. Throwing himself backwards into the water, he almost felt as if he were throwing himself backwards in time. He sank down into the cool water and kept himself submerged by propelling himself with his hands until he lay in the green weeds at the bottom. He watched as bubbles rose from his nose, wobbling their way to the brighter surface. He was content.

When John's head finally broke the surface once more, Miss Edgemont was in front of him, her grey dress ballooning out around her as she stood waist deep in the lake with a look of pale terror on her face. John stood as the water rushed down past his shoulders through the linen of his shirt making a shushing sound as it returned to the lake below.

"Miss Edgemont?" he said with some concern.

"You didn't come back up," was all she said. "I thought . . ." Then, looking around her as if she had not realised until that moment where she was, "I've never been in so deep."

John reached out a hand for hers, then thought better of it, but before he could pull it back, she had grasped him quite firmly.

She was afraid of the deep water. She couldn't swim. Yet she had waded all the way out here in the fear that he may be drowning!

"Come, let us head back to the shore," he said taking a slow step in that direction. Miss Edgemont didn't move.

"I don't like this," she said. He thought she meant the deep water, but then she said, "Show me how to go under."

It's not the water, John thought. *She doesn't like being afraid.* John fought the urge to pull her to him, embrace her. He wanted to know her, truly know her, to explore every inch of her body and soul.

"Under? Are you sure?" he asked.

"Yes," she said resolutely.

Keeping her hand in his, he led her out a little deeper, until they were submerged to the chest.

"Oh," she said.

That word from her lips. John closed his eyes for a moment to steady himself. He turned to face her, helped her to press her inflated dress down into the water, and took her other hand in his. They took their time. He showed her how to bring her mouth to the surface and blow bubbles. She would mirror him, always holding his outstretched hands, never releasing her grip. Then after some patient instruction, they dunked under, a quick up and down together.

"How was that?" asked John.

"Can we try for longer?" asked Miss Edgemont.

"Of course. You lead, and I will follow."

They tried again, but Miss Edgemont could not stay under for very long.

"I'm too buoyant," she said, laughing now—the fear was gone. "I need you closer. As an anchor."

Releasing her grip on his hands, she shifted hers to his wrists then slid her hands along his forearms to his elbows, drawing herself in towards him. His hands curled around her soft upper arms, bare in her summer dress. They locked eyes for a moment, his pale blue with her dark brown. John held his breath.

"You're a patient man," said Miss Edgemont. Her pink lips were wet and shining in the sunlight.

"I wasn't always," he said peeling his gaze from her lips back up to her eyes.

The Devil Himself

"Shall we try again?" she asked with a smile.

He nodded.

This time, she held herself in place easily using her new leverage against him. Underwater, John opened his eyes to see her face with eyes closed. Her hair strained against its pins, trying to release itself to float up above her. Her dress swirled about her, lifting itself to reveal her lower legs, her white chemise that was practically transparent in the water. She opened her eyes and was startled to see him gazing back at her in the gloomy underworld of the lake. John kept a grip on Miss Edgemont and an even firmer grip on himself.

She is without artifice, he thought. *So completely herself.* He would never mistake her trust, her openness as any kind of invitation. To do so might be to lose her trust entirely, to lose her. And that was something he could not risk. When they rose up out of the water together, Miss Edgemont was elated, beaming up into the rippling of crimson scars across his face.

"Oh!" She lost her footing and reached one arm to his shoulder. He circled an arm about her waist and pulled her to him.

"I have you," he said.

Her toes brushed against the bare skin of his lower leg as he set her back down. It was almost too much for him. Almost, but not quite. He could survive it. When he made to release her, she said with some concern, "Don't let me go," as she found both of his hands once more.

They stood there like that for nearly a minute. Miss Edgemont's hair, now weighted with water, was breaking free of its pins. She was looking at him. At his face, his neck, the red scars of his chest now visible through his wet white shirt that was clinging to him like a second skin.

A Dangerous Man to Trust?

"How can you bear to look at me?" he asked. "I must look like the Devil himself recently climbed up from the fires of Hell. And do not say that this is not the case, for you know it is the truth."

"The truth, Mr. Thornton? Is that what you're after?"

"Always."

She tightened her grip on his hands.

"I think you are wrong about the Devil. I don't think he looks anything like you. I imagine he is deceptively perfect and handsome. In fact, it would not surprise me if he were the spitting image of Mr. Cross."

She let that comment settle for a moment, then stepped in closer to inspect his face. He could see her steeling herself as if before a plunge beneath the water.

"If you want the full truth Mr. Thornton, I like to see your face because I like *you*. Correct me if I'm wrong, but I do believe we have become friends."

From anyone else in any other situation, this would seem an extremely forward statement made by a lady. But John took it completely at face value.

"I should like to think we are friends, Miss Edgemont," he said with a snarl of a smile.

"If we are friends, then you should call me Serafina."

John's heart melted into his belly.

"And you must call me John."

Serafina laughed. "Oh, I think that is perhaps a step too far. You are, after all, my employer. Miss Browning would definitely disapprove."

"When we are on our own then," said John.

Serafina held her silence for a moment as if thinking it over, then said, "All right . . . John." But she said it so quietly it was almost a whisper.

Afterwards, they stretched themselves out on the grass in an attempt to dry out in the sun. They lay an arm's distance from each other. Serafina's palms rested on her ribs, and her thin grey dress clung damply to the outline of her thighs.

"That was fun," she said, directing her comment up into the blue sky. She flung an arm out towards John and turned her head to see him. "Next summer, you should teach Molly to swim. She should not be afraid of the water."

"That is an excellent idea," said John. "Would you like to learn as well?"

"You know that I would," replied Serafina. "There are so many experiences denied a woman out of some pointless notion of propriety."

"We must be proper, Serafina," said John with mock seriousness.

"In company," added Serafina.

"But at home we make up our own rules," said John.

They both laughed.

"Do you think I might slip back into the house without Miss Browning or the servants noticing how wet I am?" asked Serafina.

John turned on his side to face her, and she withdrew her arm.

"If it comes to it, I shall tell Miss Browning that Rupert knocked you into the lake."

Upon hearing his name, Rupert had come over to sniff at their hands and lick Serafina's face.

A Dangerous Man to Trust?

"Ugh! Rupert! I'm wet enough as it is!"

John watched Serafina sit up and tussle with his dog as her dark wet hair tumbled free of its pins. He could not recall a moment in his life when he had been happier.

The day of the picnic with the Pembertons approached. Serafina had known it would be awkward, but she had not calculated how much more awkward it would feel under the appraising eye of Miss Browning. Serafina, standing outside the drawing room door, had overheard the stern old woman attempting some clarification with John on the matter of preparations.

"Miss Edgemont shall be joining you all on this picnic?"

"Well, they are *her* friends," John had replied.

"And Miss Thornton?"

"Yes, children too—it is a picnic after all. So that makes seven."

"I see," said Miss Browning.

"I'm sure you shall arrange everything perfectly," John added.

He hadn't needed to say this, thought Serafina, but it was a wise choice. Miss Browning seemed startled by the compliment.

"Well, I . . . yes . . . thank you, Mr. Thornton. I will do my best."

Serafina did not have time to hide or make herself look busy before Miss Browning strode business-like from the drawing room. The housekeeper caught her eye in the hallway.

"There is to be a picnic," she said. And then narrowing her eyes, "But I suppose you know this already."

The Devil Himself

Serafina felt as if she'd been caught in some sort of illicit activity. *Why was she feeling this way? It was only a picnic for heaven's sake.*

"Mr. Thornton insisted," she said apologetically and by way of explanation. "He could not be talked out of it."

"Indeed," said Miss Browning.

The housekeeper proceeded to step in closer to Serafina and lowered her voice.

"You must be careful, Miss Edgemont."

"Careful?"

"Mr. Thornton is sometimes . . . unorthodox in his decisions, his behaviour. The appearance is the thing," she said emphatically. "How will it appear? I know you are without fault, that you are devoted to Miss Thornton, but the servants will inevitably talk."

Serafina was not entirely sure as to what Miss Browning was alluding to here.

"They will talk about the picnic?" she asked slowly.

"Yes," said Miss Browning, "and what do you think they will say?"

She did not wait for a response, but in one swift movement, smoothed down the skirt of her black dress before striding off down the hallway.

What would they say? Serafina wondered. She would be firmly ensconced in the middle of the picnic before she figured that one out.

The day arrived. It was not a blue-sky day, but there was no rain, and that was the most anyone could hope for this close to

October. It was a joy to see the Pembertons once more. Lord Pemberton was still in London, but Lady Pemberton passed on his apologies and his regards.

"He was sorry to miss it," said Lady Pemberton looking around the grand entrance hall where they had been received.

"Really?" asked Patience with a suspicious look.

"Really," said Lady Pemberton darting an icy glare towards her daughter.

"Nevermind," said John. "I should think we shall see you all again in London soon, and perhaps Lord Pemberton will join us then."

"The Season will have an early start this year," said Lady Pemberton, her eyes lighting up as she glanced somewhat hopefully at Patience and then George. "Parliament will not wait until January to sit, so everyone who is anyone shall be in London by November."

"Well, we won't be there *for* the Season, as it were," said John. "I am not looking for a wife."

At this, he laughed a bit self-consciously, and Lady Pemberton attempted a smile, but it came out as more of a grimace.

"I have some business to attend, and Molly will not be left behind again, so she and Miss Edgemont shall be coming as well."

"How exciting," said Lady Pemberton.

Serafina leaned in close to Patience and whispered, "You can perhaps hint to your mother that I shall not be attending anymore balls." Patience reached for her hand and gave it a squeeze.

It was not long before they were all outside and seated on blankets and cushions under a white awning that had been raised to protect them from the non-existent sun. Two of the maids brought out the food, and Serafina could see that John was hopeless at giving them direction. He looked to her pleadingly, and she stepped in to coordinate placement of food and drink, sending the maids back with instructions for serviettes, cutlery, and the type of glasses that would suit the occasion. Inevitably, her instructions conflicted with the instructions already given them by Miss Browning.

"But Miss, we were told to bring the crystal."

"We don't need anything so fancy—it's a picnic on the grass, not dinner at the table," replied Serafina.

The maids looked at each other, and it was then that Serafina realised what they would say.

She behaves as if she is lady of the house!

Mr. Thornton gives her free rein!

It was not a long leap from there to, *A governess is not exactly chaperoned*. And all that that implied.

"Oh!" said Serafina as the maids scurried off.

"Is everything all right?" asked John.

"Yes," said Serafina absently.

John gave her a hard stare, but they were called back to their guests before he could question her. Although Serafina now felt as if she had a stone in her stomach, she managed to carry on as if nothing were the matter. *And was there really a matter? Or was she overthinking things?*

If one subtracted this tiny little poison pill from the day, it was actually quite a merry affair. Grace and Molly got on splendidly despite their different interests. They spent a great deal of time comparing notes on older brothers. (Grace felt George had much to learn from Mr. Thornton.) And George and John, for that matter, had taken off together on a stroll of the grounds.

A Dangerous Man to Trust?

"They get on nicely, don't they?" asked Lady Pemberton of no one in particular.

Serafina made an affirmative sound.

"And you, my dear girl, are absolutely radiant as hostess of this little picnic!"

"Oh, no," said Serafina, "I was only helping out. I would not consider myself the hostess. It isn't my place."

Lady Pemberton and Patience exchanged a look.

"Of course," said Lady Pemberton. "I only meant to say how good it is to see you so comfortable here at Bosworth Manor."

"In London, you shall meet my father," said George as he and John ambled through the gardens.

A bank of grey cloud hung low over their heads in direct opposition to the garden which was alight with red and yellow flowers—one last flurry of floral excitement before the winter.

"I've already made his acquaintance," said John.

"You've shaken his hand," said George.

They walked on in silence for a time.

"Have you given it any thought?" asked George.

"Excuse me?" John did not know to what he referred.

"Marriage to Miss Edgemont," said George stopping short and fixing John with his grey eyes. He pressed a hand back through his hair setting it on end.

"Yes. I mean, no. Actually what I mean to say is that I fear the question might scare her off. Things are quite fine as they stand. She is content. I would not want to risk . . ." he trailed off.

"All may be fine now," said George, "but what of her future?

The Devil Himself

How shall she fare when Miss Thornton is grown? Would you ask her then? And if so, why not now?"

"I understand your concern," said John carefully. "It is my own. I shall see to it that Miss Edgemont wants for nothing."

"Mr. Thornton. John. May I call you John?" John gave a nod, and George continued. "What if what Miss Edgemont truly wants is you?"

John was stunned by the direct nature of George's question.

"Has she said so?" His voice was almost a whisper.

"She need not," said George. "It's apparent in the way she speaks of you."

John felt hope rising like a feathered thing within him, but he beat it down before it could take flight.

"You must be mistaken. She is kind in the way she speaks of me because we are friends, but she does not see me in the way that you suggest. It is impossible."

"Why impossible?" pressed George.

John said nothing, but he thought, *Because I am a monster, inside and out.*

As the two men approached the picnickers from a distance, Serafina noticed them and waved. John waved back.

Ten

A Real Choice

London was all that Serafina had expected it to be. It was sooty and noisy and full of the smell of smoke and horses and their dung. As their carriage passed through some of the shabbier areas of town, Molly, who had never been to London before, was practically buzzing with excitement.

"I've never seen so many people! Is that boy selling newspapers? Why is that lady tipping water from her window? If I dressed up as a boy, do you think I could sell newspapers? My voice is very loud, so I would probably be quite good at it."

She was beaming at Serafina who was seated beside her. Serafina forced a queasy kind of smile. By the time their carriage rounded a corner into Mayfair, she was feeling sensorily overwhelmed and not a little like crawling under a blanket and curling up into a tiny ball.

"I think Miss Edgemont is in need of a rest," said John. "It's

A Real Choice

been a long journey."

Serafina had noticed that ever since the picnic, he had refrained from calling her by her Christian name, even when they were alone. It was as if he had retreated a little from their friendship. It made her sad in a way that she did not fully understand, and she often found herself gazing forlornly at the side of his exposed face or the back of his neck.

Finally inside the London house, Serafina was unpacking her things in her room when a knock at the door brought her face-to-face with two servant boys and an enormous copper tub.

"Mr. Thornton asked us to bring it up," said the first young man by way of explanation.

The two of them shuffled in with the tub and plunked it down in front of the hearth. By and by, a maid came to light the hearth and coax a warm fire to life, heating the room to a cozy temperature. Two footmen came back and forth with buckets, one hot and one cold, to fill the tub while the maid stayed to heat a kettle over the fire in order to top up the tub and keep it hot while the footmen shuffled in and out. When the tub was entirely full and steaming, the maid moved a screen into place in front of it, laid out some towels and fragrant soaps, and left.

A bath. It was exactly what she needed right now. Serafina slipped out of her travelling dress and petticoat, untied her stay, and allowed her chemise to drop to the carpet. She stood barefoot on the cold floor beside the steaming tub taking a moment to anticipate the delicious pleasure of a hot bath after a long and tiring trip. As she slowly sank her body into the soothing heat of the water, Serafina nearly wept with relief. She unpinned her hair and let it float around her, feeling for one tiny moment unencumbered and without a care.

She sank in up to her neck allowing her arms to float out in front of her. Closing her eyes, she saw John—Mr. Thornton, she corrected herself (if he wasn't going to use her Christian name, then she certainly wouldn't be using his). The bath was a thoughtful gesture. Somehow, he always knew what she needed. Serafina wondered if he was sitting in his own bath just then. She could see him wrestling impatiently with his cravat before pulling it clean away from his neck to allow his shirt to fall open. He would cross his arms to grab the bottom of his shirt and pull it up over his head in one strong movement. Serafina took a breath and slipped under the water as John had taught her to do.

John, for his part, was busy giving instructions to the household staff. He looked up from his conversation with a footman when a maid entered the room.

"Has Miss Edgemont's bath been drawn?" he asked briskly.

"Yes, Sir." The maid looked down at the carpet.

"Good." And then even though he knew he shouldn't ask it of a servant: "Was she pleased?"

"I couldn't rightly say, Sir," was the maid's reply to the carpet.

"Nevermind," said John as much to himself as to anyone else. The maid took the opportunity to flee the room.

Since the picnic, John had decided to keep Serafina's friendship at some distance. He was not entirely sure why, but he half-suspected in his more lucid moments that it had something to do with that fluttering feeling of hope he was trying to keep at bay.

When she has a choice, a real choice, she will not choose to stay with me. That is something she does out of necessity, out of practicality, and let's be honest, out of a fear for her very precarious future.

At the same time, he could not help but think of her, wishing to please her somehow, to lift the corners of her mouth. As it was, he found himself in the unenviable position of being neither here nor there—neither fully her friend nor simply her employer. He was constantly performing this balancing act of push and pull which he found exhausting in the extreme. Somehow, though, he did not know how to stop.

Later that evening after Molly had been ushered off to bed, John sat with a candle in his study taking stock of his calendar and all that needed to be done in London before their return home. There was a soft knock at the door.

"Come," he said, not taking his eyes from his calendar.

He had thought it to be a servant, his valet perhaps, but when he looked up, Serafina was standing tall in the doorway holding a candle of her own and waiting for him to acknowledge her.

"Miss Edgemont," he said standing and coming around the front of the desk.

An almost imperceptible pained expression flitted across her face in the space of a second and was gone.

"Mr. Thornton," she said with some emphasis, "I wanted to say goodnight." She paused. "And to thank you for the bath—it was very thoughtful."

John tried forcing himself not to think of her naked in the

tub but was woefully unsuccessful.

"It was nothing," he said dismissively.

Serafina stepped into his office and put her candle down on his desk. She had to reach around him slightly to do so, then stepped back. John closed his eyes for a brief moment, steeled himself.

"I went all the way under," she said looking up into his face with her big brown eyes.

He didn't understand, and for some reason removed his mask as if removing that barrier would make her statement clearer.

"Under the water," she said with a little smile. "The way you taught me . . . Sir," she added.

John winced.

"I told you not to call me that."

Serafina looked for some reason pleased with his reaction, then angry in swift succession. Her face flushed, and John was surprised at the emotion contained in her voice.

"And I asked you to call me Serafina, but it's all Miss Edgemont this and Miss Edgemont that!" She had stepped closer to him as if to better attack him with her words. "What has changed?" she asked, quieter now.

John could feel that tiny bird of hope flapping its wings against the inside of his chest, and he was afraid—more afraid than he had ever been in his life. *Kill the bird*, he thought, *kill the fear.*

"I think you should go to bed, Miss Edgemont. It has been a long day."

She stared at him. But she didn't leave. She stepped even closer. John's breath caught in his chest.

"Do you think, Mr. Thornton—Sir—that you are the only

A Real Choice

one who can read faces?"

She peered exaggeratedly into his, and he could feel her breath on his lips.

"I thought what you appreciated most was the truth. And now for some reason, you are hiding it. I thought we were friends."

At this last word, 'friends', her voice cracked with emotion. Serafina reached for her candle.

It is for the best, thought John. *Whatever she had said about never leaving, she would change her mind when her circumstances changed.*

John was in London to do just that—to give her a real gift, a real choice. To put them on an even footing. He would not be able to live with himself, live with her, if he did not. Ironically, it was more than likely that the gift itself would spur her departure. If this were to happen, it was possible that his heart would rupture irreparably, but it was nothing less than he deserved. He would tend to Molly. He would place his love and attention there. And it would have to be enough.

"Goodnight, Mr. Thornton."

Serafina's eyes were glistening, and it was all John could do not to pull her into his arms. He gave her a nod, fearing that if he spoke, his voice might betray him. She left taking her light with her.

John disappeared early the following morning without so much as a goodbye, and Serafina found herself alone with Molly and feeling not a little out of sorts.

Where had Mr. Thornton gone? It was strange for him to leave without any explanation. Was he upset with her because of what she'd said the evening before? He had always appreciated her speaking the truth to him in the past. Would he return by nightfall, or would he stay away as he had done before? She thought back to his first disappearance to London all those months ago. *He wouldn't do that to Molly again, surely.*

"I should like to go out!" said Molly enthusiastically, ignoring the maths exercises that graced the page in front of her.

"Out?"

"Into the street!" said Molly. "To see all the people," she added.

"I don't think Mr. Thornton—"

"*Mr. Thornton* isn't here," said Molly with a mischievous grin.

"It wouldn't be proper to go out unescorted. This isn't Bosworth Manor. It's London," said Serafina with some finality.

She certainly did not need an escort for herself, but to take Molly out into London? She would not feel comfortable unless she saw to the young lady's safety first and foremost.

"We could ask Spencer," said Molly.

She really wasn't going to let this go.

Serafina considered the footman.

"I suppose . . ."

"SPENCER!" called Molly loudly.

"Molly! Don't shout. Ring the bell."

"Sorry."

A Real Choice

Spencer was a young man with a prematurely receding hairline who was not given to expressing any opinions verbally or otherwise. "Very good, Sir," was his catch-all phrase. And today it was "Very good, Miss," to Serafina's request that he accompany them on a walk.

"Hyde Park, I should think," said Serafina.

She was actually warming to the idea of going out. It might take her mind off Mr. Thornton and his mysterious whereabouts.

Once she had coerced Molly into a pair of gloves, a bonnet, and a coat, they set off for the park which was not terribly far from Mr. Thornton's house. Molly was less than impressed with what they found there.

"The lake is quite dirty, isn't it?" she said. "Why do you suppose all these ladies are walking such miniature dogs? What is the point of a dog like that? It could hardly guard a house or retrieve a pheasant now, could it? What I really wanted to see, Serafina, was all the *people*."

"There are people here," said Serafina looking around.

"No. These are just pretend people," said Molly gesturing at the well-dressed ladies and gentlemen promenading along the park path. "I wanted to see the news boys and the ladies selling apples by the side of the road, and a man with no legs in a cart being pushed by a woman with a baby on her hip. People!"

"Ah," said Serafina, "you wanted to go downtown."

"Yes!"

"Well, that's not going to happen, Molly. It isn't safe there, and your brother would never allow it. Anyway, these are real people too."

"No they're not," said Molly.

A Dangerous Man to Trust?

"What about us?" asked Serafina. "Are we pretend people as well?"

"No," said Molly defensively. "We're just pretending to be pretend people with our bonnets and gloves (she gestured behind them) and our Spencer."

Serafina laughed. *The girl was too much!*

"I should think," said Serafina lowering her voice and leaning in close, "that several of the other people at the park are also pretending to be pretend people, just like us."

"Really?" said Molly looking around. "Which ones, do you think?"

The rest of the morning was spent inventing wild stories about the people around them—their hidden interests and hobbies, their secret loves, their impolite habits. It was odd for Molly to enjoy such a thing since she was not overly fond of stories.

Perhaps, thought Serafina, *it is the peeling back of appearances that appeals to her.*

By the time they arrived back at the house, they were laughing and in high spirits. They were surprised to see that John—Mr. Thornton—was waiting for them like a thundercloud in the foyer. His voice was like boulders rumbling down a hill.

"Where have you been?!"

When John had returned home that morning, Serafina and Molly were nowhere to be found. He went from room to room searching them out, but they were gone. It was as if they had only ever been figments of his imagination. There was no

A Real Choice

note, and the servants were clueless as to their whereabouts. Panic rose up in John's chest until he felt he might choke on it. Serafina and Molly were out walking in London—God knew where and with whom.

Did Serafina think they were still at Bosworth Manor? That they could go gallivanting about town where and when they pleased with no concern for their own safety? Without a word to him or anyone else?

As is so often the case with gentlemen, John's fear and concern soon turned to anger, and that anger was only heightened when, standing in the foyer, he heard Serafina's laughter rising up the steps to the front door. She and Molly stepped in through the doorway still laughing.

"Where have you been?!" John heard himself speak as if he were outside himself. The sound of his voice was like thunder. Their laughter fell to the marble floor, scattering like a broken string of pearls.

"For a walk to the park," replied Serafina in a calm and even tone. "We took Spencer," she added.

"You must not go out without me," said John, angrily eyeing Spencer.

"Very good, Sir," said Spencer.

"Is that what you would like me to say?" asked Serafina, her calm demeanour beginning to crack.

"Excuse me?" said John.

"Very good, Sir," said Serafina mimicking Spencer. "Is that what you would like me to say?"

John gave her a hard look.

"I was worried for your and Molly's safety. You left no note. I did not know where you were or when you would return!"

"Well, then, now you know what it's like!" said Serafina, her voice increasing in volume to match his.

John glanced to Molly and Spencer who appeared to be taking in the scene with a mixture of curiosity and amusement. He took Serafina gently but firmly by the arm and led her into a small reception room off the main foyer. He closed the door.

"I will thank you not to speak to me like that in front of the servants," he said, his hand still gripping her arm.

"I will thank you to take your hand off me," said Serafina looking to where he held her.

John released her immediately and stepped back. She advanced on him.

"And where were *you* all morning? I did not know where *you* were or when *you* would return!"

John was taken aback. He had never known anyone to be particularly concerned for his whereabouts. Certainly no one had ever expressed a care for his return over the course of a single morning.

"Miss Edgemont . . . I . . ."

Serafina appeared to come completely untethered. "If you call me Miss Edgemont one more time, I swear I will scream!"

"Miss . . . Serafina?"

John could see tears welling up in her eyes, and the sight of her like that caused him to lose control of his limbs. He watched as his right arm reached out for her hand and tugged her towards him. He was like a silent observer as his left arm wrapped itself around behind her, pulling her into an embrace. She came softly, willingly, pressing the side of her face to his chest. He could feel her shudder as she sobbed quietly into his waistcoat.

Dear God, thought John, *I can't even begin to understand what is happening right now.*

A Real Choice

He had held women before, but never like this. This was something altogether different. He felt warm and protective, and he realised that he had never before offered anyone comfort. His childhood both at home and at school had inculcated a kind of detachment from his own feelings and from those of others. He had never received comfort from anyone, and he had certainly never thought to offer it. He tipped his face down so that his lips brushed the top of her head.

When the sobbing subsided, he held her by the shoulders pressing her back to look into her face, but she would not meet his eyes.

"Sorry," she said in a quiet voice. "My behaviour has been quite deplorable."

"Not at all," said John. "I consider it a gift each time you share your feelings with me."

At that, she looked up. Her eyes were pink around the edges, her cheeks flushed, and her lips were almost red. John felt rather hot in his jacket. He pulled absently at his cravat.

"I will tell you where I was this morning, but you must promise to hear me out. Do not respond before you have a chance to think properly on the matter."

"What matter?" asked Serafina as she accepted a handkerchief from John.

"I have been to see my solicitor, my father's solicitor, about your inheritance."

"Inheritance?"

"Hear me out, Serafina," said John with a stern look. "My father's gift of a dowry—"

Serafina waved the thought away with her hand.

"—No. Listen. The dowry was not an appropriate gift, so

A Dangerous Man to Trust?

I have amended it. It was my father's intention to leave you with something in order to secure your future. My solicitor is drawing up the papers now. It is the same amount as the dowry, but it will be put in your name. It is a sum that will see you living quite comfortably. You will not have to rely on the kindness of anyone else, you will not ever have to marry out of financial concern, and (here John paused to suck in his breath as a sharp pain pierced its way through his chest) . . . and your position with regards to your employment here with me and Molly will be entirely of your choosing."

Serafina stared at him for an uncomfortable length of time.

"Have I done something?" she finally asked. "I know I have behaved poorly at times, but I didn't think . . ."

"Excuse me?"

"Do you wish me to leave? Are you paying me to leave?" There was panic in her voice.

"No," said John emphatically. "No, you misunderstand."

"The truth then," said Serafina. "What is this?"

"The truth is simple," said John. "I had hoped to offer you freedom to choose how you would like to live. In thinking about your situation—"

"You think about my situation?"

"All the time," said John reflexively. His throat felt thick and constricted. His voice was hoarse. "In thinking about it, it became obvious to me that you are trapped. Between a marriage you clearly would like to avoid and your employment here. I do not wish for you to leave us—far from it—but if you stay, I would like to know that it is because given every other option, this is the choice you would make. I am your employer, yes, but the more I thought about it, the more it felt as if I were your captor . . . in a sense. You chose employment with my father, not me. The current circumstance is perhaps not the situation you had anticipated when you first came to Bosworth Manor."

Serafina said nothing for some time. The silence settled over them like a heavy blanket, and John felt as if he might be smothered by it. The longer she did not speak, the faster his heart beat.

Finally, she said, "You know I cannot talk to you properly with your mask on."

He removed it and placed it on a low table. Serafina stepped up to him, peered into his mangled face. Hers was still flushed from crying.

"You are unlike any other man I've ever met," she said.

"We are still friends?" asked John tentatively.

"I should ask you the same question," said Serafina quietly, looking down at the handkerchief in her hands. "Lately, it has not always seemed that way on your part."

"Serafina," he said. "Look at me, Serafina." She lifted her gaze. "You're right. I apologise. I have no explanation for my behaviour except that I am a damaged man, both inside and out. You will never have to question my friendship again. I promise you."

"Oh."

She seemed at a loss for words, fiddling nervously with the handkerchief he had given her. John felt he could say no more. Finally, Serafina's hands went still. She dropped them to her sides and lifted her eyes to his.

"I think . . ." she said, " I think that once someone has soaked your waistcoat with her tears, you are friends forever." She gave him an awkward, almost embarrassed smile.

"Forever," said John in a whisper. He liked the sound of that.

She had not exactly said she would stay, but neither did it sound like she was leaving. John felt as if he were soaring like a kite. He did not entirely understand all that had happened there in the little reception room, but as far as he was concerned, it had ended well. He could not be more grateful.

Eleven

The Ship of Theseus

The last thing Serafina wanted to do was to leave John alone in the reception room. She wanted to stay with him. She wanted him to hold her again. But she left nonetheless, casually mounting the stairs to her room as if her entire life had not been upended in a single morning. Everything was different now.

She entered her bed chamber and closed the door, leaning into it with her back. There was a large rug on her floor—a sky blue expanse covered in blooming yellow vines. Serafina paced slowly up and down the rug from the bureau to the window and back again. She replayed everything in her head a hundred times—John's angry greeting at the door, her defiant response, the way he pulled her into the reception room (and closed the door!).

Why had she cried? What was that overwhelming feeling that had welled up within her?

A Dangerous Man to Trust?

She stopped to lean on the window sill and gaze down into the street. It was the mounting feeling of loss, she realised. Loss of her friendship with John, the closeness they had cultivated over these last several months.

It was the loss of him!

Down in the street, two well-dressed ladies passed beneath Serafina's window. A maid trailed after them carrying a large covered basket. Everything seemed so normal, so everyday, and yet not ten minutes ago John had pulled her to him and wrapped his arms around her as she wept. She had never felt so safe as in his arms, against his hard body.

And the inheritance? Serafina still could not believe what had just happened. *John thought of her situation all the time?!*

He had given her the world—her freedom to do as she wished. She had been suspicious of his motives at first, but then she saw it in his face: he wanted her to stay but had given her true freedom to leave and expected absolutely nothing in return. It was a gift, pure and simple. They were friends.

Serafina threw herself onto the bed, rolled onto her back, and unbuttoned her coat. Of course, she wouldn't leave no matter how large the inheritance (and it was very large!). She could not even contemplate it. Her life was here with Molly and John. Her heart was inexplicably tethered to this little girl and this damaged man in a way that defied mere words. She smiled to herself. She certainly wasn't going to tell John that she could not leave no matter the size of the inheritance. She had embarrassed herself enough as it was with her emotional outbursts and her weeping. She needed to regain an air of composure and calm.

But how to do that? she thought as she rolled herself once across the bed, sat up, and wriggled out of her coat. *Carry on as normal. As if nothing has changed. John is my friend and nothing more. If he wanted something more, he would ask.*

"What happened with John?" asked Molly casually as she hovered her hand over a plate of biscuits.

Serafina sipped a steaming cup of tea. They were seated in the main drawing room of the London house, the afternoon of 'the event' as Serafina had come to think of it.

"Whatever do you mean?" Serafina bounced back.

"It looked like you and John were having an argument." Molly's eyes were wide and the corners of her mouth twitched with contained amusement.

"I would not argue with Mr. Thornton, Molly. He is my employer."

"I could hear you yelling through the door," said Molly taking a bite out of an iced lemon shortbread and chewing with exaggerated enthusiasm.

Serafina placed her teacup in its saucer and put it on the table beside her.

"Are you enjoying your biscuit?" she asked, eyes narrowed.

"Very much!" said Molly shoving the remaining shortbread into her mouth. She swallowed her snack and dabbed at the corners of her mouth with a napkin.

"I don't know much about gentlemen—" started Molly.

"—No. You don't," interrupted Serafina.

"—but I do know that as a rule, they do not like being yelled at by their employees," added Molly with a grin. "And yet, for some reason, John emerged from that room looking happier than I have ever seen him."

A Dangerous Man to Trust?

"Molly! Were you listening at the door?"

"No!" countered Molly defensively. "Spencer made me leave . . . but I snuck back a little later."

"John—Mr. Thornton—looked happy?"

Molly nodded. She had reached for a second biscuit, and was eyeing it thoughtfully. Keeping her eyes on the biscuit, Molly asked, "Does that make *you* happy?"

Serafina looked at the little girl in front of her. Her dark brown hair pinned up in ringlets, her intense blue eyes so like her brother's. She loved this little girl with all her heart.

"You are too much, Molly. You know that, don't you?"

"I know it," said Molly leaning forward with her teacup so that Serafina might refill it from the silver pot on the table.

Serafina smiled. Molly was quick, and she was observant. A proper little scientist. Just like her, Molly had experienced a great loss—both her parents gone at such a young age. Serafina knew what that could do to a person, and she counted it a privilege to be able to soften that blow for Molly in any way that she could. With her unwavering love. With her unconditional presence.

Very early the following morning, in fact, just as the sun had cleared the horizon, John stepped out of his study to see Serafina in a coat heading for the front door with a pair of gloves in her hands.

"Off for a walk before Molly wakes up?"

She turned, a little surprised to see him.

"Yes, that's the idea."

John did not like the thought of her walking about London

The Ship of Theseus

unescorted. *She wasn't even taking Spencer this time!*

"Would you mind if I join you?" he asked.

"On the street?"

"Yes," said John, a little confused by the question. "London is full of streets."

"Would that be . . . I mean . . . without Molly . . ." Serafina did not seem able to finish her thought.

"Without Molly, it will be a nice quiet walk," said John with a grin.

"Yes, I suppose . . . Yes, all right."

John left Serafina waiting in a splash of buttery yellow light that streamed in through the glass above the front door. He went to fetch his coat and hat. When he reentered the foyer, she turned to him, and her face was lit golden in the morning light making her appear as she had in the candlelight of that darkened hallway so many months ago—like some kind of apparition. John stopped short in his tracks.

"Is something the matter?" she asked.

"It's the light," said John.

"It's wonderful, is it not? I like to wake up early to catch it—first a rose pink as the sun peers over the horizon, then it turns gold. It will be gone soon. Not the light, but the colour for some reason."

"If you do not know the reason for the change of colour, then no one does," said John putting on his hat. "You seem to know everything. You certainly appear to have read every scientific book in my father's collection."

"It is entirely likely that someone does know the reason for the change in colour. Sir Isaac Newton comes to mind."

"He's dead," said John with amusement.

Serafina rolled her eyes. "I do not need your compliments,"

she said putting on her gloves.

Of course she didn't need them, but John could see from her face that she liked them. He had only said what he thought. She was perhaps the most intelligent woman he had ever met. His father had struck gold when he had hired her as governess for Molly.

If she were a man, thought John, *she would be giving lectures, not babysitting small children.*

They stepped outside together into the crisp autumn air.

"Take my arm," said John.

Serafina gave him an odd look, but she slid her hand into the crook of his arm. Her fierce little grip brought a smile to his face.

"Hyde Park?" he asked.

"I don't mind," said Serafina.

John could feel her capitulating to his takeover of the walk, and he didn't like it.

"Serafina," he said. She was quick to respond to her name, looking to his face in an instant. He even thought he saw her pupils dilate despite the bright morning light. "Where would you have gone if I hadn't joined you?"

"I would have probably wandered," she said. "Aimlessly," she added.

"Right then," said John. "Aimless wandering it is. You lead."

Serafina seemed pleased. John had expected she would lead with verbal directions—"Let's take a left here," or "Carry on straight ahead,"—but instead, she led through touch. Her strong grip on his arm nudged him one way and then another. Eventually, he came to realise that a squeeze of his arm meant he should come to a stop so that she could decide how to proceed. Standing at one corner waiting for his next tactile

The Ship of Theseus

instruction, John felt as a horse might beneath a rider. He shook his head, but he could not shake off the image of her as his rider, her thighs wrapped around him, holding him in place . . .

They ambled past a trickle of early morning activity. A man driving a horse and cart over the cobbles—deliveries perhaps. Two maids running errands. A fine carriage returning a fine gentleman home after a long night of entertainment. John had been that man once upon a time. How pointless his life had been. Every conversation had been a competition, every beautiful woman a game. He had been truly unhappy, and he had carried that unhappiness like a disease, infecting those with whom he came into contact.

And now? thought John. *How is it different now?*

Serafina tugged him to the left and led him across one more street.

"We appear to have found our way to the park nonetheless," she said looking delightedly up into his face. "John?"

John brought himself back to the present, but he could feel the shadow of his past self hovering over him, haunting him.

"Are you all right?" asked Serafina.

"Never better."

"Why is it I don't believe you?" she asked.

"It's nothing," said John. "Our walk has brought back some old memories—that's all."

"Bad memories," said Serafina.

John looked at her. He felt as if he was made of ice, and he was melting under her warm gaze. He wanted her to know. To know him, the true him. Not some version of himself that he presented for show. *She should know*, he thought.

"I have not always been . . ." started John, but he couldn't

A Dangerous Man to Trust?

finish his sentence.

Serafina was looking at him strangely, as if gauging her next move. He had to look away. She thought she saw him because she had seen him unmasked, but that was just his body. She did not see his spirit—not properly. If she did, she would not be here in a practically empty park first thing in the morning clinging hold of his arm.

"Come," she said, sliding her hand from the crook of his elbow down to his wrist. She led him over to a bench where they sat. "What is it?" she asked. "What is bothering you?"

"You should know," said John, "that I used to be . . . that is, I have not always been . . ." He truly did not know how to say what he should say. And if he was honest with himself, he feared her judgment, he feared losing her esteem.

Serafina surprised him by reading his mind: "Do you mean to say that you used to be unlikeable? That you have not always been particularly thoughtful?" asked Serafina.

"Yes. That," said John. "How did you know?"

"As you said earlier, I know everything." She looked to him to see if her little attempt at humour was working, but she didn't want to sound dismissive, so she added, "And you are my friend. I'm very sensitive when it comes to my friends."

She seemed to think that enough of an explanation.

"Also," said John, taking a breath as if readying himself for a plunge, "I have . . . I had . . . well, I probably have . . ." he trailed off.

"A reputation with women?" supplied Serafina matter-of-factly.

John looked at her with incredulity.

"I have been told as much," said Serafina, "and I could surmise."

The Ship of Theseus

"Does this not bother you?" asked John. "Do you not feel uncomfortable in my employ . . . as my friend?"

Serafina placed her hands in her lap, and her lips parted to speak once more. John would never forget what she said next.

"I only know the man I see in front of me. I do not know this other man from the past. I've never met him."

"But we are one and the same," said John.

"In one sense, yes," said Serafina. "But in another sense, not at all." He looked at her quizzically. She smiled and said as if by way of explanation. "As you know, I read a lot." When John opened his mouth to speak, she raised a finger to silence him. "There are several books of philosophy in your father's collection," she said. "Not natural philosophy, but the philosophy of the ancients. There is a paradox referred to as The Ship of Theseus."

"Theseus? You mean the prince who killed the Minotaur?" John could not imagine where she was going with this.

"The very same," said Serafina. "After Theseus killed the Minotaur on the island of Crete, he escaped on a ship to the island of Delos and then home to Athens. To commemorate Theseus's achievement, each year the Athenians would sail Theseus's ship on a pilgrimage to Delos. They did this regularly for hundreds of years. As you can imagine, Theseus's ship fell into disrepair. Floor boards needed to be replaced, new sails sewn, and eventually after hundreds of years, the entire ship had been replaced, piece by piece." Serafina looked up at John with a triumphant look in her eye. "The question is," she said, "can we still say that this is the same ship? Theseus's ship?"

The light of understanding began to settle over John's face. Serafina continued to drive her point home.

A Dangerous Man to Trust?

"And what of you, John Thornton? If, over the years, you have replaced one inclination with another, one habit or behaviour with another, can we say you are still the same man? In a sense, yes, your identity as John Thornton remains intact, but in a sense, no since your constituent parts are entirely different. Therein lies the paradox. I choose to see you as you are now with your new component parts. I don't know this other person from the past who was also called John Thornton."

John did not know how he was looking at Serafina just then, but it made her blush. She looked down at her hands, and he had to resist the urge to reach for her chin, to lift it up and turn her gaze to his once more. He had thought she was special, but he had not realised just how special. He wanted her with him. Always. Forever. Seated beside him on a bench. Tugging him down the street. Yelling at him in the reception room.

Dear Lord, what have I done to have this woman placed not simply in my path but in my house?

He desperately wanted her as his wife, but how could he ask, and would she even agree? She might be his friend, but he was still something quite hideous to behold. Sure, she did not mind his face, but it was not simply his face—his body was a horror. Even if they married, she could never want. . . He could never ask it of her. John's mind darted from one thought to the next. Just the day before he had offered her a gift of freedom. The inheritance. If he asked her to marry him now, it would seem as if he had paid for the privilege, as if it had all been some scheme to soften her towards him. And it wasn't. It truly wasn't.

"John?"

Serafina was looking at him again. He had been silent a little

The Ship of Theseus

too long.

"Thank you," said John in all earnestness.

"Do you feel any better?"

John recovered his composure. "I feel like a new man." He said it with a wink and smile and was gratified when Serafina's face appeared to bloom with happiness.

"Good," she said. "I could not bear it if you were sad."

She could not bear it?

Again, John thought of asking her to marry him. Again, good sense overrode his impulse.

Serafina had been thrown off-guard by the idea that John wished to accompany her out into the street. Without Molly. Just the two of them. Of course, they often strolled the grounds of Bosworth Manor together, but this was different. This was public. It was certainly not how an employer behaved with a governess.

But it was how a friend might behave with a friend, thought Serafina.

John was nothing if not true to his word. The outing had certainly been friendly. That John had chosen to open up to her about his past was no small thing, and Serafina still cradled that feeling of intimacy close to her heart. It had been such a lovely outing until Lady Langley had arrived.

After Serafina had told the story about the ship of Theseus, she and John had continued sitting on that bench for some time. Soon their conversation turned to Molly as it so often did. How was she faring with her tutors? What little and not-so-little projects was she contemplating now? Serafina

A Dangerous Man to Trust?

would tell John something shocking that Molly had said, and they would both laugh. John would counter with his own amusing tale of his sister. They made a kind of game of it, and their laughter rang out over the park that stretched away like a green carpet in front of them. So taken were they with their own company that they did not even notice the park was beginning to fill. It was not crowded as it would be during the fashionable hour of the day, but it was certainly no longer empty. They paid no attention when a lady slowed her step as she approached them along the path in front of their bench. They barely noticed that she had stopped entirely.

"John?!"

Both Serafina and John looked up in surprise to see the most exquisite creature standing in front of them—a beautiful young lady who was wearing the most expensive and fashionable clothing. The ringlets that hung down from beneath her bonnet looked like they had been spun from pure golden sunlight. Her face was the face of a porcelain doll. Skin like the smoothest alabaster and eyes so large and green it almost felt as if you might fall in if you did not occasionally look away. Serafina usually did not spend much time thinking about her own appearance, but faced with the radiance of this lady, she could not help feeling like a clod of dirt in comparison. Serafina glanced behind the lady, and sure enough, there was her maid waiting at a respectable distance.

John scrabbled to his feet immediately. Serafina followed a little more hesitantly.

"Eleanor," he said in a voice that was pure gravel.

He was nervous! Serafina could sense the quick shift in his demeanour. It did not escape Serafina that they were using each other's Christian names.

The Ship of Theseus

They know each other well, thought Serafina. *Very well.*

"Ah, this . . ." said John dipping his head toward Serafina, ". . . this is my friend Miss Edgemont. Miss Edgemont this is Miss—"

"—I'm no longer a Miss, interrupted the lady. If you will forgive me making my own introduction," she said to Serafina, "I am Lady Langley."

"Pleased to meet you," was all Serafina could muster.

"You married," said John.

"Yes. The Viscount Langley. But I have not had much luck with husbands. He passed on just under two years ago. His heart, you see. I am widowed."

"My condolences," said John.

Lady Langley accepted his sentiment with a tiny nod.

"I was sorry to hear of your father," said Lady Langley.

"I've returned to Bosworth Manor," said John a little awkwardly. "My sister is there."

"Yes. You have a sister."

Serafina could only watch as the two of them looked at each other for what she felt was an extended length of time.

"It's good to see you, John. I'm so glad you have chosen to join the land of the living once more."

"Yes," said John without smiling.

"I am hosting a ball next week. If I had known you were in town, I would have sent an invitation."

"That's quite all right," said John quickly.

"No. You should come. I will have an invitation delivered to make it official."

Lady Langley looked to Serafina as if she might extend the same invitation her way, but Serafina could see that she wasn't looking at her but instead past her.

A Dangerous Man to Trust?

She is looking for my lady's maid, thought Serafina. *My chaperone. And now that she does not see a lady's maid, she is deciding who or what I am.*

"Nice to meet you . . . Miss Edgemont, was it?"

"Likewise," Serafina nodded.

Lady Langley looked to John. "I hope to see you next week. Don't even think of disappointing me, John."

"It has been good to see you," he said.

Lady Langley left, taking her dazzling eyes and her perfect skin with her down the path. The maid trailed after her offering John and Serafina a nod as she passed by. Serafina lifted her hand to acknowledge the maid. John stared after Lady Langley as if deep in thought.

"Shall we make our way back?" asked Serafina.

"Pardon? Uh . . . yes . . . rather . . . I should think." John's mind was clearly elsewhere, and Serafina for some reason felt as if she were sinking, disappearing down into the earth.

John took her hand distractedly and placed it to his arm. There was no "Lead the way," or "How should you like to return?" He simply led her home in silence. When they arrived back at the house. He turned to her just inside the front door.

"I'm sorry about that," he said.

"Not at all," said Serafina. "It's always nice to see an old friend."

"I shall have to attend her ball," said John staring off into space.

"It would be the polite thing to do," said Serafina. "Though it should not be a chore. Lady Langley is likely an excellent hostess." Serafina forced herself to follow up this statement with, "You might enjoy yourself."

She smiled, trying her best to make sure her smile reached

her eyes, so that he would not see the disappointment, the hurt in her face.

Twelve

London Gossip

The Pembertons were soon in touch and inviting the Thornton household (of which they clearly considered Serafina to be a member) over to their house for tea.

"I'm excited to see their new dog!" said Molly as she ran up the front steps of the Pemberton house, ringlets bouncing.

"They have a dog?" asked Serafina.

"Grace sent me a note," said Molly. She turned at the top of the steps to address John and Serafina. "I get all the London gossip through my various contacts."

John and Serafina looked to each other reflexively, eyebrows raised.

Most of the Pembertons were waiting for them in a vibrant

yellow drawing room.

"Mother did not think one yellow room was enough," whispered Patience as she took Serafina by the arm and led her to a low couch upholstered in yet more yellow.

Molly dashed across the room to see Grace and her new dog.

"Is this it?" she asked Grace, gesturing to the small tan-coloured pug on the carpet.

"Yes, isn't she lovely? She is very affectionate. I've named her Potato."

"Potato," said Molly slowly. "The name fits . . . I mean she does look a bit like a potato."

"Doesn't she though?" said Grace, enthusiastically petting the tiny dog so that it started to yip and run in little circles.

Molly gave Serafina a wide-eyed look, and Serafina had to repress a small chuckle. Potato was not a dog according to Molly's system of classification, but Molly was certainly being polite about it, so Serafina thought she ought to count that as a win.

John had been waylaid on his way in through the drawing-room doors. George was taking the time to re-introduce him to Lord Pemberton, and Lord Pemberton appeared to be taking the interaction very seriously. He always did when it came to other gentlemen.

"And how was the trip down?" asked Lord Pemberton.

"The usual," said John. "The roads were dry, so that was something for which to be thankful. Although I daresay Miss Edgemont could do without several hours in a rattling carriage. She looked practically green by the time we arrived."

Why would he say that? thought Serafina. It seemed unnecessary.

A Dangerous Man to Trust?

"It's the wheels," said Lord Pemberton. "Some are better than others at cushioning the impact of a rough voyage."

"I doubt it's the wheels!" called Molly across the room.

"Molly!" hissed Serafina.

"This is your sister," said Lord Pemberton to John.

Serafina could see the baron disguise the initial shock of being so addressed by a child from across the room. Lord Pemberton cared a lot for manners. Serafina had quickly learned that fact when living in his home after her parents had died. He appreciated good manners, common sense, a stiff upper lip, and order. Serafina had qualified on all those counts and so had risen in his esteem during her stay with his family.

"Yes, Miss Molly Thornton," said John. "Please excuse her enthusiasm."

Molly jumped up and made a deep curtsy. "I am ever-so-pleased to make your acquaintance Your Lordship. You have a very fine canine here," she said gesturing to Potato who was gnawing on Grace's shoe.

Serafina pressed a hand to her mouth to keep from laughing.

"As I was saying," said Molly. "I doubt very much that it is the wheels. The comfort of the journey will rest on the manner in which those wheels are attached to the carriage. There needs to be some mechanism to absorb the shock, the force of movement. There needs to be some give, some flexibility. Otherwise the force with which the wheels are impacted will travel up into the carriage."

Lord Pemberton stared at Molly in silence. Potato let up a low whine until Grace fed her a biscuit.

"Miss Molly Thornton is it? Well. I do believe you are correct. Here is a young lady filled to the brim with sense!"

said Lord Pemberton to his children.

"He does not think that I am filled with sense," whispered Patience into Serafina's ear. "But he loves me anyway." Serafina grinned at her friend.

Just then, Lady Pemberton bustled into the room, all apologies for her tardiness.

"Mr. Thornton. So wonderful of you to come. And you have met my husband of course the last time you were in town. George, I am so pleased you could come as well. All the family together at last! Come. Sit. Sit. Has no one called for the tea yet? Patience?"

"We were waiting for you," said Patience.

"Right. Well, we're all here now."

Patience hopped up to ring the bell and call for tea. John took a seat beside Serafina on the couch and opposite George. Lord Pemberton rested himself in a large wingback at the top of the low tea table near George and John.

Tea was a jolly affair, though perhaps not quite as jolly as it might have been without Lord Pemberton present. Serafina could sense the slight edge of tension with which George held himself in his father's presence. Patience and Grace, however, did not seem to notice. They were themselves whether their father was present or not. And Lady Pemberton was shining in the company of her husband. It was clear she had missed him for those weeks they had been apart. Serafina remembered theirs as a loving marriage—something she had not experienced with her own parents. Staying with the Pembertons offered her a glimpse into what a marriage might be like. Certainly, it was not perfect. Lord Pemberton was a bit stiff, and he appeared to have some trouble reading the emotions of others—this sometimes caused problems. On the other hand, Lady Pemberton was perhaps too loose in her associations. She was so gregarious and open with her friendship, and this had on many occasions complicated their lives significantly.

Just think of me, for one, thought Serafina. *To take me in, just like that, without a second thought.*

Lord Pemberton had not initially been pleased with his wife's choice to bring yet another young person into the family home, but he had allowed it nevertheless. Serafina had felt his reticence behind his polite words. But he had warmed to her over the months she had stayed with them, and when she had finally decided to leave to take employment with Mr. Thornton, Lord Pemberton had called her into his study for a quiet word.

"Miss Edgemont," (he always called her Miss Edgemont) "I would be remiss if I did not say that your absence will be felt."

"Oh. Well. That is kind of you to say. I hope I have not been too much of a burden."

"No. Not *too* much," he said.

"I shall make my own way from now on."

"If that is your wish. However, I hope you are not leaving on my account. Lady Pemberton tells me that I do not give off the most welcome manner. It is an affliction I am afraid."

"Not at all," said Serafina not really knowing what to say.

"You are welcome to return at any time," said Lord Pemberton.

"Thank you, my lord."

"Very well, then. I wish you the best of luck."

Serafina was brought back to the yellow drawing room by Potato who had abandoned Grace's shoes and was now trying to make a meal of hers. She picked up the little dog, put it in

London Gossip

her lap, and stroked it gently along the neck and behind the ears. Potato settled down and leaned into her ministrations.

"Miss Edgemont has a way with animals," said John. "My mastiff Rupert follows her wherever she goes."

"Does he now?" said Lord Pemberton.

"I do believe that dogs serve the opposite purpose to a canary in a coalmine. They are there to tell us where to find the best circumstances in life," said Lady Pemberton who was beaming at Serafina and John. "And clearly, Potato knows where it will be best."

Serafina felt herself to be on display and tried desperately to think of a way to shift the conversation. Patience came to her rescue.

"I am so looking forward to Lady Langley's ball," she said.

Serafina knew full well that she wasn't. She never looked forward to balls. So this was Patience trying to divert her mother. *What a friend!* Serafina looked towards her gratefully, and Patience widened her eyes and lifted her eyebrows in a playful manner to acknowledge Serafina's unspoken thanks.

"That is heartening to hear, my dear," said Lady Pemberton excitedly. "It should be one of the highlights of the early Season and an opportunity to meet some of the most eligible gentlemen of the ton."

She turned to John. "I hear you have also been extended an invitation, Mr. Thornton."

News travels fast in London, thought Serafina.

"I . . . ah . . ." John looked at Serafina before he answered properly. "Yes, Lady Langley happened upon me at Hyde Park, and there was no escape."

At this, Lord Pemberton gave a low chuckle. Lady Pemberton looked at Serafina and back to John.

A Dangerous Man to Trust?

Grace reached into Serafina's lap to pet Potato as she said, "Lady Langley is perhaps the most beautiful lady in London, maybe the world. She looks as if she has just stepped out of a fairytale. Perhaps she *is* a fairy."

Lady Pemberton gave Grace an oddly stern look, but Grace continued: "Were you not engaged to be married to Lady Langley, Mr. Thornton?"

Serafina's heart felt as if it had dropped down into her lap with Potato. Her breath caught in her chest.

"Grace!" scolded Lady Pemberton.

Grace looked confused by the scolding. "But that's what *you* were saying, Mama."

Lady Pemberton flushed a pale pink.

"It's all right," said John. "It's no secret. We were to be married, but it is all in the past now."

"It's like a novel," said Grace. "Mama said that Lady Langley called the wedding off after your accident."

"Grace! Mr. Thornton, I apologise profusely for my daughter."

"Sorry," said Grace a bit belatedly. She turned to her mother, "He just now said it wasn't a secret, so I thought . . ."

"I will be speaking with you later," hissed Lady Pemberton in a loud whisper.

Serafina looked at John whose hand had made its way to his neck and was fiddling with his cravat. He avoided her gaze. The image of Lady Langley floated into her mind—a vision of absolute feminine perfection. As Lady Pemberton made a valiant attempt to change the subject of the conversation, Serafina's mind was collapsing in on itself.

Lady Langley broke it off with him. He had intended to marry her. He had loved her. That would explain his nervousness at their meeting in the park, the way he went completely silent on the way home. Oh Serafina, you are such a fool. If he wanted more, he would ask, and he hasn't asked. But he did ask her once upon a time. He wanted more from her. And now here she was again. Widowed and inviting him to her ball, insisting he come. Whatever happened between them to call off the engagement, it was clearly water under the bridge. Lady Langley had extended an olive branch with her oh-so-delicate fingers.

Serafina thought of her life at Bosworth Manor with John and Molly. If things simply continued as they were for the rest of her life, she would be happy. It would be enough. But if John took a wife . . . Serafina knew she would have to leave. Thinking these thoughts, Serafina began to notice that the yellow room was wobbling around her. It was almost as if the room itself were breathing. The voices of the company came to her like an echo, all fuzzy at the edges. She carefully lifted Potato and placed the dog on Grace's lap. Then leaned over Grace and whispered to Patience.

"Patience, I have come over all strange. I do believe I will be sick."

Patience registered the situation immediately (so did Grace, but Patience gave her wrist a little squeeze, and this seemed to be a cue to remain silent).

Standing, Patience said, "If you will excuse us for a moment, I would like to have Serafina's opinion on a painting." She took Serafina by the arm and hurried her from the room. Serafina could just make out Lady Pemberton saying something about artists being, as a rule, impulsive creatures.

Patience rushed Serafina down the hall, around the corner, and into some sort of storage room for linens and other household items. Serafina was immediately sick into a cerulean blue porcelain wash basin. Patience was at her side, passing her a cloth to clean her face.

"Would you like some water?"

Serafina nodded. Patience disappeared and soon returned with a blue porcelain pitcher that matched the basin.

"There aren't any cups in here. You'll have to drink directly from the pitcher."

Serafina rinsed her mouth, and as she spat the water out into the basin, the door to the room opened.

"Serafina!" It was John, followed closely by Lady Pemberton.

"It's nothing. I'm fine," said Serafina sitting down on a stool that Patience had pushed forward.

"It's not nothing," said John. He sounded quite cross. "You are not fine."

John stepped through the room to lower himself down onto one knee in front of Serafina so that they might be at eye level. She couldn't look at him. She was looking at her lap.

"Serafina, look at me," he said sternly.

She lifted her eyes to his.

"Do you need to lie down?"

"No. I told you I'm fine."

"Right. Well. I think you've had enough tea for today. Lady Pemberton," he said without taking his eyes from Serafina, "unfortunately we will have to cut our visit short. I will have to call a physician."

"No, really," said Serafina. She was about to say it was nothing again, but John was looking so vexed that she thought she'd better not.

London Gossip

Lady Pemberton had insisted on keeping Molly for the rest of the day.

"She will amuse herself with Grace and Potato. It will give you some time to rest and recover," she had said.

John was staring across to Serafina in the carriage as they rode home. He was feeling quite exasperated with her. Exasperated and worried. It was an unfamiliar combination, and he was struggling to get a hold of himself. He had never before been so concerned for someone else's health. Here was a circumstance completely beyond his control. It was an altogether unpleasant sensation, and he almost felt like Serafina should not have been sick, that she was to blame somehow. He knew it was irrational, but he felt it nonetheless.

"Why?" he asked with some agitation. "I was sitting right beside you. Why would you not tell me if you were feeling unwell?"

Serafina gave him a queasy glance, then shifted her gaze out the window.

"I didn't want to disturb the tea," she said flatly.

"Well, I will be calling a physician when we arrive back at the house," said John in a clipped tone.

"No need," said Serafina, still looking out the window.

"I will decide that," said John.

Serafina finally looked at him.

"And why will *you* decide that?" she asked. A hint of colour was slowly rising in her cheeks. "I am the one who is unwell, and I have said that there is no need."

"I will decide because I am in charge here," said John irritably.

"I see," said Serafina in a derisive tone. "I forgot. You are my employer. And you are also a man. Of course you are

A Dangerous Man to Trust?

in charge. I will have to do as you say, won't I? Or face the consequences."

John could feel his hackles rising. *She was so incredibly stubborn!*

"I'm glad you understand the situation," said John, leaning into the role she had laid out for him.

When the carriage pulled up to the house, John alighted and reached out his hand for Serafina. She refused to take it, attempting to disembark on her own. John could see that she was still quite unsteady on her feet.

"Serafina! For God's sake, take my hand. I will not have you falling in the street!"

Serafina gave him a fierce look, but she took his hand. He did not let it go as they mounted the steps to the entrance. Spencer greeted them at the door, but John could only manage the barest of nods as they passed him by. He kept her hand in his as they crossed the foyer. And he did not let go as he led her up the staircase and to her room. All he could think about was putting her to bed and calling a physician.

As he entered her bed chamber with her, Serafina turned to him quizzically.

"What are you doing?"

"Putting you to bed," said John matter-of-factly. "Here. Let me help you off with your coat." He could see that she was still a bit dizzy from the way she rested a hand to the bureau to steady herself.

"I'm fine," she said. Then, "Oh," as she pressed a hand to her forehead.

John fumbled with the buttons on her coat, and leaned in towards her as he slid it from her shoulders. He made her sit on the side of the bed and crouched down at her feet.

London Gossip

"What are you doing?" she asked him again.

"Removing your boots," said John. "Unless you think you will not plant your face in the floor if you lean over," he added.

Serafina responded with silence.

Tugging at the laces of her boots reminded him of the night he had slipped his hands down her dress to loosen her corset . . . which made him think.

"Are you wearing a corset?" asked John.

"Why do you ask?"

"Because if you are, it should come off. I can call a maid."

"No. No corset," said Serafina.

"Good," said John as he slid one hand behind her lower leg in order to remove her boot with the other. "Corsets are such foolish devices."

Once he had removed both her boots, he stood and appraised his patient.

"Time to lie down. Can you manage that?"

"Yes," said Serafina peevishly.

Once she was lying on top of the bed covers, John moved quickly to fetch a blanket from a chair across the room and pulled it up over her body.

"Comfortable?" It was a question, but he barked it like an order. *Why was his heart racing?*

Serafina simply nodded. She closed her eyes which for some reason sent John into a panic.

"Serafina!"

Her eyes popped open.

"What?"

"Nothing. I just thought . . . I thought perhaps you had fainted."

"I'm only resting," said Serafina. "That is what you want,

A Dangerous Man to Trust?

isn't it?"

John pressed a palm to her forehead.

"I'm not feverish if that's what you're thinking."

"We shall let the physician decide," said John. And with that, he left the room.

He took the stairs two at a time to the ground floor, shouting for Spencer and cursing himself for not instructing him to call a physician at the outset.

"Very good, Sir."

"Sharpish!" barked John when he noticed that his internal panic was not translating into quicker action on Spencer's part.

Serafina had known that the physician would be of no use. She was not truly ill. It was simply the physical manifestation of the emotion she had felt when she thought of the possibility that John might marry, that she might have to leave Bosworth Manor. Nevertheless, the physician—a Dr. Thompson—made a fuss of taking her pulse and looking into her eyes and mouth.

"No fever," he asserted looking to John as if for approval. John *was* paying the bill after all. "It's likely nothing serious. Perhaps something she ate. Since she is no longer expelling her stomach contents and is simply fatigued, I would say that she is likely on the upswing. Have the maid bring her some peppermint water. I would be very surprised if she wasn't up and about by this evening."

Dr. Thompson stood and picked up his black leather case.

"Are you sure?" asked John. "She is looking very peaked."

"Nothing that a little rest will not fix," said the physician.

London Gossip

"And remember the peppermint water." Serafina shifted herself up in her bed. "I shall send you the bill in due course, Mr. Thornton," said Dr. Thompson to John before saying his farewells. "Send for me if anything changes."

When the physician left, Serafina was left alone in her bed chamber with John who was staring out the door. It had taken some time for the physician to arrive, and in that time, Serafina felt as if she was at least partially recovered from the initial shock of her previous realisation.

"Peppermint water!" said Serafina. "You could have stopped any woman on the street, and she would have offered the same advice."

"But he is a physician," said John.

"I'm sure he shall charge you a pretty penny for that fact," said Serafina.

"I'm happy to pay for the peace of mind," said John.

"I would have felt better if you hadn't," said Serafina sliding back down on her pillows. She *was* feeling a little tired.

She closed her eyes, and when she woke, the light had changed. The sun had set, and only a hint of its luminous spirit remained—a kind of purplish twilight cast itself through the window and into her room. When she rolled over on the bed, there was John sitting in a chair watching her.

"Your peppermint water," he said picking up a cup from the bedside table.

Thirteen

Nip it in the Bud

J ohn did not know what to think of Serafina's demeanour. She had recovered from her illness quickly just as the physician had predicted, but she seemed to build each of the following days upon a foundation of melancholy. Not that she advertised the fact. No. She smiled and even laughed. She teased Molly, played cards, and visited with Patience.

She is trying her best to disguise her feelings, thought John. *She didn't want to come to London. Perhaps, it has been too long away from home. Of course she would not say anything. It is just a few more days until the solicitor finishes up the papers for her inheritance. Then we can be rid of this wretched city.*

The evening of Lady Langley's ball arrived, and John steeled himself for a night of polite and trivial conversation. His valet had done a marvellous job of outfitting him for the occasion, but John was feeling anxious in anticipation of the evening and had been pulling at his cravat all the way down the stairs

Nip it in the Bud

to the front door. Serafina was standing by a table in the foyer with a letter in her hand.

"You look quite fine," said Serafina. Her face was solemn.

"I never look fine," said John. "I look like the Devil, but I suppose yours is a relative statement, so I will accept it."

"It is an absolute statement," said Serafina seriously. "Except for your cravat. Lady Langley will think you a boor if you walk into her ball like that."

Serafina stepped up to John and reached her little hands up to fix his cravat. Not something a governess would normally do, but theirs was a friendship that had crossed those bounds of propriety on several occasions, leaving them with a sense of relaxed familiarity in each other's presence. John closed both his eyes for just a moment.

"Lady Langley already thinks me a boor," said John, "so no further harm would be done."

"That is not the impression I received when she spoke to you in the park."

"She is excessively polite," said John.

"Hm." Serafina stood back. "There. Now you are ready to go. Enjoy your evening."

John thought her eyes looked sad.

"What will you do this evening without a third for Whist?"

"I imagine Molly will entertain herself writing yet another note to Grace," said Serafina. "And I shall read."

"Of course," said John. "Of course."

The ball was as he had expected it would be—a glorious twinkling affair, humming with conversation and reeling with music. Young ladies circled the outside edges of the room like flower petals waiting to fall into the arms of a would-be dance partner or a would-be husband. John spied Lady Leveson-Gower doing the rounds and a few other acquaintances he had run into the last time he had been in town. He could see Lord Pemberton speaking with a few older gentlemen on the other side of the room.

"John—I'm so glad you could come."

Eleanor had glided up behind him. As John turned to face her, his eyes caught on a man he thought he would never see again—Theodore Cross. He had to take control of the bile that was rising in his throat in order to divert his attention and address the hostess of the ball. She was standing in front of him in a green silk dress as thin as gossamer and clinging to the outline of her silhouette. A chemise worn as a dress would have offered her more coverage, but it was clear she wasn't wearing one of those at all. John forced his eyes to Eleanor's face which was beaming at him like a star.

"I would not have missed it," he said.

"If I had not been so insistent, you might have," said Eleanor with a cheeky smile. "I hear you are a changed man, John Thornton."

"Where would you hear that?" asked John.

"Here and there. It seems you are quite the father figure to your little sister Molly. Staying with her at Bosworth Manor, hiring tutors."

"Ah, the tutors are the gossips, are they? Or is it the servants?"

"Everyone's a gossip," said Eleanor leaning in towards him.

There had been a lull in the music as they spoke, but it started up once more. Lady Leveson-Gower had made her way over once she had registered John and his mask (they were hard to miss).

"So good to see you again, John," she said, and the sentiment sounded genuine. "The evening will be an interesting one now that you're here." John didn't know what to make of that statement at all.

"Yes," said Eleanor, "He was just asking me to dance." John turned his face sharply in Eleanor's direction.

"Of course," he said with a bow and lifted an open palm for her hand.

Her silky white glove slid against his skin, and he led her mechanically out onto the dance floor. They began to dance, and it seemed to John that Eleanor was manoeuvering herself a little too close to his body—well, not *too* close—but certainly closer than expected.

She is not the woman she was before—shy and innocent, he thought.

She was a widow now, and if he knew one thing about widows, it was that they knew what they wanted, and they knew how to ask for it.

It has all been leading up to this moment, thought John. He simply had to maintain his courage and say what he needed to say.

"Eleanor," he began.

"Mmhmm," was her murmured reply as she slid gracefully along with him in time to the music.

"I want to apologise . . . for the manner in which I behaved during our engagement."

"You do?"

"Yes. I was like poison, tainting every good thing in my path. I have no excuse for it."

A Dangerous Man to Trust?

"I see."

He was momentarily distracted by the way his hand slipped over the thin silk at her waist. He could feel every curve of her through the practically non-existent fabric. *My God, it had been a long time since he'd been with a woman.* John forced himself back to his purpose.

"And your brother William."

At the mention of her brother, Eleanor missed a step, and John had to catch her as she fell in towards him. He righted her, and they picked up the dance once more.

"Not a day goes by that I do not wish I had taken his place in that fire," said John in all earnestness.

Eleanor's green eyes burned into his.

"Are you trying to butter me up, John?"

"What? No! I'm trying to apologise. I've owed you an apology for the last six years. I want you to know that I regret how I treated you . . . that I honestly regret living when William did not. To me, the passage of time has been nothing: I feel as cursed as the day it happened. I dream about that fire every night, and every night I am damned once more to relive that terrible day. If I could trade my life to give you your brother I would."

Eleanor twirled away from him and spun into him once more. They were dancing now with her back to his chest. He could feel the soft curve of her bottom against his thighs.

"John?" said Eleanor questioningly. "Your apology sounds heartfelt."

"That's because it is," said John.

Eleanor turned to face him. Her eyes were glistening.

"You hurt me."

"I know. You deserved better."

"Do you want me to say that I forgive you?"

"Of course not," said John. "I only needed for you to hear my apology."

"It's possible you have changed," said Eleanor in a wondering kind of tone, "but you are still quite clueless when it comes to society."

"What do you mean by that?"

"Let me give you a word of advice," said Eleanor, "as a way of accepting your apology."

John looked at her quizzically.

"When I saw you in the park the other day laughing so uproariously with that woman on the bench, I imagined you were having a little dalliance with an actress. It would not be out of character, would it?" she asked, but she did not wait for a reply. "I was not the only one to notice your antics at the park. You are very distinctive with your black mask." Eleanor paused as if in thought. "She *did* look like an actress—an interesting face."

"Miss Edgemont?"

"There were other ladies and gentlemen about, John. People saw you together in that park behaving the way that you did."

"Laughing?"

"Being overly familiar," replied Lady Langley. "With no chaperone present."

"I told you she is my friend . . . and she is Molly's governess." John could hear how this sounded and cringed.

"I *know* she's your sister's governess," said Eleanor.

"How do you know?" asked John.

"Because people are talking," said Eleanor. "This is my advice: you must be more careful than to carry on with the governess. It will not go well for her or for your sister."

A Dangerous Man to Trust?

"I'm not carrying on with her!" John could feel his control slipping away. "What do you mean, it will not go well?"

"How long have you been in hiding, John? This is London—London society. A governess is only as good as her blemish-free reputation. There are entire books written on the subject, though I doubt you have read any since you are a man. The governess is a model for your sister to emulate. If her reputation is questionable, then your sister shall suffer. People shall talk. I'm telling you now that they *are* talking. It would be best if you nipped this thing in the bud—be rid of the governess before any more harm can be done to your sister's reputation."

John continued their dance in a mechanical fashion. His mind was reeling. *We should never have left Bosworth Manor.*

"It's good advice," said Eleanor smiling faintly. "Probably not what you want to hear, but it's good advice. You can be forgiven for not understanding, but the situation remains. If Molly's mother were still alive, she would never have allowed this to happen. She certainly would not have hired . . . Miss Edgemont, was it? No. She would have hired someone considerably older and more homely. Someone who liked reading the Bible and wearing black dresses. Miss Edgemont is entirely too desirable to be a governess. Just ask Mr. Cross."

John's face flushed red just as their dance came to an end. He stood facing Eleanor.

"What does Mr. Cross have to say?"

"This and that," said Eleanor vaguely. "Apparently, he is in love with your governess."

"He is, is he?"

"He thinks she needs protecting . . . from you," she added.

"But Theodore Cross is a weasel of a man," said John.

"A weasel with connections," replied Eleanor. She glanced

down at John's hands which had curled into fists at his side. "Threatening Mr. Cross will not get you out of this one, John," she said as if reading his mind. "The horse has left the gate. The rumours are already spreading."

Serafina had lingered in the foyer after John had left.

He did look very fine in his tailcoat.

She had thought nothing of fixing his cravat for him. The gesture would be nothing to him anyway—they were friends, pure and simple. She conjured Lady Langley's ball in her mind, and in her vision Lady Langley looked the picture of a princess as she glided about the dance floor with John's hand on her waist.

Serafina could never have imagined how ravishing Lady Langley did, in fact, look in her green dress so thin it might have been made of spider's silk. It would have been a scandalous outfit for a young lady making her debut, but for a widow, it was simply a way to advertise her independence and the fact that she could now make her own decisions.

The Pembertons would be at the ball, remembered Serafina. She hoped that Patience would not tell her about it afterward. She did not need to hear how lovely an evening it had been for John and Lady Langley. And she certainly did not need to hear about what Lady Langley had worn or how many dances they had entertained together. One dance would be expected—it would only be polite. Two would mean something else entirely. And three would be unheard of, almost scandalous in the way it would demonstrate the couple's lack of restraint with each other. Serafina had been to a ball in her youth at which a young lady had answered in the affirmative three times when a particular gentleman had asked her to dance—whether she understood what she was doing or was simply being polite, Serafina did not know. Regardless, the resulting social fallout was such that the couple were forced to marry in order to put any rumours of the young lady's reputation to rest. Of course, that would never happen with Lady Langley. She was a widow, and widows were afforded more leeway in their interactions.

"Are you sad?" It was Molly standing on the stairs.

Serafina turned and smiled reflexively.

"Of course not."

"You look sad," said Molly. "Is it because you weren't invited to the ball?"

"Molly," said Serafina with exaggerated patience, "I would not go to another ball if I were invited to do so by a prince."

"But what if John were doing the inviting?" asked Molly.

Dear Lord, the child was sharp.

"Mr. Thornton could not invite the governess to a ball," said Serafina. "It would not be proper, and I think you know that."

"Perhaps we could have a ball at home!" said Molly brightly. "We make up our own rules at home, so governesses would be invited . . . along with children. Grace and I have been talking, and we think it is entirely unreasonable that children are excluded from so many exciting events." Molly gave Serafina a look. "So we know how you feel."

Serafina forced a laugh. "I do not feel excluded, Molly. Put your mind to rest. I am quite happy to be here with you."

"In which case," said Molly, "would you like to hear some of the latest gossip from one of my very credible sources?"

"Why do I have the feeling that you will tell me whether I

say yes or no?"

"If you can believe it, Potato, the so-called dog, has eaten all of Grace's shoes!"

Serafina raised her eyebrows.

"Well not *eaten* eaten, but certainly *ruined* all of Grace's shoes. Lady Pemberton is taking her shopping tomorrow so that she can buy some new ones. They're going to keep them in their boxes on a high shelf. Do you think I could go with them?"

"Have you been invited?" asked Serafina.

"Yes—I wouldn't invite myself!" said Molly as if that were so entirely out of the question it did not deserve a question.

"All right then. I'll send a note to Lady Pemberton first thing in the morning."

"Thank you, Serafina!"

Molly skipped down the steps and threw her arms around her governess. Serafina held the little girl to her. They stayed like that, in their embrace, for over a minute until Molly lifted her head.

"I love you, Serafina."

Molly had never said those words before, and upon hearing them, Serafina felt a sharp pang in her breast.

"I love you too. With all my heart."

"I know," said Molly with a grin.

When Molly skipped back up the stairs, Serafina waited a moment in the foyer, staring forlornly after her. Then she mounted the stairs slowly to her own bed chamber. There, she closed the door and sat gingerly on the bed before leaning her face down into a pillow. She wept quietly so that no one would hear.

A Dangerous Man to Trust?

After Lady Langley parted with John to see to her other guests, he felt stranded and completely at a loss. He cast about the room before his eyes alighted on Patience dancing with a most clumsy gentleman who was stepping all over her feet. The man looked to be apologising, and Patience had that forced look of politeness that did not disguise her distaste for the situation. John strode through the dancers and tapped Patience's dance partner on the shoulder.

"May I cut in?"

The man was flustered to see John's masked face looming over him.

I must actually look dangerous, thought John.

"Why, yes, yes, Mr. Thornton," stammered the man, looking to Patience with some sense of wonder that she had attracted this very wealthy and very forbidding man from across the room.

"Mr. Thornton," said Patience as she took his hand.

"Miss Pemberton."

"To what do I owe this surprise?"

"You seemed in need of a rescue," said John.

"You are observant. Serafina says as much."

"Does she?"

"She speaks of you all the time."

John was momentarily heartened by this fact, but he was done with small talk. Fear was rising up from his feet, and he needed to act fast before it reached his brain and rendered him entirely senseless.

"I need to find your mother," said John. "Now."

Nip it in the Bud

John ushered Lady Pemberton out of the ballroom and into a hallway. Lady Pemberton was already well aware of the situation which was certainly not a good thing. Rumours were indeed spreading.

"We must be quick, Mr. Thornton. People will notice we're missing," said Lady Pemberton. "I had intended to speak to you after the ball."

"I cannot wait that long," said John. "What do you make of the circumstance, Lady Pemberton? Is it as bad as all that?"

"I hate to say it, Mr. Thornton, but yes, it is as bad as all that. It seems to be the topic of conversation all around the ballroom. The subject was brought up less-than-surreptitiously at a tea I attended yesterday. I even heard our upstairs maid whispering about it with Lord Pemberton's valet. You are of interest, Mr. Thornton—it is your history, your dramatic and mysterious appearance. People want to know about you, and if they can't know about you, they will make things up for the simple reason that they enjoy thinking about you. It adds some excitement to their exceedingly tedious routines. It is such a shame that so many women's lives are upended by a bit of gossip. I truly feel for your sister, Mr. Thornton, not to mention Serafina."

"What is there to be done?" asked John.

"The most obvious solution is to dispense with your governess, Mr. Thornton." Lady Pemberton looked into John's face curiously as she said this. "But I can see that that is not the answer you are looking for. Am I right?"

"Molly needs Serafina like a fish needs water," said John. "I could not do that to her."

"Perhaps it is not just Molly who needs Serafina," said Lady Pemberton.

A Dangerous Man to Trust?

John reddened.

"I have treated Miss Edgemont with the utmost respect, Lady Pemberton. I am a gentleman, and she is a lady in my house. I take my position as her protector very seriously."

"Yes," said Lady Pemberton. "George has told me as much."

John pulled at his cravat. He couldn't breathe properly.

"You have only one other option, Mr. Thornton," said Lady Pemberton.

"What would that be?"

"A wedding," said Lady Pemberton. "Marry Serafina. That would put an end to the rumours. Serafina's reputation would remain intact as would your sister's. And people would certainly stop talking once you are no longer a mysterious and eligible gentleman. There is nothing so boring to society as a man wedded to the woman he loves."

"Marry her? Marry her?" John was reeling again. "Lady Pemberton, you make it sound so very simple. Serafina, as we both know, wants nothing to do with marriage."

"You have not asked her," said Lady Pemberton pertly, "so you cannot know that for certain. And . . . the situation has changed . . . Perhaps the current circumstance will force her hand."

"But I don't want to force her hand!" said John. He felt completely exasperated. "I want her to make a free choice."

"So you *do* love her," said Lady Pemberton. "That is a start. But you must remember, Mr. Thornton, no choices are free choices for a lady. We are always compelled in one way or another."

Fourteen

Our Own Rules

John left the ball in haste. By the time his carriage pulled up outside the London house, his cravat had been ripped from his neck and dropped to the seat beside him. He left it behind along with his hat and gloves as he practically leapt from the carriage. Spencer did not know what to make of his master's arrival home so early in the evening.

"Is all well, Sir?"

"No, all is not well!" said John. "Has Miss Edgemont retired to her chamber for the evening?"

"I believe so, Sir. Shall I send a maid to fetch her?"

"No," said John struggling a little manically with the buttons of his coat and shrugging it off. Spencer had to dive to catch it before it hit the floor. "I will be in my study. Do not disturb me."

"Very good, Sir."

John closed himself into his study and paced the room a

half dozen times. He was feeling excessively constricted, as if he couldn't breathe properly, but he had no cravat to loosen, so he undid his cufflinks and let them clatter to the desk. He removed his jacket and waistcoat, and then he lifted his mask from his face and angrily threw it across the room.

Molly. He had to protect Molly. *And* Serafina. This was his only job, the only real purpose in his life.

I will not force her hand, thought John. *I cannot have her marry me like that.*

Whichever way he looked, however, he found himself trapped in a box of his own making. *Perhaps if he had not taken Serafina out walking in London or if he had not been so severe with Mr. Cross . . . It is all past and done,* thought John. *The only moment to think of is now.*

John continued to pace the room, thinking, trying to find a way out. He needed a way to save Serafina from becoming trapped in a marriage with him or separated from the little girl whom she loved and who loved her. Eventually, an idea came to him. It was not the best idea, but it was the only idea he had. *We can make up our own rules*, he thought. *But I certainly cannot wait for morning.* His gaze slid up to the ceiling, to the second floor, where Serafina lay sleeping.

Serafina had gone to bed early. She had wept until she thought she could not weep anymore, and then she had wept again. She had released all of her pent-up feelings into her pillow, and when she had felt entirely empty—of tears, and hope, and happiness—she had slept. It was a kind of dead sleep. Deep and dreamless. So when John came to knock gently at her bed chamber door, it did not rouse her. He knocked again—this time even louder. Serafina slept on.

"Serafina. Serafina."

She opened her eyes in the middle of the night to find John in her room, gently shaking her awake by the shoulder. He had placed a candle by her bedside, and she could see his unmasked face in the golden glow of the light. The look on his face scared her. He looked frantic.

"Is Molly all right?!" asked Serafina, bolting up in her bed.

"Shh, yes," whispered John, lowering himself down on one knee. "Molly is fine. I need to talk to you."

"In the middle of the night?"

John was looking at her in the most painful way, as if he thought she might be dying . . . or he might be.

"Serafina. I am going to say some things, and I need you to listen."

She shifted herself to seated and lifting the bed covers, swung her legs out over the side of the bed so that she might face him. She took him in. His shirt was undone at the collar and cuffs, partially untucked at the waist. His hand moved reflexively to his throat, but finding no cravat to tug at, he pulled at his shirt as if it might be throttling him.

"John, what's wrong?"

"I came home early from the ball . . ." he started. And he proceeded to tell her everything. About the park and Mr. Cross and the rumours. About Lady Pemberton's confirmation of the seriousness of the situation for Molly and for her. "I am so sorry, Serafina. I have been too cavalier with my actions. I did not mean to cause you or Molly any harm."

Serafina opened her mouth to speak, but John lifted a hand

to silence her.

"Listen to me, Serafina. There are only two possible solutions to this problem. One solution would be for you to leave my employment, but I cannot abide that—it would destroy Molly, and I . . . I . . . have grown attached to you. We are friends, are we not? You would wish to stay?"

Serafina nodded slowly, her mind reaching out into the darkness for solution number two. She could not find one, so when John finally broached the subject of marriage, she was rendered completely speechless.

"I know you do not want to marry," said John preemptively. "You have made that very clear. But perhaps we could come to an arrangement, make up our own rules so to speak. It could be a partnership, a proper partnership so that we may continue as we are under the protective umbrella of wedlock. I would put your inheritance into trust for you. That money would remain yours should you wish to leave at any time and use it to set up your own household. And I certainly would not . . . I mean I could not expect . . . you would be under no obligation . . . that is—" (he took a breath) "—I would not burden you with my body. You should have no fear of that. And I would never . . . you spoke of your father's mistress previously . . . I would never humiliate you in that way. You have my solemn promise on that count."

He was already down on one knee on the carpet in front of her, but now he reached for her hand.

"Do you think it a viable solution?" he asked.

Serafina felt as she might if she had been knocked over by a wave at the seaside. She was surprised and disoriented, and she could not quite square the situation in front of her with the situation she had imagined.

Our Own Rules

"What about Lady Langley?" asked Serafina.

"What about her?" said John, clearly nonplussed.

"I thought . . . it's just you seemed . . ."

"Did you think I was interested in Lady Langley?" asked John.

"Well, it did occur to me . . . that a previous attachment may have been reignited."

"I have never had an attachment with Eleanor," said John. "She was engaged to another John Thornton as you well know. Someone entirely different. And he did not have a proper attachment to her either."

"So you do not love Lady Langley?"

"Love? Good gracious, no."

"And you would like to enter into a . . . partnership . . . with me?"

"It is a viable solution."

"We shall make up our own rules," said Serafina as if to herself.

"Whatever rules you like," said John. "We can do this any way you like. I do not want you to feel trapped."

"But I shall be your wife," said Serafina.

"And I shall be your husband," said John.

They stayed like that, John's hand clasping hers in her lap, for several moments in the flickering candlelight.

"Fine," said Serafina releasing his hand and swinging her feet back up onto the bed. She pulled up the covers.

"Fine?" asked John. "Is that a 'yes'?"

"It's a yes," said Serafina rolling over and away from him. "It is, as you say, a viable solution."

Serafina rested in stillness facing away from John. She waited quietly as he stood, paused over her, then left the room.

A Dangerous Man to Trust?

Once the door had clicked shut, Serafina rolled onto her back and kicked off all the covers.

What had just happened? Was that even a proposal? He cared enough to marry her, but he would not—what were his words?—burden her with his body? What did that even mean? The phrase made her think of his body. So hard and strong. She had liked the way it felt to be held against him. She liked the smell of him. Serafina drew in a deep breath from the darkness and let it all out again.

John walked with his candle along the darkened corridor to his room. She had answered him quickly—of course she had: there were only two choices. What had Lady Pemberton said? A lady's choices are always compelled. He felt relieved that Serafina had answered in the affirmative, but the way she had done so . . . turning away from him in her bed—it left him feeling a bit wounded.

What had he expected? That she would throw herself into his arms? Lavish him with kisses? Start undressing on the spot? No. He had not thought any of those things. But he was thinking them now . . . John quietly reprimanded himself . . . *He would have to maintain control of both his thoughts and his actions.*

It will have to be enough, thought John. *The status quo maintained. She may leave if ever she sees fit. She is under no obligation on any front. I have made that clear.*

As John undressed for bed, he saw her again in his mind as he had seen her in her bed chamber. Her pale sleeping face lying quiet amidst a storm of dark hair that swirled about her pillow. It was all he could do not to bend down and press his lips to the corner of her delicate little mouth.

When she had sat up in bed, her first thought was for Molly's welfare. Of course it was.

He could see again her bare feet reaching the floor with her toes and her white night dress nearly transparent in the candlelight. Seeing the shadows and shape of her body had made it difficult for him to speak.

She had not a thought to cover herself, to reach for a dressing gown. She trusted him implicitly in that regard. And she had agreed! She would be his wife.

John promised himself that he would not let her down. He would offer her every freedom to live alongside him as an equal partner. He would give her her space, and he would never, ever impose himself upon her in any way. John slid under the bed covers and soon fell asleep. As always, he dreamed that he was trapped in a burning building. He dreamed someone was dead, and it was all his fault.

In the morning, John dressed, wrote a note to be delivered to Lady Pemberton, and made for his solicitor's office. Serafina's inheritance would have to be put into trust. A marriage contract would need to be drawn up.

Serafina should not agree to anything without a contract. Lord Pemberton could take the place of her father and discuss it with her, offer his advice.

Mr. Cavendish the solicitor was all smiles as usual. He put a hand up to smooth a few wisps of hair across his balding head.

"It doesn't rain, but it pours, Mr. Thornton. First the matter of the inheritance. And now . . . putting it into trust will be an expensive affair."

"I am aware," said John curtly.

"A marriage contract as well? My, my. And this is all to do with the same Miss Edgemont, I presume."

"Yes."

"You are to be wed?"

"That is how it appears, does it not?" John was starting to feel a little impatient. "I assume that all my dealings with you are kept as private matters, Mr. Cavendish. It would be bad business for a solicitor to begin spreading gossip."

"Now, now, Mr. Thornton. I may be curious myself—it is a weakness of mine—but I would never betray the privilege of a client such as yourself. Even my wife does not hear of the matters that pass through this office."

"I will take your word for it."

"Is there a date for the wedding?"

"No. But I would like these papers to take precedence over your other business—I can pay for the trouble that may cause you. I would like them by tomorrow."

"Tomorrow?! Mr. Thornton, you will have to apply for a special license if you would like to be wed so soon."

"Do not worry yourself," said John flatly. "It is all in hand. The trust and the contract—that is all I will be needing from you tomorrow."

John left the solicitor's office in a state of heightened tension. His limbs were practically buzzing with it. He felt like one of those electric lamps he had once witnessed at a very expensive party—a glass bulb that housed a filament humming with light. He only hoped he could contain the surge of his emotions so that he would not shatter.

Serafina had callers by that afternoon—Lady Pemberton and Patience.

"Congratulations on your engagement, my dear! Is Mr. Thornton not about?"

Lady Pemberton looked around as if he might be hiding somewhere in the drawing room. Patience rushed past her mother to envelope Serafina in a warm embrace.

"He has been out all day," said Serafina over Patience's shoulder.

"Well, there is much to be done, and time is of the essence."

"Are you not happy?" asked Patience looking carefully at her friend.

"Yes, I . . . it is all a bit sudden. That's all," said Serafina. "I'm still recovering from the shock."

"He loves you, you know," said Patience.

"You should have seen him at the ball, my dear. He was beside himself. So concerned for you and Molly. Knowing that you have been dead set against marriage, he practically bit my head off when I suggested that the circumstance might force your hand. He wanted you to make a free choice. Those were his words—a free choice."

"Is that what he said?" asked Serafina. She tried to replay the words he had spoken the night before. The way he had asked her to marry him. *We can make up our own rules.*

Had he been attempting to soften the blow? Help her to feel less cornered? Or did he want a different kind of marriage altogether?

"I told him there is no such thing for a lady," said Lady Pemberton with a chuckle. "No such thing. But I think you will be happy with him, my dear. You have truly blossomed in his company, if I may say so. And you will see what a comfort a marriage can be, especially one built on a foundation of love.

A Dangerous Man to Trust?

Your husband will be a soft place to fall in a world of hard edges." Lady Pemberton looked to Patience. "Oh dear, I have come over all poetic."

"Don't worry, Mother—I don't think you're in danger of making a name for yourself as a poet."

Serafina smiled. Patience could always make her smile.

"And what about a dress?" asked Lady Pemberton. Serafina didn't understand the question. "A dress for the wedding!"

"Oh. I hadn't thought of it. Perhaps I shall wear one of the dresses you were kind enough to gift me."

"Yes, that is an excellent idea," said Lady Pemberton. "There won't be time to have a new one made."

"It wouldn't be necessary anyway," said Serafina.

"What do you think, Mr. Thornton? Which dress should Serafina wear?" asked Lady Pemberton.

John was standing in the doorway to the drawing room, and when Serafina realised this, her heart gave a little jolt.

"That is not for me to say," said John, striding in and taking a seat across from Serafina. "I will take her as she comes."

He gave Serafina a look she had not seen before. It was unnerving in its warmth, and she had to look away for fear that she might melt under his gaze. Lady Pemberton's eyebrows lifted. She was grinning ear to ear.

"What did I tell you?" she said to Serafina. Then turning to John, "Mr. Thornton, you can rest well knowing that I have secured the special license."

"So quickly?" said John.

"I have connections," said Lady Pemberton looking pleased with herself. "You may both be married as soon as the day after tomorrow."

Serafina drew her eyes back to John who was now looking

at Lady Pemberton.

He would be her husband. How was that even possible? How had she taken the place of someone like Lady Langley? Patience and Lady Pemberton kept saying he loved her—they were adamant for some reason. But John hadn't used that word, not even when it had come up the night before in connection with Lady Langley. And yet, the way he had been looking at her just a few moments ago . . .

John turned his masked face to Serafina.

"The day after tomorrow then. Is that all right with you, Serafina?"

Serafina hadn't expected to be consulted.

"Oh . . . Mm. Yes."

John narrowed his eyes ever-so-slightly. When Lady Pemberton and Patience finally left, he kept Serafina in the drawing room and gave her a long hard look.

"What?" asked Serafina, feeling a bit flustered under his gaze.

"Are you having second thoughts? Because that is permitted, you know? I would understand—I'm not exactly the most appealing prospect as a husband."

John pulled at his cravat. Serafina was surprised to note that he looked nervous.

"You'll do," said Serafina, not wishing to give away too much before she understood how he really felt about her. "I have not had a second thought yet. Why? Have you?"

"Never!" said John clearly taken aback. "What would make you think that?"

"What would make *you* think that *I* was having second thoughts?" countered Serafina.

It felt good to be arguing with him. It felt normal.

"You just seemed . . . a bit reticent," said John. "I don't want you to feel trapped."

"Do *you* feel trapped?" asked Serafina.

She knew she was pushing out at the edges of this conversation, but she couldn't help it. She had expected him to counter with some kind of witty retort or perhaps another question, but instead his eyes softened, and he said in a quiet voice, "No, Serafina. I never feel trapped with you."

"Oh." Serafina dropped her eyes down to her lap. "Then we should be married the day after tomorrow."

"If it pleases you," said John.

"It pleases me," said Serafina, her eyes still on her lap.

Fifteen

The Key to her Heart

The day before the wedding, Serafina found herself ushered into Lord Pemberton's study. The baron stood up stiffly behind his desk and gestured to the chair opposite him.

"Please, Miss Edgemont, take a seat."

"Thank you, my lord," said Serafina sitting down.

"First of all, may I extend my congratulations to you on your upcoming wedding to Mr. Thornton."

Serafina thanked the baron once more.

"Mr. Thornton has come to me to act in place of your father, God rest his soul." When Serafina said nothing, the baron continued. "I have your settlement papers here on my desk, and I have read them over."

"Oh!" Serafina had not had a thought for the legal aspects of her marriage despite the fact that it was obligatory practice.

"It is . . . unusual," said Lord Pemberton rubbing his chin

thoughtfully. "Mr. Thornton has not stipulated an amount of pin money that would be due to you on an annual basis."

"Really?" This surprised Serafina. It would be the most basic assurance in the settlement.

"This is because he has granted you full access to all his accounts. You may take what you need as you need it."

The baron paused for this piece of information to sink in. Serafina was confused.

"You should understand that nothing of his can legally be your property. However, he has granted you legal access once you become his wife. He has also put your name to his various estates and holdings as someone who may take decisions on his behalf. Should he predecease you, his entire estate falls to you and his sister Miss Thornton. There are various other stipulations to account for all contingencies, but as it stands, I think you have the general idea."

Serafina realised her mouth was open and quickly closed it. The baron gave her a curious look.

"I have not heard of a settlement like this in all my years, Miss Edgemont."

"It . . . it is very generous," said Serafina as she attempted to grapple with the meaning of it all.

"As you may be aware," said Lord Pemberton, "I do not find it easy to glean the emotions of others." He raised a hand when Serafina opened her mouth to protest politely. "Lady Pemberton is a patient woman. I doubt another would be so understanding. Now. If I am to stand in place of your father and offer you my advice, I must take great care to offer you the best advice. I would have to say that you could hardly do better in terms of a marriage settlement—that is a fact. Lady Pemberton insists that yours is a love

The Key to her Heart

match. Normally, I would find that difficult to discern, but the contract I have in my hands appears to be proof of this, at least on Mr. Thornton's part. There is not a man in London who would open all of his accounts to his wife or permit her to take financial or business decisions on his behalf in perpetuity."

"So your advice is . . ."

"I would marry the man," said Lord Pemberton simply. "Granted, he is not entirely sensible, but in this case, that works to your advantage."

"I hardly want to take advantage," said Serafina.

"Of course, Miss Edgemont. I did not mean to imply . . . I am merely pointing out the facts."

"Yes, I know," said Serafina. "I very much appreciate it."

While Serafina was at the Pembertons', John had been at home pacing in his study. *Had he done enough to make it clear that he was hoping for an equal partnership? The law was not on his side when it came to that particular concept.* Hearing the front door open, he strode from his study and into the foyer where Serafina was removing her gloves and bonnet.

"Well?" said John.

"Well what?" asked Serafina.

"Are we still . . . that is . . . are you still in agreement about the wedding tomorrow?"

"Why would you think otherwise?"

"I don't know," said John. His fingers reached for his throat, but he let his hand fall once more to his side. "I find it hard to believe it's happening at all."

Serafina smiled, and John's heart gave a little lift.

"Lord Pemberton thinks that you are not entirely sensible," said Serafina as she undid the buttons on her coat. "I fear you have perhaps plummeted in his esteem."

She's teasing me, thought John. *This is good.*

"I promised you an equal partnership. It's the best I could do given the law."

John stepped behind her and helped her off with her coat. She turned to him and tilted her face up to his. She looked suddenly quite earnest.

"Are you sure, John? Are you absolutely sure?"

"About what?"

"About marrying me."

"Of course."

Serafina held John's gaze. She was breathing softly in his direction. She had brought the cool autumn air in with her, and she smelled crisp and bright like an apple. John wanted to take her in his arms. Hold her. Kiss her. Tell her he loved her.

They were friends. He knew that much, but he could not, would not, assume more. He had promised himself. She should not feel obligated to match his feelings, to pretend he was anything more to her than a very good friend.

"Where is Molly?" asked Serafina, her face brightening.

"She is upstairs planning her new life as your sister," said John. "I have never seen her so happy."

"Well, there you go," said Serafina. "We are doing the right thing."

She started to climb the stairs, leaving John in the foyer holding her coat.

"Serafina."

She turned on the stairs.

"Yes."

The Key to her Heart

"The ceremony is in the afternoon. Tomorrow. We should leave here by two o'clock."

"I'll be ready."

"Yes. All right then."

"Was there anything else?" asked Serafina.

Yes. I love you, thought John. *I love you, I love you, I love you.* But he said, "No, that's all."

Serafina moved through the day as if moving through a dream. Each moment seemed to arise and subside, and she had not the faintest recollection of what she had just said or done. All she could think of was John, that he would be her husband by this time tomorrow. If she were to judge the man by his actions, it would seem that Lord Pemberton was right: he did love her. He offered her more in terms of a relationship than she had ever dreamed possible before. However, if she were to judge him by his words, he was simply her friend. Tomorrow. Tomorrow everything would start anew. Perhaps things would be clearer then.

What she had to do now was to pick out a dress. There was the silver-blue silk she had worn to the Pemberton ball, but that was not a night she preferred to remember. Or there was the white muslin dress decorated with tiny yellow embroidered flowers scattered over the skirt. Patience had said she looked dazzling in white. There was one more dress that Lady Pemberton had gifted her: it was a pale lavender silk trimmed in a delicate white lace. Serafina tried it on and gazed at her reflection in the mirror. The dress looked expensive and beautiful, fitting her to perfection.

A Dangerous Man to Trust?

It was two o'clock in the afternoon the following day, and John and Molly were waiting for Serafina by the front door.

"Maybe you should run up and see if she is ready," suggested John.

"Maybe *you* should run up and see if she is ready," said Molly.

Despite his nerves, John couldn't help but smile. His sister's sharp mouth never failed to amuse him.

"There she is!" said Molly.

John's breath caught in his chest. She was wearing the pale grey dress she had worn the day they had submerged themselves together in the pond. It was a simple cotton dress no one would ever think to wear to their own wedding—no one but Serafina. She had paired it with a pale pink Spencer jacket for warmth. John remembered that dress well, his hands holding her bare arms. The way the grey skirt had ballooned around her in the water. He had helped her to press it down. But the dress was not the most striking thing about her. She had worn her hair down, neatly tying a long lock from each temple together at the back of her head to keep her dark tresses from falling in towards her face.

"Serafina," whispered John when she reached the bottom of the stairs.

"Are we ready?" she asked.

"We've been ready for awhile," said Molly.

"Sorry to keep you waiting."

John couldn't speak as he helped Serafina into the waiting carriage outside, and he couldn't speak as they rode along the bumpy cobbled streets. His heart was beating a drum inside his chest.

She had chosen to wear something meaningful. Could it be an accident that she chose the grey dress? And her hair down! It was

The Key to her Heart

unheard of. He could picture her in his mind standing in the darkened hallway with a candle so many months ago. The pins had been removed from her hair, and it fell to her waist. She was on her way to bed. He had not been wearing a mask when he encountered her in the hall. What had she said?

It's a shame we must wait for all the world to be asleep in order to simply be ourselves.

She had touched him with her words in a way he had not been touched before.

When they arrived at the church, the Pembertons were waiting.

"My dear girl, what are you wearing?" asked Lady Pemberton with a furrowed brow. She quickly caught herself. "I mean to say you look lovely—it is an interesting choice is it not, Patience?"

"She looks like herself, Mother. I believe that is the choice."

Patience gave Serafina a wink, but when John looked at Serafina, she was neither smiling nor relaxed. She kept looking to him as if for reassurance, but he did not know how to give it to her.

The priest greeted them and ushered them into the empty church. He was a youngish man, clean-shaven with a kind face. He did not seem at ease which may have been due to the presence of Lord Pemberton. He kept looking nervously in the baron's direction.

"I don't have much time, unfortunately. We will have to do without some of the prayers. But it will be a marriage nonetheless!" said the priest with forced cheer. "And that is something to celebrate."

Serafina stood with John facing the priest as Molly and the Pembertons looked on. When the priest asked if there was anyone who might declare an impediment to why they may not be coupled together in matrimony, there was silence in the church.

John could think of one impediment. Serafina had come as herself. It seemed only right that he meet her on their marriage day without any artifice or concealment.

He interrupted the priest: "May I just . . . before we continue, I should like to . . ." He reached up and removed his mask, tucking it into his jacket pocket.

The priest started back ever so slightly at the sight, but John turned to see Serafina's face light up like a summer's day. He had made the right decision.

It was not long before John was clasping Serafina's hand in his at the priest's instruction. He could hear himself pledging his troth: ". . . to love and to cherish . . ."

His throat had gone all dry and sticky.

Then Serafina spoke the same words: ". . . to have and to hold . . ."

She kept her eyes on his, and the entire church seemed to fall away, leaving them standing all alone as if at the top of a mountain. When the priest intruded upon them with further instructions, John did not even hear him.

"Mr. Thornton . . . Mr. Thornton? The ring."

"The ring?" asked John. Then the realisation dawned upon him, "The ring!"

"Have you forgotten a ring?" asked Serafina, her eyes dancing with amusement.

"Forgive me," said John. "It completely slipped my mind." Turning to the priest, he asked, "Is it entirely necessary?"

"The ceremony is not complete without it," said the priest quietly, "But here." He slipped one hand beneath his robes

The Key to her Heart

and pulled forth a small brass key. Handing it to John, he said, "You may use this."

John looked down at the key in his hand. It had a loop at the top.

"That will be perfect," said Serafina.

John was grateful for her understanding. Despite the fact that she was marrying one of the wealthiest men in town, she was doing so in a simple grey dress with a brass key on her finger. He doubted very much that he would be able to find another woman who would be as content to do so.

"Place the key . . . the ring on her finger," instructed the priest, and repeat after me. "With this ring I thee wed, with my body I thee worship, and with all my worldly goods I thee endow . . ."

John spoke the words and slipped the key along the fourth finger of Serafina's left hand. By the time the priest pronounced them man and wife, Serafina was smiling. She gave his hand a squeeze, and this immediately set him at ease.

"I should probably . . . so as not to upset the little girls . . ." He reached for his mask in his pocket and replaced it on his face, transforming himself into the handsome man from the masquerade once more.

The priest leaned in towards Serafina, "I'll be needing that key back, Mrs. Thornton."

"Mrs. Thornton? Oh . . . yes . . . thank you. It was a very creative solution," said Serafina.

Once she'd returned the key to the priest, John said quietly, "I'm so sorry. About the ring."

Serafina had not let go of his hand. She gave it another little squeeze.

"Do not think of it, John. This was more memorable."

A Dangerous Man to Trust?

John could not quite believe his fortune. *Serafina was his wife.*

Lady Pemberton had arranged an elaborate tea at her home to celebrate the occasion. It was an intimate but festive affair. John conversed at length with Lord Pemberton and George on matters of business and state. Lady Pemberton spent time pouring tea and calling for more sandwiches while intermittently drawing the men back into the ladies' conversation and scolding Grace for the way that Potato was behaving. Molly spent most of the afternoon speaking about Serafina as "my older sister," and Patience kept looking to Serafina as if wanting to say something.

Finally, Patience was able to pull Serafina into a quiet corner of the yellow drawing room.

"How does it feel?" asked Patience.

"Nice," said Serafina.

She did not want to elaborate. Her emotions were overwhelming her, and it was all she could do to drink tea and make conversation when her husband was sitting at the other corner of the room. He would cast his eyes over to catch hers every so often, and every time he did so, she felt a buzzing sensation through each of her limbs and down into the very core of her.

"Just nice? Why don't I believe you?" asked Patience playfully. "I wanted to say, Serafina, that it was the most magical ceremony I have ever witnessed. The love you share is quite visible to anyone looking on."

"Is it?"

"He can't stop looking at you," said Patience. "I dare say he may get up right now and carry you off to bed." Patience laughed.

"Patience!"

"Sorry. It's just. I am so happy for you. I love you, Serafina."

"I could not wish for a better friend," said Serafina.

But she was thinking, *And what exactly would we do there in bed? I'm sure Patience doesn't really know either.*

Serafina had some idea of a more intimate encounter between man and wife, but she no longer had a mother who might offer her detailed explanations or advice for her wedding night. Lady Pemberton had not broached the topic, and Serafina was not sure if she would have been able to survive the embarrassment if she had.

The subject was moot anyway as John had made it clear he would not burden her with his body. Was the marriage act a hardship for women? Serafina could hardly believe that she would find John's body burdensome in any way.

"Serafina!" said Patience, calling her back to the present, to the tea and the yellow drawing room. "You were off gathering wool," said Patience with a smile.

Sixteen

Lady of the House

That evening, Serafina tucked Molly into her bed.

"I don't really mind Potato," she said sleepily. "She's quite funny sometimes."

Serafina stroked the hair from her forehead.

"Serafina?"

"Yes."

"I hope that one day I will have a wedding like yours. With a key for a ring and a tea party . . . He's your best friend, isn't he?"

"John?" Molly nodded. "I suppose he is," said Serafina. "Although Patience shouldn't like to hear that."

"She can be your best *girl* friend," said Molly. "I'm sure that would be fine."

"You're probably right."

Serafina pulled up the covers and kissed her little sister on the forehead. She had never done so before with the sense of security she did now, knowing that they would be bound together forever as one family.

When she emerged from Molly's room, John was approaching her down the red-carpeted hall. He was in shirt and trousers, but he had lost his cravat and jacket. His shirt fell open at the neck, and it was not lost on Serafina that he had removed his mask once more.

"It was a long day for her," he said.

"Mm."

"It is customary," said John stopping in front of her, "for the lady of the house to have better chambers than the governess."

"That is not necessary . . ." began Serafina.

"I know," said John. "You don't need anything fancy. But the servants will think it strange if you do not take the appropriate bed chamber. We cannot afford any more gossip. Here, let me show you."

He led her along the hall and around the corner, opening a carved wooden door onto an enormous room. At the centre of the room was a large four-poster bed covered in a silver-green bedspread and hung with gauzy white curtains that were tied loosely to the posts of the bed. There was an ornate wardrobe, a bureau, a writing desk, a couch, as well as a decorative screen and wash stand in one corner, and on the floor, green and white vines swirled, and pale pink flowers budded across the most delicately woven rugs. A fire was burning in the fireplace.

"I shall have the servants bring up your things . . . if you are in agreement, that is."

Serafina stepped into the room. She sat down on the bed and looked at him.

"Yes, all right."

Serafina looked around, trying to imagine herself becoming accustomed to a room like this. She noticed another door at the far side of the chamber.

"Is that a closet?" she asked.

John reddened. "No. That door connects this room with mine." He hastened to add, "But I've had a bolt fitted on your side. You will have complete privacy. I can promise you that."

"Oh."

"Goodnight, Serafina." John turned to leave.

"John?" She wanted him to stay. "I appreciated . . . the . . . well . . . everything today," she said.

"I will give you a proper ring," he said. "That was an egregious oversight on my part."

Serafina dismissed the thought with a shake of her head and a wave of her hand.

"I much preferred the key," she said with amusement in her voice.

Just the thought of him sliding the key onto her finger filled her with the most effervescent kind of joy. It had been an unexpected and somewhat silly interruption to what had been an overly solemn ritual. The key, she felt, was just as symbolic as a ring might have been.

John smiled his snarl of a smile, and Serafina felt that now familiar buzzing sensation deep down in her belly. The feeling sank down deeper between her thighs. She stood up.

"Goodnight," she said.

"Goodnight," said John, and he left.

Spencer and two of the maids brought up Serafina's things to

Lady of the House

her new room.

"I'll unpack them. Not to worry," she said to the maids who looked as if they might spend the rest of the evening putting her things away. "It's late. You should get some rest. I know you have an early start in the morning."

When the maids had gone, Serafina removed her blushing pink jacket and hung it in the wardrobe. Slipping out of the pale grey dress, she stripped down to her skin, then looked over at the door that separated her room from John's.

He had a bolt fitted! On my side. He didn't say anything about a bolt on his side.

She slipped on a thin white night dress over her head and wriggled her way into it, doing up a few buttons at the front. The room was pleasantly warm with the fire burning merrily in the hearth. Serafina pulled back the expensive covers of her new bed and slid her legs down between the silky smooth white sheets. She lay there for what felt like an eternity staring up at the four corners of her four-poster bed.

She was thinking about John. His lip pulled up in a permanent snarl. His pale blue eyes like a winter sky. The way he stood, the shape of his hands. She rolled over onto her side and gazed out across the room at the door, the bolted door between them. *His actions said that he loved her. He probably loved her. Could she even bring herself to ask him? And how might he know that she loved him? Could she simply say so?*

Having remained awake for several hours like this, Serafina made a decision, slipped out from under the covers and padded across the rugs to the bolted door. She very quietly slid the bolt back, unlocking the door.

There! She would not have the door locked against him as if he were some sort of criminal. He was her husband, and if he wished to enter her room, then . . . well, then, he could. It was as forward an action as she was willing to take. She knew she wanted something more from John, something closer, but exactly what that was, beyond a kiss or an embrace, she couldn't say.

As she turned back to her bed, she heard a sound beyond the door. It sounded like a cry.

"John?" she said his name hesitantly though the door.

And then she heard it again. It was as if he were crying out in pain. It was a disturbing sound—guttural and desperate—and it tugged at her heart in a way that made her anxious for his safety. She opened the door. His room was much like hers, but his bed was bigger, his furniture heavier, his fire built higher. In the golden glow of the firelight, she could see him sleeping on top of his bed in the shirt and trousers he had been wearing the day before. His body was making small jerking movements, and the sounds that came from his mouth—they were sounds of sheer panic and distress.

He's having a nightmare, thought Serafina. *But what a nightmare!*

Serafina had once been told that you must never awaken someone who is in the middle of a dream, for doing so might split their soul in two. She didn't truly believe this, but as a child she had been awakened on several occasions from within a dream, and she found it an altogether unpleasant and disorienting experience. So when she stepped up beside John's bed, she had no intention of waking him, simply calming him so that he might sleep properly. She sat down beside him on the bed and placed a hand to his chest. The twitching of his body immediately subsided, his cries came quieter.

"It's all right," she whispered. "I'm here with you."

Eventually, he went completely quiet, but when Serafina

stood to return to her room, the nightmare seemed to start all over again. *He was in so much distress!* Once more, she sat on the bed, placed her hand to his chest. By now, she had been awake for hours and hours, and she could feel the weight of sleep descend upon her like a heavy quilt.

I'll just rest my head until he is calm, she thought, lifting both legs up onto the bed beside John. He was lying on his back, and she rested her head on the pillow by his shoulder. She stretched one arm across his chest, curling herself into him. He became very still and silent as she breathed softly into his scarred neck. Her eyelids were so heavy. *I'll just close them for a moment*, she thought, and she fell into a deep and restful sleep. The room was quiet but for the crackle of the fire in the hearth behind her.

When John woke the next morning, he thought he must still be asleep and dreaming. Serafina was curled around him like a cat. She had one bare arm thrown across his chest and one leg across his thigh. Being careful not to wake her, he carefully looked down to where her leg looked as if it were attempting to climb across him. Her thin white night dress had shifted up to her thigh, and she was exposed all the way from her upper thigh down to her pretty toes. The soft sound of her breathing into the side of his neck was as soothing as the purr of cat.

Dear God, thought John. *What has happened?*

He looked across the room to the door that separated their chambers. It had been swung wide open. He could see her bed from where he lay, the coverlets disturbed as if she had slept there for a time, then for some reason, come here to his bed.

She stirred and rolled away from him onto her back. Still asleep. Her nightdress was so thin, he could see the dark outline of her nipples. He reached for her hem and tugged it down over her legs.

"Serafina," he whispered, lifting a hand up to move a lock of hair from her face.

She opened her eyes. It took her a moment, but when she realised where she was, she bolted up in the bed.

"Is your chamber not to your liking?" asked John with a hint of amusement.

"I'm so sorry," said Serafina looking entirely embarrassed. She was flushing pink across her cheeks. "I didn't think I'd fall asleep. It's just that . . . I heard you cry out . . . You were having a nightmare. You seemed terribly distressed."

"So you decided to lie down in my bed?"

She gave him a scolding kind of look.

"I decided to stay to make sure the nightmare had passed. I must have fallen asleep." She looked at him apologetically. "I'm sorry. You must think me very forward."

"I'm your husband, Serafina. Nothing is too forward."

The look on her face when John said those words melted his heart.

"Nothing?" she said quietly.

"Nothing."

To John's surprise, she lay back down against the pillow and turned to him. She seemed somehow softer first thing in the morning. He wanted to touch her cheek, kiss her throat.

"Then can I ask you, why are you sleeping on top of the bed in the clothes you were wearing yesterday?"

"I did not think I would sleep at all, so I made no preparations for bed," said John.

"I couldn't sleep either," said Serafina.

"It was an eventful day," said John.

"There's no bolt on your side of the door," said Serafina slowly. "Do you not need your privacy?"

"Not from you," said John.

"Because I am your friend?" asked Serafina.

"Because you are my wife," corrected John.

"Oh."

Serafina looked at him then drawing her eyes down to his throat, his chest. She placed the palm of her hand over his heart.

"What was the nightmare?" she asked.

"It was nothing," said John dismissively.

"I thought you didn't need your privacy from me," she said.

Quick as a whip, thought John. He smiled a half smile.

"I dreamed I was trapped in a burning building. Someone died, and there was nothing I could do."

"Your accident?"

John nodded.

"Who died?"

"Eleanor's brother William," said John rolling onto his back and away from her hand. "It was not nightmare enough for it to happen once. He dies every night. I can never save him."

"You mean to say you have this dream every night?! How do you sleep at all?"

"There's no need to be upset about it, Serafina. It's no less than I deserve."

John could sense Serafina becoming increasingly agitated.

"What? Do you think it's your due punishment? It's not as if you killed him."

A Dangerous Man to Trust?

"I may as well have," said John.

When Serafina had laid back down in his bed, this was not how John had anticipated the morning going. She seemed angry with him now, and this made him want her all the more. Her fierce little face, her practically transparent nightdress, the instinctive way she had placed her hand to his chest. He had some faint memory of her doing so last night. It was the nicest feeling to be touched like that. A comfort.

Serafina sat up and swung her legs from the bed. As she did so, her nightdress rode up to her thighs once more. She made no move to pull it down.

"Are you leaving?" asked John.

"I'm never leaving," said Serafina turning in her seat on the edge of the bed. "I'm your wife. But I *am* going to get dressed and eat breakfast."

She stood, and John watched her walk across the room in her bare feet. At the open door to her bed chamber, she turned back.

"I do *not* like the bolt on the door," she said curtly. "Have it removed."

Then she stepped into her own room and left the door open behind her.

John was left alone in his room not knowing which way was up. She appeared to be quite cross with him . . . but she had left the door to her room wide open . . . and she was intending to get dressed! The messages he was receiving were not exactly crystal clear. He had promised himself he would not impose on her in any way. He was certainly not going to step foot inside her room without an overt invitation.

He watched through the doorway as she padded over to her bed and started adjusting the pillows and struggling with the covers in a furious way. *Was she making the bed?!*

"The maid will make the bed, Serafina!" he called out to her across the threshold. "Leave it as it is."

She gave him a hard look, but abandoned her efforts nonetheless. He watched as she walked over to the wardrobe and pulled out a pale blue muslin morning dress and chemise, then disappeared beyond the doorframe in the direction of the screen and wash stand. She reappeared wearing the dress with her hair still tumbling down past her shoulders. John watched as she fumbled in one of the cases the servants had brought up the night before. Her hands emerged with a hairbrush. She disappeared once more with the brush, then after some time, emerged in the doorway with her hair pinned neatly to her head.

"Aren't you going to get dressed?" She asked.

John didn't know what to say. He was sat up in the bed not truly understanding what was going on.

"Well, usually, my valet . . ."

"I can attach a cuff link," said Serafina in a matter-of-fact tone of voice.

She walked over to the wardrobe and pulled out a shirt and a pair of trousers and brought them over to the bed. John stood.

"Serafina, what are you—"

"Take off your shirt," she said.

Well, that was certainly crystal clear, thought John. So he obliged, pulling his shirt up over his head. He couldn't help but grimace as he anticipated her reaction to seeing his body as damaged as it was.

"Oh," she said, looking at the crimson ripples of his scarred chest, his shoulder, his arm. Her gaze followed the scarring all the way down to his belly.

She placed her hand to the damaged side of his chest and trailed her fingers up the scarring of his neck to his face. John held his breath as she stepped in close and pressed the side of her face into his chest the way she had done when he had held her weeping. This time, however, it was her skin against his and the sensation made every muscle in his body relax. John let out his breath and slowly, hesitantly wrapped his arms around her. After a few moments, she pulled away and looked him in the face. He felt he should kiss her. This would be the moment. Now. But he could not quite believe that she was inviting him to do so, and he was terrified of making a mistake with her. She was simply too precious.

"Call me when you need help with your cufflinks," she said.

Then she strode back into her own room and set about unpacking her things.

Serafina was upset. *John had been having nightmares every night for the past six years, and he thought this was perfectly all right—in fact, he thought it was something he deserved!* She felt the way she had when he had harmed himself with a pin for Molly's entertainment all those months ago. No. She felt worse this time.

She was also upset for a different reason.

Why had he not kissed her? It didn't make any sense. He had left his side of the door unbolted. He had said he did not need his privacy from her. He had seemed pleased to wake up with her in his bed. And what else had he said?

"I'm your husband, Serafina. Nothing is too forward."

But how forward could she possibly be?

Does he think I don't want to be here? That I would prefer not to be his wife?

Serafina dropped a sheaf of paper on her writing desk and strode back over to the doorway that connected the two bed chambers. *Nothing is too forward, apparently.* John was standing in shirt and trousers. He held out his arms towards her with a smile.

"I'm ready for my cufflinks."

"John," said Serafina from the doorway. "Will you not kiss me?"

His eyes went wide.

"Serafina, you should not feel obliged . . . It's not necessary . . ."

"Why do you think I should feel obliged?" Serafina was beginning to feel impatient with him—impatient and frustrated in a way she couldn't quite explain.

"This is something you would like?" asked John somewhat disbelievingly.

"Very much," said Serafina quietly, still standing in the doorway. "But only if it is something you would like as well."

"Come here then," said John. His voice was a soft rumble.

Serafina walked across the room to where John waited for her. Her entire body was humming with anticipation. She stepped right up to him and tilted her face to his. He stroked his fingers up along her throat and placed one large hand against the side of her face. She liked the rough feel of his palm against her skin, and she leaned her cheek into it as she closed her eyes. He brought his other hand up to hold both sides of her face in a way that made her feel treasured. His lips touched hers gently at first, then pressed in more urgently. It was a sensation of pure release for her. The kiss went on and on—hot and wet and desperate. Her hands reached around to his shoulders, then up to his head where her fingers combed their way through his thick mass of dark hair. Serafina instinctively pressed her body against his. She could feel herself matching the way his mouth moved, trying to take him in, taste him, consume him.

He pulled away before she was anywhere near done with him.

"How was that?" he asked.

Serafina felt breathless and quite weak in the knees. She needed more.

"It was all right," she said trying to look and sound more collected than she felt.

"Just all right?" asked John cocking his head to one side with amusement.

"Yes," said Serafina. "Just all right."

"I see," said John. "That's a shame because it was the best kiss of my entire life."

"Was it?" asked Serafina quietly. She couldn't quite look him in the eye.

"Perhaps I should try again . . . if you are willing," he said.

Serafina didn't want to seem too eager. It didn't seem ladylike.

"What would you do differently this time?" she asked, as if she might withhold her participation based on his answer.

"I should kiss your throat," said John stroking a finger along the side of her neck and up to her ear, "take your earlobe in my mouth, and then move on to your lips." He touched two fingers to her lips, and they parted.

"Oh."

Lady of the House

There came a hard knock at the door. John reached for his mask and placed it over his face.

"Come," said John, not taking his ice blue eyes from Serafina.

Molly stepped into the room and sat down on John's bed.

"Are you two not coming down for breakfast? I've been waiting and waiting... It's our first breakfast as a family."

"Sorry, Molly," said John. "I was having a little trouble with my cufflinks. We'll meet you at the table in a minute. I promise."

"They're going to have to boil the water for tea again," said Molly. "It will be cold by now."

"Right," said John. "Why don't you tell them to put the kettle on again."

Molly looked to Serafina.

"Are you feeling all right, Serafina? You look a bit hot."

John smiled.

"I'm fine," said Serafina.

"Off you go!" John shooed Molly from the room and closed the door behind her.

John looked at Serafina who could not take her eyes from him. This wonderful man was her husband.

"We only have a minute," he said apologetically.

Serafina picked up his cufflinks from the bedside table in one hand. He held out a cuff for her, but she took his hand in hers and pressed her lips to his knuckles. Then turned his hand over and kissed his palm.

"Serafina," John whispered.

"Let me do up your cuffs," she said.

Seventeen

Raspberry Jam

As they made their way to breakfast, John noticed that Serafina's face was still flushed from the kiss. She kept looking over at him, and John took each step as if he were walking on air.

The sheer impossibility of it! That she would spend the night in his bed in her (very) thin nightdress. That she would demand the bolt be removed from her side of the door! That she would set about getting dressed with the door wide open . . . and then come right out and ask him (quite angrily) for a kiss!

It occurred to him then that it had probably been her first kiss, and he was momentarily shot through with the shock of that realisation. He would follow her lead. He would give her whatever she wanted as and when she wanted it. He looked at the side of her face, the small permanent pout of her lower lip. John's desire for his wife threatened to overwhelm him, but he was nothing if not a man in control of himself. More than anything, he had been touched by the way she had kissed his hand. No woman had ever done that before. She had done it so reverently, he had felt almost embarrassed to witness it. He felt as if there was nothing he had done or could do to deserve such a devotional gesture. This woman was his wife, and the very fact was a wonder.

"There you are! Finally!" said Molly as they entered the morning room and took their seats at the breakfast table.

Molly was practically bouncing in her seat.

"What do you think we should do today?" asked Serafina as she reached for the tea pot and poured a cup of tea for John and then for herself.

"We should do something special," said Molly. "Something we've never done before . . . as a family."

"I have an idea," said John, passing Serafina a rack of toast, the butter dish, and a bowl of raspberry jam.

Serafina looked at the jam, then at him.

"Well, what is it?" asked Molly excitedly.

"Would you," asked John leaning in towards Molly, "like to go to the museum?"

John's father, being as unwell as he was in his later years, had never taken Molly to London let alone the museum, so John knew for a fact that her answer would be yes, but he had not anticipated the scream of delight that would precede it. Spencer appeared at the door to make sure everything was all right.

"Molly!" said Serafina as if to scold her, but she was laughing at the same time. She looked at John. "You certainly know your sister well."

After breakfast, as Serafina and John made their way back to their adjoining rooms to dress properly for their outing,

A Dangerous Man to Trust?

John could sense Serafina looking at him.

"What is it?" he asked, stopping just outside the door to his room.

"How do you know I like raspberry jam?" she asked.

John could feel his face splitting into a grin. He leaned in close and whispered into her ear.

"I could smell it on your breath. Raspberry jam and fresh-baked bread."

"When?" asked Serafina looking confused.

"In the woods," said John. "When you were so kind as to help me back to my horse."

Serafina's eyes went wide in surprise.

"Your breath smells the same right now," said John. "I imagine you taste just as nice."

Serafina blushed, and John slipped his hand into hers and tugged her into his room. Serafina reached up with tentative fingers and removed his mask. She tilted her face to his, leaning in for a kiss, but John withheld it. He used a finger to tilt her chin to the side and bent down to brush her neck lightly with his lips. He could hear her tremulous breath as he slid his lips up to her ear, licked her earlobe gently, then took it in his mouth.

She let out a pant of breath. Her lips parted, and that was when he finally offered her the kiss she was so breathlessly anticipating.

Dear Lord, she was ready for him this time!

There was no hesitation on her part. He could feel the desire coursing through her, and it lit a fire within him that he was very careful to contain. Her arms wrapped around him, and she held him to her with that same fierce grip he had come to expect when she took his arm. He pulled her even closer to

Raspberry Jam

him, his hand at the small of her back, and she lifted up onto her toes as he tasted her neck once more. She lifted her head, and he nearly lost himself as he kissed her passionately across the delicate soft skin of her breast right down to the scooped line of her dress.

When John pulled away from his bride, she stood looking at him, her breath coming heavily, her lips wet and shining.

"You'll need a bonnet," he said. "And I'll need a jacket." Serafina sat down on his bed, and John smiled to himself at the thought that she needed to recover from his ministrations. "Molly will not forgive us if we make her wait again," he added.

"You're right," she said as she stood and stepped up to him once more. She walked herself right up to his body and planted a small kiss on his chest. He couldn't really feel it though his shirt, but the gesture touched him to his core. If that was the only kiss she had ever given him, he would die a happy man.

"Don't forget gloves!" he called after her as she walked through to her own chamber.

"When have I ever forgotten gloves?" she asked without looking back. He could tell she was smiling.

Serafina was not entirely sure she would be able to make it through a morning at the museum *not* touching John. She had never imagined a kiss could be . . . so . . . all-encompassing. Her entire body had responded to him in a way she had not anticipated, and she only wished she had received some instruction from someone before her wedding. She certainly wanted more from him, but what that *more* entailed, she was not entirely sure.

Of course, John would know what that more entailed. He was an expert at undoing corsets after all.

While his experience was clearly of some benefit to her, Serafina couldn't help feeling less than thrilled with the idea of John engaging like this with anyone else, even if it may have been in the past. The thought set her on edge, and she wondered if she would measure up, or if, perhaps, he would eventually find her lacking in some way.

Serafina soon realised that their trip to the museum was not a spur-of-the-moment plan. Montagu House—the mansion that hosted the museum's collections—had fairly restricted hours, and John had acquired tickets sometime in advance. John caught Serafina looking curiously at him as he presented their tickets at the gate.

"I made the arrangement some time ago," he said answering her unspoken question.

"Before we were to be wed?"

"Well before that," said John. "I knew Molly would enjoy it, and I thought it would perhaps make your stay in London a little more tolerable."

He was so thoughtful.

"Come," he said, offering her his arm.

They strolled leisurely through the ornamental gardens as Molly ran on ahead toward the main building. A fountain spilled forth into a pool of green water, and a breeze sent a mist from the fountain across Serafina's face.

"This was a nice idea," she said looking up at him with her damp face.

Molly was waiting for them at the top of the steps by the front door.

"You two do spend a lot of time mooning about," she said

Raspberry Jam

with her hands on her hips. "Do you think they have curiosities like the ones you have at home?" she asked John. "The sea creatures turned to stone?"

"I know for a fact that they do," said John.

Molly could barely contain herself. Serafina had to take her hand when they entered the building so as to prevent her from running up the great stairs and making a spectacle of herself. Other well-to-do ladies and gentlemen were browsing their way through the museum, talking in hushed voices, and looking about—some with an air of excitement and curiosity, others with an affected look of boredom.

Molly could not get enough! Even climbing the stairs was an adventure as there was at least one mounted and stuffed beast on every landing.

"Is that an ibex?!" exclaimed Molly.

At one juncture, Serafina had to coax her new sister past an exceptionally ferocious tiger.

"I know it's not alive," said Molly. "But I can't help thinking it may come alive just as I walk near. It looks ready to pounce!"

She squealed and squeezed Serafina's hand as she picked up her pace and walked past the snarling creature. By the time they reached the room of curiosities, they were laughing. They spent a good deal of time peering methodically into one display case after another—fossilised seashells, an ancient stone tortoise, tiny little sea monsters who had left their imprints in the rock. John wandered off to the other end of the gallery, but Molly became stuck at one particular display—a stone tooth.

"What's a mamout?" she asked, reading the label within the display case.

"Ah," replied Serafina excitedly. "It is a kind of ancient

elephant."

"But elephants don't live in Siberia," said Molly, still reading what had been written within the display case.

"Not anymore," said Serafina. "But they did once."

As Molly turned, mouth open to ask another question, Serafina could see out of the corner of her eye that a lady had stepped up beside her.

"Is this your little charge?" asked a familiar voice. It was Sophia Crampton.

Serafina had been bent over the glass cabinet, but she stood up now.

"How *are* you, Sophia?"

"Well," said Sophia.

And Serafina had to admit to herself that she did look well. Elegant and beautiful and poised. She was wearing the most elaborate bonnet Serafina had ever seen—feathers and flowers tumbled across her head, and a wide satin ribbon in the most luminous shade of magenta was tied beneath her chin.

"But how are *you* doing?" asked Sophia with exaggerated concern. "These rumours must be quite worrying. A lady's reputation is everything." She turned to address Molly: "You will find that out soon enough, Miss Thornton."

"Is your bonnet not very heavy?" interrupted Molly.

Molly's mouth was open and she was peering around the side of Sophia to get a better look at her headdress. Serafina had never felt like smiling in Sophia's presence before, but she was smiling now. Molly was examining her as if she were one more curiosity in a cabinet.

And that was when Sophia's mother joined them.

"Miss Edgemont!" she said. "How have you been? Sophia and I have been so concerned for you. Sometimes people will talk whether there is a story to tell or not."

Serafina wasn't sure what to say to this, but John saved her from having to decide. He appeared quite suddenly at her side as if materialising out of the air. Serafina saw the look on the ladies' faces shift as they registered his presence.

He does come across as somewhat forbidding, thought Serafina looking up at him.

"Lady Crampton," he said. "Miss Crampton." He nodded in their direction then reached an arm around Serafina's shoulder. "I did not know you were acquainted with my wife."

"Your wife?" spat out Sophia in some confusion.

"Yes," said John with a grin pulling Serafina warmly in towards his side. "I still cannot believe it. I am perhaps the luckiest man in London."

"Not perhaps." said Molly looking from the Cramptons to John. "You *are* the luckiest man in London."

"There you have it," said John giving Molly an acquiescent nod. "My sister, Miss Molly Thornton," he said introducing her, "but it seems you have already met."

"Well, this is certainly happy news!" said Lady Crampton offering her surprised congratulations. "No longer Miss Edgemont, then," she said to Serafina. "Mrs. Thornton from now on."

"Yes, thank you," said Serafina smiling.

"Isn't that wonderful?" said Lady Crampton to her daughter who was looking quite stunned and remained completely silent. "And here we were so anxious for your future, Mrs. Thornton. What a delight! I hope you will not mind if I tell all my friends."

"Of course. It is news we do not mind sharing," said John.

"There has been much speculation as to how long you would

remain a bachelor once you were returned to society, Mr. Thornton. I'm afraid you will have disappointed a fair few young ladies," said Lady Crampton, tittering at the thought.

"You are too generous in your assessment," said John.

"Well, I hope you will enjoy the rest of your morning," said Lady Crampton. "Come, Sophia, we should be getting on."

Sophia said nothing. Just stared at Serafina.

"It was a pleasure seeing you again," offered up Serafina.

John had seen Serafina's face from across the gallery when Miss Crampton had approached her, and he'd known immediately that this was not a lady with whom she cared to speak. The room was large, the ceilings high, and there was no carpeting, so Miss Crampton's voice travelled across to him like an echo. He did not like the way she was talking to his wife, and he took great pleasure in striding over to correct her assumptions.

John kept his arm around Serafina's shoulder until the Cramptons had left them alone once more in the gallery.

"That should do it," he said.

"Do what?" asked Serafina.

"Lady Crampton is not a terrible woman, but she does have a weakness for gossip. Our marriage should be a known quantity around London by the end of tomorrow."

"Oh."

"You're not the scheming sort, are you?" asked John with a wry smile. "Lucky for you, I am."

"So am I!" piped in Molly. "What are we talking about?"

"Nothing you need to worry about," said John.

Raspberry Jam

As Molly wandered off to make sure she had not missed anything in the gallery, Serafina took John's arm, not wanting to let him go.

"Miss Crampton has always been one to dig her heel into someone else's wound," she said.

"Yes, the swan is not so swan-like in her demeanour, is she?"

"The swan?" asked Serafina.

"In my mind," said John. "Miss Crampton is the swan and Lady Crampton the goose."

Serafina laughed.

"The image fits!" she said. "And what am I if not a swan or a goose."

"Why, you are a chicken of course," said John lifting an eyebrow.

"A chicken! Somehow it doesn't seem a compliment," said Serafina pretending offence.

"A duck then," offered John.

"That is no better," said Serafina laughing and making a show of pushing him away.

"I'm sorry," said John with a grin.

"Do you not think me swan-like?" asked Serafina.

"No," said John quite seriously now. "Swans may be beautiful and graceful, but they always seem to me to be showing off."

"Well if you're going to put it like that, I should not mind being a duck," said Serafina.

John laughed, then leaned in close and whispered into her ear, "You are my soft little dove, Serafina."

"Oh."

The look that she gave him just then made his chest ache, but in a good way.

Once Molly's curiosity was sated at the museum, John had

their carriage stop at a local pastry-cook shop on the way home. Molly was only too thrilled to eat out. The shop was warm and smelled divine. It was humming with well-dressed people, mainly gentlemen, taking a pause in their day to have a bite before dinnertime rolled around.

"I shall have a sticky bun," said Molly brightly, "and a tart, and could I also have a glass of whey?"

"Whatever you want," said John. "It's your special day out."

John couldn't help feeling eyes on them. He was certainly conspicuous in his black mask. Normally, he would hate the attention, but today it served them well to be visible. He took Serafina by the arm and led her over to a table where they enjoyed their pastries and coffee.

"I think I should like to do this again on my birthday," said Molly looking around. "Who were those ladies at the museum?"

"Lady and Miss Crampton," said John. "Society people."

"Did you get a good look at that bonnet? " asked Molly. "There were so many decorations attached to it, I thought the lady would fall over. Top heavy, you see—never a good idea, structurally speaking."

John and Serafina shared a look of amusement at Molly's commentary. The day had turned out splendidly. On the way home, Molly insisted on stopping to feed the remains of her sticky bun to the ducks at Hyde Park, and they all returned home quite spent.

John was anticipating some time alone with Serafina that night, but on his way up to bed, Spencer waylaid him. There was a messenger at the door from his solicitor who needed a timely response. It was just a few loose ends that needed tying up, but it required his immediate attention. It took him some time to sort the matter, and when he finally stepped through the door to his bed chamber, Serafina was fast asleep in his bed. He could see through the open adjoining door to her room and her untouched bed. She was wearing that thin nightdress again, her face as peaceful as an angel, one arm thrown up alongside her head. John felt his heart fit to burst.

John undressed quietly, being careful not to wake his wife. Normally, he would sleep naked (he didn't even own a nightshirt), but tonight he only stripped down to his drawers. He didn't want to scare Serafina or pressure her in any way. As he slipped in beside her, she murmured something sleepily and rolled towards him. John could hear her soft breathing alongside the crackle of the fire, and he wondered once more what he had done to deserve anything like this.

By the time John woke in the morning, the covers had somehow been kicked clear, and Serafina was wrapped around him like a vine.

"You had that dream again," she said softly when he opened his eyes.

"It's always the same," he said. "I hope I didn't disturb your sleep."

Serafina slid her fingers along the scarring of John's chest as if examining it intently.

"John."

"Yes."

"I think you should know . . . I mean it's possible you've guessed . . . but I think you should know that I have not a clue what I am doing."

A Dangerous Man to Trust?

"What do you mean?"

"Usually, before a wedding, the bride's mother will speak to her on matters relating to . . . the wedding night. I had no one to speak with me. And while you may think I am very clever and know everything, that simply isn't true."

John reached a hand up to stroke her hair from her face. He could hear the concern in her voice. *She was actually anxious.*

"Don't worry yourself, Serafina. I'm here, and I know what to do. We will take things as slowly as you like. I will follow your lead."

"How can I lead if I don't know where we are going?" asked Serafina quite pointedly.

"What do you feel? What do you have the urge to do?" asked John.

"I want to be close to you all the time," said Serafina. "I want to touch you and taste you and have you touch me."

John was touched at how open she was with him. He felt trusted.

"Well that's certainly a start," said John smiling. "May I touch you?"

Serafina seemed surprised by the question.

"You don't have to ask, John. You may touch me anywhere you like."

He looked down her body to her leg that had been thrown across his in the night. Her nightdress was still covering her to the knee. John reached down with a finger and gently pulled her nightdress up her leg all the way to her hip exposing the round flesh of her bottom. She quivered against him as his finger stroked its way up her leg. Instinctively, she rolled onto her back, and he propped himself up on a forearm, leaning over her.

Raspberry Jam

"You'd like to taste me?" he asked.

"Mm," was her response.

He leaned in and brushed his lips against hers gently before pressing them to her hot mouth for a kiss. And what a kiss! Her mouth was open, and she was taking him in with a hunger he could not quite understand. He probed her mouth with his tongue, and she returned the favour. Her arms reached around him, and her fingers slid gently along his back. John was a man in control, but this was testing his limits. His arousal strained against his drawers, and she could feel him pressing into the side of her. When he pulled away from the kiss, she looked down at his drawers wide-eyed.

"Oh," was all she said.

"It's nothing you need to worry about right now," he said, hoping to sound somewhat soothing.

"But later?" she asked with a furrowed brow.

"It's nothing you need to worry about later either," he said. "We will go at your pace, Serafina. Whatever you want."

"But I don't know what I want," said Serafina quietly.

"I think you do," said John. "Where would you like me to touch you? Take my hand and place it there."

She looked down at his hand on her bare hip. Her nightdress had been pulled up so high, she was nearly exposed.

"If I am honest, you will think me too forward," said Serafina looking embarrassed.

"I told you. I'm your husband. Nothing is too forward. Now where would you like me to touch you?"

She locked eyes with him as she reached down, took his hand, and slipped it between her legs.

"There. You see? You know exactly what to do," said John.

She was so incredibly wet already.

A Dangerous Man to Trust?

Serafina rested her head to the pillow. She was looking at him expectantly, needfully, and John had to focus on keeping his breath steady as he pressed his fingers to her tender flesh. He dropped his face to hers and kissed her once more as he began to move his fingers in a circular motion, keeping up a gentle pressure between her legs. He could hear her breath become ragged as she arched her back and spread her legs wider. He kissed her neck, her chest above the neckline of her nightdress.

She did not seem to know what to do with her hands. She had brought a hand up to hold him, but as he continued the rhythmic movement of his fingers against her, she had to drop her hand back down to the bed. He could see her grip the sheets. Her breath was coming fast now. It wouldn't be long. John placed his lips to her open mouth to feel her hot breath within him. Then he slipped his tongue once more past her lips. At that very moment, she came apart, arching her back and releasing a long moan of pleasure. Her entire body spasmed beneath him. When her muscles softened once more, he slid down her body and kissed her on the insides of her soft thighs. His own body was screaming at him like some kind of caged animal—it wanted more.

Maintain control. Keep it together, he thought. *This is just for her.*

John thought he might lose himself if he continued as he was, so he sat up, and so did she. She placed her hands to the side of his face and kissed him once more on the mouth, pulling him back down to the bed with her. She stroked his face, kissed his neck, his damaged shoulder. The way she was moving against him . . . her body certainly knew what to do even if she did not, but he didn't want to push things too far too soon. He kissed her gently on the lips.

"How was that?" he asked.

She smiled openly.

"It was unexpected," she said with a little shrug. "I wouldn't complain if we did it again."

"So you liked it?"

"I think you know that I did," said Serafina.

"If we are not downstairs for breakfast in a timely manner," said John, "Molly shall be up soon and beating upon the door."

"I never knew having children would be so difficult," said Serafina with a laugh. "They are such a nuisance."

Eighteen

Chemistry

Serafina was feeling both energised and relaxed after her time with John in bed that morning.

She smiled to herself thinking of the sensitive and compassionate way he had spoken to her. Even now, seated in the drawing room across from Lady Pemberton and Patience, she could see his pale eyes set within his familiar face—smooth and handsome on one side, red and damaged on the other. She loved both sides of his face equally.

The way he had pulled her nightdress up her leg...

She knew there was more to the marriage act than what he had done with her that morning (she was familiar with the basics of animal reproduction), but the details of how exactly it might be done were unclear to her. What she wanted most of all was to be able to give John the ecstatic feeling she had had that morning. She liked the way he had simply come out and asked her where she wanted to be touched. *Perhaps, she*

Chemistry

could do the same—she could ask him what he wanted.

"I do believe our little plan is working!" said Lady Pemberton delightedly.

"Excuse me?" said Serafina. Her mind was miles away.

"News of your marriage is spreading like wildfire across London. I'm not sure if you were aware, Serafina, but Mr. Thornton was one of the most sought-after bachelors in London. You are the envy of the town, which I should point out is not a good thing. Of all the deadly sins, envy is the only one that is no fun at all."

Lady Pemberton laughed at her own commentary and jostled Patience beside her who lifted her eyebrows and gave a little smile and upward tilt of her head. Patience looked over to Serafina and rolled her eyes up to the ceiling.

Lady Pemberton continued, "The rumour mill is often fuelled by envy, so we must be careful to shape the narrative in our favour. As it stands, I think things are going well. I, for my part, have been planting the seeds of a Cinderella storyline. Everyone loves Cinderella, do they not? A gentle lady fallen on hard times. She works hard and is mistreated by those who now feel themselves above her—I'm thinking of Sophia Crampton and her lot, but I would not name names. Eventually, her prince finds her and saves her from her hardship, whisking her off to the palace to live happily ever after."

"And I'm Cinderella in this story?" asked Serafina with amusement.

"Yes, my girl."

"And the palace is . . ."

"Bosworth Manor, of course," offered up Patience with a grin.

A Dangerous Man to Trust?

"Is Molly my evil stepsister?"

"Gracious no, child," said Lady Pemberton taking each of Serafina's words as seriously as the last. "Molly is the sad little girl in need of a mother. Who would begrudge her that?"

"You see," said Patience. "It is all sorted, Serafina. Your story is winging its way around town. It is sure to bump aside those previous rumours. Cinderella's reputation was never in question."

"Lady Pemberton, I must thank you," said Serafina.

"Marriage is not so terrible, is it?" asked Lady Pemberton with a sly look.

"Marriage *to John* is not so terrible," said Serafina smiling.

"Good afternoon, ladies," interrupted John from the doorway of the drawing room. His voice was deep, and it rumbled across the room.

Serafina's heart gave a start.

"Mr. Thornton!"

"Lady Pemberton. Patience. I hate to curtail your visit, but I had planned a surprise for my wife, and we need to be leaving shortly."

This was news to Serafina.

"Oh my!" said Lady Pemberton looking to Serafina. "Your husband has a surprise for you." She grinned. "That is not so terrible, is it?"

Serafina wished Lady Pemberton had not repeated her earlier words in front of John. She looked to him, but he was smiling brightly at her.

"We are due to attend a chemistry lecture at the Royal Society. Humphry Davy will be speaking about how he has isolated a few new elements," said John.

"What!?" Serafina was standing now. "What did you say?"

Chemistry

"I said we are due to attend a chemistry lecture."

"I heard what you said," said Serafina.

"Then why did you ask me to repeat it?" asked John, his eyes dancing.

"Are women even allowed to attend?" asked Patience.

"I was careful not to ask that question," said John. "But I—a man—shall be attending the lecture, and I have informed the organisers that my wife shall be accompanying me." He looked to Serafina, "To be honest, I do not truly understand what the lecture is about, but perhaps you could explain it to me afterwards."

Serafina could not find the words. *Her husband had organised for her to attend an actual science lecture at the Royal Society!* She felt like Molly had upon finding out they would visit the museum—she felt like screaming. Instead, she sat herself down once more in her chair, knees together, hands in her lap.

"That would be lovely," she said.

"I think it would be more than lovely," said Patience under her breath.

"Well, then," said Lady Pemberton. "We shall happily take our leave. I hope you enjoy yourselves at the lecture." She didn't sound convinced that it would be something she herself would enjoy.

On her way out, Patience nodded her head to Serafina. "Cinderella," she said. Then she turned and curtsied to John: "Your Majesty, it has been a pleasure."

"What was all that about?" asked John when they had left.

"Nothing. Just a story that's been making the rounds."

"Patience is quite funny, isn't she?" said John.

"That is one of the many things I love about her," said

A Dangerous Man to Trust?

Serafina staring out into the empty hallway after her friend.

She did not notice the way John's expression shifted when she said the word 'love'.

The room in which the chemistry lecture was to be held was a heaving mass of black jackets and coats and top hats. The murmur of the crowd rose and fell like a wave as gentlemen made their introductions and took their seats. Several gentlemen had come over to see John. They knew him from school or the club. Each time, he introduced her to them as his wife, and each time they took her in with careful smiles and appraising eyes. There was only one other lady in attendance, and once she spied Serafina and John, she appeared to pull her husband in their direction.

The gentleman with whom John had been speaking looked up as the couple approached.

"This is Mr. Alexander Marcet and his wife Mrs. Marcet."

"Jane," said the lady, reaching a hand out to Serafina. "Jane Marcet."

"Mr. Thornton, your reputation precedes you," said her husband.

"And what reputation is that?" asked John with some irritation.

"I didn't mean..." said Mr. Marcet. "It is only that there has been much talk of how you have taken over the estate, the care of your sister... and certainly your happy new marriage."

"Nevermind him," interrupted Mrs. Marcet. "He always says the wrong thing. We are so happy to make your acquaintance." Serafina had never heard someone say that phrase in such a genuine and heartfelt manner. Mrs. Marcet turned to her, "Are you interested in chemistry, Mrs. Thornton?"

"Very much so, but I never imagined I would be attending a lecture at the Royal Society."

"Well, you should use your imagination more often," said Mrs Marcet good-naturedly. "There are many things you might be able to do if only you imagine them first."

Serafina was immediately taken with this older, more confident woman in front of her. She wanted Molly to meet her.

"My wife has a mind for mathematics and science," said John to Mrs. Marcet. "She has an especial knack for explaining the terribly complex in the most simple and intuitive manner. My younger sister Molly has benefitted not insignificantly from her many creative lessons in natural philosophy, mathematics, and logic. Serafina is always in the library reading dusty old books, so I thought it might make a change to abandon the books for a day and take in some bright new ideas."

Serafina could feel her cheeks burning. Mrs. Marcet was looking at John in wonder.

"Well," she said to Serafina. "I think we shall get along quite fine. Would you care to sit with us?"

The lecture itself was fantastic. Mr. Humphry Davy was a good-looking young man, rosy-cheeked and full of enthusiasm for his subject. He interrupted the lecture periodically with electrochemical demonstrations and ended (somewhat unusually, Serafina thought) with an invitation for members of the audience to test out the effects of nitrous oxide for themselves. Mr. Davy appeared to be already coasting on the effects of the so-called laughing gas which may have been why his lecture had been such a jovial affair.

"He is never without his nitrous oxide," said Mrs. Marcet in a low voice.

"Have you tested it?" asked Serafina.

Mrs. Marcet nodded with a bright open face.

When the lecture ended, Serafina turned to John excitedly. "I should like to try it—the nitrous oxide."

John had spent most of the lecture taking sidelong glances at Serafina's face. She was enthralled to this Mr. Davy in a manner he had not seen her display before. The man was strikingly handsome, beyond intelligent, and he had a charisma one rarely encountered in a man of science. Serafina laughed openly at each of his little jokes, and John could hear her sharp intake of breath as Mr Davy demonstrated this or that electrochemical process. John couldn't help but wonder if this was the man Serafina had been waiting for when she had held out against marriage for so many years.

Of course, John thought, *she will make do with me. She is my friend and cares for me, is even (surprisingly) physically willing as my wife* . . . but watching Mr. Davy up at the lectern, John knew that he could never be this handsome, clever man. He could never be what Serafina truly needed.

Why was he even thinking these things? Before they had left the house, Serafina had mentioned her love for Patience. Love—she had used that very word, and John had felt struck as if by a brick thrown through the window: he had been so concerned to put a stop to the rumours and so concerned that Serafina say yes to his marriage proposal that he had not even considered that once married, he might need her to love

Chemistry

him. He thought back to the night she had agreed to be his wife. The way she had rolled away from him in her bed. He could not help the feeling that she was making the best of a less-than-perfect situation, one in which she found herself to some extent trapped.

As Mr. Davy finished his lecture, John brought a hand up to rub his chest.

Serafina turned to him eagerly: "I should like to try it—the nitrous oxide," she said.

John didn't like the idea of his wife taking strange chemicals into her body, but it was her body, and her decision, so he said nothing, only nodded.

John noticed with irritation that Mr. Davy had saved his widest smile for Serafina as she stepped up to him and his tank of laughing gas. John did not like the way the man moved in close to fit the mask over his wife's face, adjusting her hair beneath the straps. He had not done so with the gentlemen, merely handing the mask to them so that they may attach it themselves.

"All your cares will fall away, if only briefly," he said. "Inhale."

When Serafina removed the mask, she was smiling.

"I see what you mean. Thank you. It was a fascinating lecture," she said, handing the mask back to Mr. Davy. John noticed that Mr. Davy brushed his hand against hers as he received the mask from her.

"I hope to see you again sometime, Miss . . ."

"Mrs. Thornton," said Serafina reaching for John's arm.

On the way home in the carriage, Serafina was buzzing with

residual excitement.

"Why did you not try the gas?" she asked.

"I wanted to have my wits about me in case you reacted poorly," he said.

Serafina moved from the seat opposite him to the seat beside him and slipped her hand in his resting it in her lap.

"This was the best surprise I could have ever imagined," she said. "Mrs Marcet has insisted we come to see them in the near future. She would like to meet Molly."

"That's nice," said John.

Serafina reached up and removed his mask.

"Serafina, what are you . . ."

"Look at me," she said. He obeyed. "What is wrong?"

"Nothing is wrong," said John forcing a smile. "I'm just tired."

That night, John could not bring himself to go up to his bed chamber with Serafina. He had thought that her willingness was enough, but he realised now it was not. He had her as his wife, and he could easily have her in his bed, but what he wanted was something deeper, something he knew he did not deserve and could never have.

"Are you not coming to bed?" asked Serafina on the stairs.

"I have some things I need to attend to first," he said. "Don't wait up."

"Oh."

By the time John made his way up to his room, it was very late. Serafina was in his bed again, her hair tossed across the pillow like a storm. He slipped into bed beside her thinking he would wake early and sneak out. She needn't have to engage physically with him simply because she was his wife. He could not help thinking that despite her protests to the contrary, she felt somewhat obliged. How would he feel in her situation? He could not even comprehend it. He imagined looking at his face every day. He imagined trying to kiss his face. It wasn't possible. She couldn't actually want . . . she could not actually love . . . him. John believed that he had been sailing along on a tide of wishful thinking and that he would be taking advantage of the situation—of her—if he continued as they were.

He slept and dreamed as always that he was trapped in a burning building. This time it was not William who died but Serafina. John cried out in real terror as he watched her burn, and he was inconsolable when he woke. His breath came quickly catching in his chest, and his face was wet with tears. Serafina was holding him in his bed.

"John. John! You're awake now. John, it's all right."

When he saw her and felt her body alive in the morning light, he was flooded with relief. But John pressed her away from him and sat up.

"I think you should sleep in your own bed from now on," he said.

"What?"

"You do not need to hold me every night. I am a grown man."

"John. I don't understand," she said reaching out to him.

He took her outstretched hand and placed it gently back at her side.

"You do not need to cater to me," he said meeting her bright eyes with some difficulty. "You should go to your own room. I'll see you at breakfast."

It was perhaps the hardest thing he had ever done, but it

was for the best. He would not be able to live with himself if there was even the remotest chance that he was imposing upon her. He loved her, respected her too much for that.

Serafina just looked at him. Then she angrily ripped the covers away from her, stomped across the room, and closed the adjoining door behind her. He could hear her banging open her wardrobe and slamming a drawer. At breakfast, however, Serafina was her normal self, joking with Molly and planning their day. John's heart was breaking, but he decided there and then that he had done the right thing.

Serafina could not begin to understand what had shifted within John. Between waking in the morning and sleeping that night, he had somehow changed. He did not want her in his bed. Nor did he want her holding him at night. Serafina felt the pain of his rejection reverberate through her all the way down to her feet. Days passed. They slept in different beds. His nightmares continued, and she could hear him crying out each and every night, but she forced herself to remain where she was, staring up at her bed curtains. She did not properly cry, but tears would make their way to the surface, and she would wipe them away with an angry hand. For days, he did not touch her, and once when she had casually reached a hand to his, he had actually flinched.

So this is it, she thought. *This is how a marriage can change from one day to the next. You imagine you know someone, think you can trust someone, but really, how can you really know anyone at all?* Serafina was reminded of her mother—the way she had slipped into a deep melancholy over her emotionally distant

Chemistry

husband, a man she continued to love but who no longer loved her. *Well, that shall not be me!* thought Serafina. *There is Molly for one. I shall not do to her what my mother did to me.*

So Serafina dressed in the mornings, pinned up her hair, and greeted John amicably at the breakfast table. She planned lessons with Molly and took her over to the Pembertons' to play with Grace and Potato. And in the evenings if they were not playing cards together, Serafina would read in the library.

As the days proceeded, one after the other, Serafina became increasingly confused by John's behaviour. He did not want to touch her, but he still seemed concerned with her well-being. He would ask after her day, share stories with her, play cards with Molly. It was as if they had reverted back to how things had been before the wedding.

One day, when she and Patience were sitting alone in Lady Pemberton's yellow drawing room while the little girls played in the nursery, Patience surprised Serafina by broaching the subject.

"Something has changed, hasn't it? With John?"

"How would you know that?" asked Serafina.

"He looks at you differently," said Patience. "It's a forlorn kind of look on his face."

"Is it?"

"He loves you," said Patience.

"His behaviour suggests otherwise," said Serafina. "He has never said he loves me. These days, he will not even touch me."

"I have never seen a man look at a woman the way he looks at you, Serafina. If he does not love you, I will eat my bonnet—no, I will eat *your* bonnet since you hate it so much."

Serafina couldn't help but smile.

A Dangerous Man to Trust?

"Perhaps," said Patience, "there is something troubling him."

"If there is, he will not speak of it," said Serafina. "It is as if a wall has gone up between us."

"Have you told him how you feel?" asked Patience.

Serafina looked down at her lap.

"No."

"Why not?"

"I don't know. It feels . . . it feels too . . ."

"Difficult?" supplied Patience.

"I feel as if I am begging him to love me," said Serafina. "It feels . . . embarrassing."

"Well, if it feels *embarrassing,* best to avoid it at all costs no matter the consequences," said Patience.

Serafina was reminded that her friend could be incredibly irritating sometimes.

"I had better get back with Molly," she said standing.

"Yes, you'd better," said Patience.

Nineteen

Cinderella

John thought Serafina seemed content. They had both slipped back into their former roles quite easily. She was no longer banging drawers or slamming doors—that had only happened the once on that first morning. She laughed with him and Molly, played cards, visited with friends, and everything seemed as it had always been. He had made the right decision. He had set her free to go about her days without having to consider him, without having to open herself up to him physically.

It is probably a relief to her, thought John.

One morning, he watched her buttering her toast methodically all the way to the edges, her face intent upon her task. Her lips were pursed together in the most appealing manner, and he felt he might die right there in his chair with the effort of containing every natural urge in his body. She looked up at him.

A Dangerous Man to Trust?

"John, could you pass the jam?" she asked.

He slid the pot of raspberry jam across to her, and she dolloped a large spoonful onto one corner of the toast but somehow managed to spill some jam onto her thumb as well. She brought her thumb to her mouth and pressed it between her lips, glancing up at him as she sucked the jam from her hand.

What was she doing?

John squirmed uncomfortably in his chair and reached a hand up to tug at his cravat.

"Where's Molly?" he asked.

"She was up early, and she was hungry, so she's already eaten. I think she's in her room trying to build a small paper fire balloon."

"A what?"

"Mrs Marcet has been filling her head with a whole fleet of new ideas. The Marcets built an enormous fire balloon some time ago. The air inside the balloon is heated, and this makes it lighter than the air outside the balloon, so if the materials used are light enough as well, then the balloon should take flight. But I think Molly's going to need some help," said Serafina taking a sip of tea. "It's too delicate a task for one little person."

"I could lend a hand," said John.

Serafina's face lit up.

"She would love that."

"Serafina," said John. "We should be heading home soon . . . to Bosworth Manor. I know you didn't wish to come to London in the first place, and I am well aware that we have perhaps stayed longer than you would have wished."

"It's all right. London has been more pleasurable than I remember it."

Cinderella

"The Marcets?" asked John.

"I *have* very much enjoyed their company. But there has been more than the Marcets. It has been so easy to visit with the Pembertons in London as they are so near. And, of course, there was the museum outing and Mr. Davy's lecture . . . and our wedding," she said.

John didn't know what to say to this last in her list of pleasurable activities.

"Serafina, I have to ask a favour of you."

"Anything," she said.

"Well, don't say that," said John impatiently. "You should not agree to something before you know what it is."

"I'll agree to whatever I like," said Serafina somewhat defiantly.

John looked at her. He wasn't entirely sure they were still talking about the same thing. He made an effort to bring things back to the point.

"I know you don't like balls, but Lady Leveson-Gower is hosting a dance in a few days, and we have been belatedly invited. She did not realise we would be in London so long, nor that we would be married. Knowing your preferences, I would decline, but she is an old family friend, and when last I spoke with Lady Pemberton, she thought it best for us to make an appearance at a large society event so as to put her Cinderella story front and centre as it were. There's nothing I despise more than the social theatre of this town, but if it is to put these rumours to rest and to reassert our social standing for Molly's sake and for yours, then I will be willing to get dressed up one last time before we head home."

"So we shall put on a show?" asked Serafina.

"Yes," said John. "Unfortunately, it appears necessary."

A Dangerous Man to Trust?

"I have just the dress," said Serafina brightly.

She ate the final bite of her toast, folded her napkin beside her plate, and pushed back her chair. John stood as she made to leave. Serafina stopped by John on her way out. She reached her hands up to his cravat, and John felt himself pull back ever so slightly.

"You'll have to try not to flinch at my touch," she said fixing his cravat. "At the ball, I mean. If we are to put on a show, you must appear to be in love."

John opened his mouth, but nothing came out.

The day of Lady Leveson-Gower's ball arrived. The Pembertons would be attending the ball as well, and Serafina had promised to save Patience from any would-be suitors who might be, according to Patience, "elderly, slow-witted, boastful, boring . . . or poetic."

"Poetic?" said Serafina. "But what's wrong with that?"

"Trust me," said Patience. "If he fancies himself a poet, I will have to listen to his poetry, and I will not put myself through that kind of torture."

Serafina rolled her eyes at her friend who slapped her playfully on the arm.

"I'm serious, Serafina—no poets!"

"Fine, fine," said Serafina laughing.

Patience had been kind enough to send her maid Delphi over to the Thornton house to do Serafina's hair for the ball. No one was quite as adept at the latest elaborate hairstyles.

"Thank you, Delphi," said Serafina. "It looks lovely. I could not have managed without you. No corset for tonight as you

Cinderella

may have noticed. Lady Pemberton's undergarments nearly killed me last time."

Delphi brought a hand up to hide a wide smile.

"Yes, Mrs. Thornton."

"Please head on down to the kitchen for some cake and some tea before you leave."

Serafina was seated at her dressing table wearing the pale lavender silk dress adorned with delicate white lace. It had not suited for her wedding, but to put on a show as Mrs. Thornton, this was certainly the dress. Cinderella was going to the ball.

There was a knock at the adjoining door between her chamber and John's. Serafina's heart began to beat a little harder. John had never knocked at her door before.

"Come," she said.

John entered in his formal black tailcoat and stopped short inside the threshold as Serafina stood to face him.

"You look . . ."

"Like Cinderella?" asked Serafina. "That's the idea, isn't it?" She looked him up and down. "And you look like my mysterious and charming prince."

John gave her a hesitant smile. He seemed to be holding himself back in some way, but then his smile grew wider, and Serafina could see him relax a little.

"Your pumpkin awaits, my lady," he said offering her his arm.

They descended the stairs, and John stopped at the front door.

"I almost forgot." He fumbled in his coat pocket and drew forth a small green velvet box.

He opened the box, and Serafina could see it was a ring. A wide yellow gold band inset with a pattern of diamonds and emeralds.

"I can have it adjusted if it does not fit properly," he said. "The jeweller used your glove size as an estimate."

John slipped the ring onto Serafina's finger.

"Oh."

"If you do not like it," said John quickly, "you do not have to wear it. It is entirely your choice. I just thought, for tonight . . ."

"I like it," said Serafina looking at him. "It was very thoughtful."

"Well, it wasn't very thoughtful of me to forget on the day," said John.

Serafina dismissed his comment with a wave of her hand.

"You really did prefer the key, didn't you?" he said, looking at her in that way that he did.

He wasn't looking at her hair or her dress or her body. Serafina could feel him looking past her appearance to her very essence. She nodded, keeping her eyes locked on his. She wanted to lift his mask, press a kiss to his mouth, feel the prickle of his stubble against her skin, but she held herself in check.

She would speak with him later. She would tell him how she felt. Tonight. After the ball. She would bare herself to him, embarrassing as it might be, and if that was not enough to help him open up to her about whatever it was that was troubling him, well then, there was nothing else she could do.

Serafina sat across from John in the carriage. The night air was cool, and a shiver rippled through her.

"Are you cold?" asked John.

"There's a little chill," said Serafina. "But I'll be fine."

John removed his coat and placed it around her shoulders.

Cinderella

"It will be warm inside," he said. "Once we get there."

Serafina could not understand her husband. He no longer wanted her to touch him, but he was still so incredibly attentive and thoughtful. He certainly cared for her . . . Patience swore up and down that he loved her.

"We should probably dance," said Serafina. "If it is to be a show, I mean. Cinderella cannot go to the ball and not be seen dancing."

Despite the ice blue of his eyes, the look John gave her was smouldering. He glanced down to the ring he had so recently placed on her finger.

"Of course," was all he said. "We shall dance." Then he started slightly in his seat. "Where are your gloves?"

"Oh!" Serafina looked down at her bare hands, her arms. "I forgot them. Do you think anyone will notice."

John laughed. "I think everyone will notice, Serafina. It's a ball. You might attract less attention if you walked in with no shoes."

"Should we turn back?"

"Nevermind about the gloves," said John leaning back in his seat. "I am sick of the theatre of it already, and we haven't even begun to put on our show."

When they arrived at Lady Leveson-Gower's ball, they were announced as Mr. and Mrs. Thornton. Serafina had never felt so conspicuous in her life, and she was kicking herself for not remembering to wear gloves. She could see them now, shiny and white, draped across her bed.

The ballroom was lit with the warm glow of candles.

A Dangerous Man to Trust?

Cream and yellow flowers adorned the spacious hall, and the musicians were sitting attentively in their chairs waiting to begin. It seemed to Serafina that all of London high society had been packed into the room. She looked about for the Pembertons, and spied them at the far side of the room speaking with Lady Crampton and a few others. She and John were immediately approached by Lady Leveson-Gower who looked just like the cat who had swallowed the cream.

"I am so delighted you could come, John. And your lovely wife as well."

John made the introductions between them. Lady Leveson-Gower looked down at Serafina's bare arms. "Are we hoping to set a new fashion, Mrs. Thornton?" she asked with some amusement.

"No," said Serafina blushing. "I simply forgot to wear my gloves."

"Ah! How refreshing," said Lady Leveson-Gower. "May I steal her from you, John?"

Serafina was taken by the arm as Lady Leveson-Gower took her on a turn about the room. She spoke with Serafina, nodding intermittently at guests as they passed them by.

"I wanted to say, Mrs. Thornton, I am so pleased that John has found you. You may have heard that he has a past that is not exactly reputable. But he was never like those other spoiled young men who felt that everything was their due. No. John always seemed a little lost, as if he was flailing about in the sea looking for something solid to hold onto, to keep him afloat. I do believe he has found that with you. I knew it when I spied him watching you at Lady Pemberton's ball."

Serafina turned sharply towards Lady Leveson-Gower.

"He was watching me?"

Cinderella

"Oh yes. He was watching you dance with the baron's son, and you should have seen the look of devastation that crossed his face. I have never seen a man look so crestfallen."

"Really?"

Serafina quickly reviewed the events of that night in her mind. John had encouraged her to stay at the Pembertons' thinking that George might marry her. *If he had been as crestfallen at losing her as Lady Leveson-Gower suggested, how could he have done so?* Serafina answered her own question: *because he thought that marrying George would be in my best interests. He does not think of himself*, she thought.

Serafina's head swung around, scanning the room.

"Are you looking for your husband?" asked Lady Leveson-Gower with a chuckle.

Serafina nodded apologetically.

"He's right over there . . . speaking with—oh my—Lady Langley. Not to worry my dear," she said patting Serafina's arm. "He only has eyes for you."

"Thank you, my lady," said Serafina. "You have been most forthright, and I truly appreciate it. To be perfectly honest, I am not terribly partial to balls at all, but I am glad to be attending yours."

"Off you go, then. Mingle with the crowd. Cinderella must be seen tonight."

Serafina gave Lady Leveson-Gower a questioning look.

She winked and said, "Lady Pemberton has been spinning a yarn for you—I suggest you play along."

John kept his eyes on Serafina as she wandered off with Lady

Leveson-Gower. She looked absolutely heavenly in that dress, like a princess stepped out of a fairytale. He could tell she wasn't wearing a corset, and it made him smile to himself. No fashion nonsense for *his* wife: no corset and no gloves. When Eleanor approached him, it was all John could do to keep the train of her conversation going. He could barely pay her any attention with one eye on Serafina across the ballroom.

"John!" said Eleanor after attempting to engage him for some time, "I'm over here." She turned to follow his line of sight. "Ah, your wife, is it?" she asked with a wide smile. "Then you are forgiven. I had not thought you in love, John."

"Excuse me?" said John, not really hearing.

"In love! I had not thought you in love!" said Eleanor raising her voice over the murmur of the crowd.

"I see," said John giving nothing away with his expression.

"Is it like that, John? Have you not told her you love her?"

John preferred not to continue with this line of questioning. He could see that Serafina had broken apart from Lady Leveson-Gower and was heading in his direction. Unfortunately, she was intercepted by a very familiar-looking and very handsome young man—Mr. Humphry Davy!

"If you will excuse me, Eleanor."

John made a small bow and started across the ballroom. He was stopped along the way by Lady Crampton who repeated her congratulations on his new marriage and set about detailing the ins and outs of trying to find a husband for her exceptionally discerning daughter. He tried to engage Lady Crampton as politely as he could while keeping an eye on Serafina. She was laughing with Mr. Davy. Talking and laughing. Mr. Davy had placed one hand on her shoulder and was gesticulating very charismatically with his other hand.

Cinderella

Serafina was wide-eyed. She looked completely delighted with whatever it was he was saying to her.

I will electrocute the bastard, thought John. *I will shove his nitrous oxide tube up his . . .*

By the time John had managed to extricate himself from Lady Crampton, he turned to find himself face to face with Mr. Davy.

"Hello, Mr. Thornton. So nice to see you again! I was just speaking with your lovely wife. It is not often one encounters a lady so versed in the mechanics of electrochemistry. She has some interesting ideas. I should like to speak to her again on the subject."

As Mr. Davy was speaking, the violins started up, and gentlemen began to lead ladies by the hand into the middle of the dance floor.

"Mr. Thornton, may I dance with your wife?" asked Mr. Davy as if coming up with the idea right there on the spot.

John curled his fingers in towards his palms. Just the thought of Mr. Davy holding Serafina by her very bare and gloveless hand set his blood boiling. *The nerve of the man! Who would ask such a thing? He must be on something.* John could not spy a nitrous oxide tank anywhere. *Perhaps he has ingested some other chemical*, thought John. The man's pupils were dilated, and he seemed to be trembling with a kind of nervous energy.

"That is something you will have to ask my wife," said John. "I cannot answer for her."

Mr. Davy spun on his heel and strode across the room to Serafina where she was now sipping a pink cordial and talking with Patience. John watched him go. He could see the man bow before Serafina and then lean in to speak closer to her ear. Serafina's eyebrows lifted. She smiled her brightest

A Dangerous Man to Trust?

smile and spoke something to Mr. Davy. John's fingernails were digging red crescents into his palm. Once Serafina had finished speaking, Mr. Davy stood back and just stared at her. Then he turned and left. At which point, Patience gave Serafina a wide-eyed look and whispered something into her ear. They both appeared to be laughing.

John unclenched his fists. He took a breath. He wanted the evening to be over.

"You look like you're having a splendid time." It was George Pemberton who had somehow sidled up beside John.

"Nice to see you, George," said John. "How have you been?"

"Busy," said George.

"But not too busy for Lady Leveson-Gower's ball?"

"Mother would have had my head if I had not attended," said George in all seriousness. "And, anyway, I wanted to be here to show my support for you and Serafina."

"My thanks," said John.

"Oh look," said George, "It's Mr. Davy. He is invited to all the best parties these days. Quite the celebrity. It doesn't hurt that he usually brings along a few tanks of laughing gas."

John grunted something in acknowledgement. Mr Davy approached them. His face was flushed, and he was beaming from ear to ear.

"Mr. Thornton, your wife will not have me," he laughed. "She says all her dances have been saved for you whether you will dance with her or not."

"She said that?" asked John.

"She's quite a catch, Thornton. And so loyal. Did you let her leave the house without gloves? I should wonder if she is not the object of more attention than mine this evening."

When Mr. Davy had left chasing after some other young

lady, George leaned in towards John. "Is she not wearing gloves?"

"She forgot them," was all John said staring out across the room.

George didn't laugh. He never did, but one corner of his mouth twitched upward ever so slightly.

Twenty

The Truth

Several dances had transpired at the ball before Serafina decided it was time to find John once more. She had been mingling in the crowd with Patience at her side for support, and now she was quite exhausted with conversation. More than a few young and not-so-young gentlemen had approached her, more out of curiosity than anything else.

"They are all wondering who the fantastic woman is who has stolen Mr. Thornton's heart," said Patience. "You must know, Serafina, that since his reappearance on the scene, he has not once asked a young lady to dance despite a whole gaggle of them mobbing him at every ball. He has seemed so disinterested in finding a wife that it is striking he has done so so quickly."

"Mm," said Serafina sifting the crowd with her eyes for John.

"You're not even listening to me, are you?" asked Patience.

The Truth

"Sorry, Patience, I was looking for John."

"He's over there with George."

Just then, the most dashing gentleman approached Patience from across the floor. He was tall and his hazel eyes twinkled in the candlelight.

"Miss Pemberton," he said bowing, "your mother introduced us last season." When Patience looked as if she had not the faintest idea who he was, he added, "I'm Lord Flemming."

Patience gave her head a little lift as if to acknowledge him. Serafina noted that his hair was a blaze of fire atop his head.

"The Earl?" asked Patience.

"Precisely."

Serafina thought this was the perfect time to sneak off. She started edging away. Patience gave her a pleading look, but Serafina shrugged her shoulders with a smile. She turned and having locked eyes with John across the room, she strode towards him as if he were reeling her in with a line.

"It's starting to get a bit much for me, John. Shall we dance? I don't think I can converse with anyone else this evening."

"Of course," was all John said, offering her his hand.

She took it, and he led her out onto the dance floor. He slipped one hand to her waist, and as the music started up once more, he guided her along, his eyes never leaving hers. It was such a nice feeling to move with him to the flow of the music. A soft rhythmic sensation, like moving with the flow of water in and out at the seaside. Serafina immediately relaxed.

"Is this better?" asked John in a low voice.

"It is the best," said Serafina quietly.

She could see John's expression register her words with some surprise, and she wondered if she should speak to him right now. Open herself up to him. She squeezed his hand.

"I like being your wife," she said.

John said nothing, but she could feel his hand on her waist tense ever so slightly.

Perhaps I shouldn't start this now, thought Serafina. *Just enjoy the dance.*

Serafina for the first time that night was happy she had forgotten her gloves. Holding John's hand would not be the same with a piece of fabric between them. It was his touch she missed the most. That feeling of skin against skin was such a comfort.

"I miss the way you touch me," she said. *Oh dear, here we go*, she thought.

"Serafina," said John firmly, "You do not need to . . ."

His words trailed off as the dance came to an end. He tried to release her, but she stared at him defiantly as she kept hold of his hand. John was forced to walk with her, hand-in-hand, from the dance floor.

Lady Leveson-Gower was radiating the most joyful energy in their direction as they approached her where she was standing with George and Lady Pemberton.

"Oh John, I had hoped against hope, but seeing you dancing together, it is apparent that this is a love match, is it not?"

John opened his mouth, but Serafina answered for him.

"It is," she said looking up at her husband. "John is the keeper of my heart. If we were ever to be separated, I think I should die for lack of a vital organ."

Lady Leveson-Gower clutched her own heart and sighed. She looked from Serafina to John and back again.

"What is it about John that you love the most, may I ask?"

"I don't think—" said John, but Serafina interrupted him.

"He makes me feel safe," said Serafina looking up into his

The Truth

face. "He is attentive with Molly, he thinks of everyone but himself—"

"Serafina," said John, tugging at her hand. "May I have a word?"

"Excuse us," said Serafina to Lady Leveson-Gower. "My husband needs a word."

John led her firmly by the hand out of the nearest doorway and into the hall which made Serafina feel a bit like a naughty child being taken for a scolding. She kept talking as they went.

"—but most of all, I love the way I can be myself with him. I can say anything, I can be honest, and I do not have to pretend."

Now that she had started, Serafina found that opening up about her feelings in front of John wasn't embarrassing at all. It was a release and a relief. In the hallway, John turned on her quite fiercely. His breathing was heavy.

"Stop talking, Serafina!"

"I was simply answering the lady's question."

"I know we are here to put on a show, but that was too much!"

John was actually angry. She could see it in the way he held his jaw, and this made Serafina quite furious herself. She refused to let go of his hand even though he was trying to release her.

"This dress is for show, John, and all the polite conversation with the various gentlemen, and having to smile at Mr. Davy even though he had the impertinence to touch me on the shoulder. That's all part of the show. But loving you, John, is not. I love you, and I will say so again and again. And if you do not like it, well, it doesn't matter because it is the truth!"

They stood staring at each other in the hallway for over a minute, and then finally, when his breathing had calmed, John spoke.

"You love me?" he asked.

Serafina threw up her hands in exasperation.

"I do not know how to say it more clearly. I love you, I love you, I love you!" She was almost shouting now, and realising this, she lowered her voice. "It hurts me that you have pulled away, that you do not want me in your bed, do not want to touch me—it is like a knife slowly twisting against my flesh each and every day. I know there is something troubling you, John, and I want you to feel as if you can share it with me. Instead of shutting me out. I'm your wife."

John just stared at her, his hands at his sides.

"Fine!" said Serafina, and she turned to leave.

John caught her hand and pulled her back to face him.

"I don't understand," he said.

"You don't have to understand. You simply have to believe me." Serafina's eyes were welling now with the emotion she had so carefully contained over the last several days.

"But you have seemed content of late," said John. "Laughing, talking, playing cards . . ."

"I would not ruin Molly's days with my heartache. You know me better than that," said Serafina.

"Serafina, I . . . I am so sorry. I never meant to hurt you. Quite the opposite. I've been such a fool. I just thought, how could you truly . . . I mean, my face and my body . . . how could you want to . . . and if you in any way felt obliged, I could not live with myself if I took advantage. I respect you—*I love you*—too much to do that to you."

Serafina felt as if she might float up to the ceiling. *He loved her.* She knew it deep down in the depths of her soul, but it was nice to hear it from his lips. She looked at his mouth, the

The Truth

way his top lip lifted up at one corner in a snarl.

"Is that what was bothering you? You thought you were taking advantage? There could be nothing further from the truth. I love your face, John, both sides of it," she said, lifting his mask. "I should be disappointed if you looked any other way. I love your body as well, scars and all. You cannot know what sweetness it is for me to touch you or . . . or have you touch me as you did the other day."

She stepped in closer, and John placed a hand to each side of her neck and jaw. She tilted her face up to his, and he stroked her throat with his thumbs as he gazed into her eyes. She revelled in this feeling of exposing herself to him. Being entirely vulnerable and at his mercy, knowing without a shadow of a doubt that she could trust him completely.

"I thought I might die the other day as I watched you butter your toast," said John. "Not touching you has been the hardest thing I've ever done."

Serafina lifted herself up onto her toes and pressed her lips against his. She took his top snarl of a lip in her mouth as John pressed a hand to the small of her back and drew her pelvis in towards him. He kissed her in a way he had not done before. There was an animal hunger to it that Serafina could feel vibrating all the way down to her toes. It lit a fire in her belly, and the heat of it sank down low between her legs. Her arms reached around him, and she clutched him to her as if in fear of losing him once more. By the time he pulled away, she was breathless and very conscious of how wet she felt beneath her dress.

"Maybe we should go home," said Serafina wishing to continue as they had begun.

"But we have a ball to attend," said John playfully. "And

A Dangerous Man to Trust?

Cinderella needs to be seen dancing with her prince."

He took her hand and turned it palm up, planting a wet and gentle kiss against her wrist.

"John . . ."

"I'm so glad you didn't wear gloves," he said with a mischievous smile as he lavished her with kisses all the way up her arm. Serafina made a small involuntary squeaking sound as John pulled her to his side, tucking her hand at his elbow.

"I do not deserve you," he said, as he allowed her to replace his mask before leading her back into the ballroom.

"I will decide what you deserve," said Serafina as John spun her out onto the dance floor to join the twirling host of dancers who appeared to be moving as one about a centre island of cream and yellow flowers.

As she danced with her husband, Serafina imagined the mesmerising pattern the dancers would make if seen from above—like dazzling planets spinning about a floral sun.

John and Serafina danced the rest of the night away. It kept them from having to converse with anyone else, and it allowed them to hold each other for the rest of the night. He felt as if he never wanted to let her go.

John could not believe how the evening had unravelled. *His wife loved him!* It did not seem possible, and his mind struggled to make sense of this new information, but it was a nice kind of struggle—exciting, joyful. He knew Serafina only spoke the truth to him . . . from the very beginning. He smiled remembering how she had yelled at him that first time he had left for London without saying goodbye—every raw feeling on

The Truth

display. *Who else would have done that? And how had she known she could trust him to do so?* It was as if she had some secret lens with which she could look into his soul. She had truly seen *him*. He knew that now. And as he revised every memory of their interactions with that in mind, what he found was a love story.

John kept his eyes on his wife. Her face was flushed, and she was quite breathless with dancing. She was looking at him intently, eyes wide as if to better hold him in her gaze.

"We appear to be the last couple on the dance floor," said John. "Perhaps it is time to take our leave."

In the carriage, on the way home, they sat across from each other.

"What?" asked Serafina after John had spent the better part of the ride home just looking at her.

"You're amazing," he said. "You are so brave and so incredibly clever and lovely. You had my heart from the beginning, Serafina. From the very beginning. I could never have imagined you would feel the same way about me."

"You tried to marry me off to George," said Serafina, softening the moment with humour.

"It seemed like a good idea at the time," said John, and they both laughed. John dropped his smile: "I was devastated to see you dancing with him."

"I was physically ill when I thought you may have an attachment to Lady Langley. Do you remember that tea at the Pembertons'?" asked Serafina.

"That was on my account? I'm so sorry, Serafina."

"I *was* being a bit foolish, but my body had somehow taken over—there was nothing I could do."

John remembered arguing about calling a doctor on the way

A Dangerous Man to Trust?

home with her in the carriage. *God, he loved arguing with her.*

By the time they arrived home, it was very late, and Serafina was nodding off against the window of the carriage. John roused her gently and led her up to her room. At the door, she seemed to come partially awake and turned to him.

"May I not sleep in your bed from now on?"

John's heart felt like it would burst.

"Yes, of course. I would love that. I just didn't want to assume."

"Assume away," said Serafina sleepily. "I want to be with you, always."

In his room, he sat her down on the bed and removed her shoes, reaching up past her knees to roll down and remove her stockings one at a time. When he stood, she turned in her seat so that he could undo the buttons at the back of her dress.

"Help me take it off," she said standing.

He slipped the dress from one shoulder and then the other, and she stepped out of it wearing only her thin chemise. Her proximity and her state of undress were sending signals to parts of his body he thought best to ignore for the time being. She looked so incredibly fatigued from the night's events. He pulled back the covers for her, and she lay down. Then John stripped down to his drawers and climbed into bed beside his wife. Her eyes were closed, but she turned to him, reaching an arm across his bare chest and resting her head on the pillow by his shoulder. He kissed her forehead, inhaling the scent of her skin, and she snuggled closer into him kissing his scarred shoulder and murmuring something he couldn't quite make out. John had never been happier in his entire life. For the first time in a very long time, he drifted off into a deep and dreamless sleep.

The Truth

It was late in the morning before John woke. Serafina was sleeping soundly in his embrace, and he lay still enjoying the feeling of her body so close to his. The covers had been thrown back sometime in the night, and when he looked down, he could see her chemise had ridden up to her waist, exposing one side of her soft round bottom to his gaze. He tried to tug her garment down, but it was wedged beneath her and it wouldn't budge.

Serafina opened her eyes. She leaned her face into his neck and he could feel her inhale him.

"I like the way you smell," she said.

"Serafina," said John. "Your chemise."

"I don't mind if you see me, John. You're my husband after all."

John was trying not to let on how desperate he was for her, but his hand reached down to grasp her thigh lightly above the knee then slowly made its way up her bare leg to rest a thumb in the crevice of her hip.

"Would you like me to take it off?" asked Serafina.

That was direct.

John nodded silently. He watched as Serafina sat up and pulled the chemise over her head. *Dear Lord, she was beautiful.* And the way she just sat there looking at him looking at her was enough to send him over the edge.

"Your pins," said John realising they had not undone her hair before bed.

He sat up and she turned her bare back to him so that he could remove some of the pins. As he gently pulled each one from her hair and placed them on the side table, she reached up to unravel the braids that came tumbling down. By the end, her hair hung down her back in rippling waves. John used a hand to sweep her silky tresses to the side, baring the back of her neck. He kissed her there, and she let out a soft moan. She shifted, turning to him in the bed and sliding down beneath him. She ran her fingers through his hair as he brought his mouth to meet hers which was sweet and wet and eagerly matched his every movement. John felt wanted in a way he had never felt before. He slid down her body, kissing her throat, her chest, then took a hard nipple in his mouth and heard her gasp. Lower still, he ran a hot tongue down her belly, and he could hear her breath become ragged as he lowered his face between her legs. He caressed her with his tongue, drinking her up in a way he had never done with anyone else. He continued as he was while sliding one hand delicately up along the side of her torso before taking her nipple between his fingers. Serafina gripped the sheets as her breath came in heavy pants. John could feel her thighs tense on either side of his face as she lost control of herself, panting and groaning as she climbed towards a climax that had her cry out in a way that made John nearly lose himself entirely.

Serafina's body went limp, and she reached for his head, tugging him gently up by his dark hair.

"John," she said as he lay down beside her.

"Serafina," he said with a smile, pressing a soft kiss to her lips and sliding a finger down between her breasts to her navel.

"I should like to see you," she said looking down at his drawers which were clearly having a difficult time containing him. "All of you."

John stood up beside the bed and dropped his drawers to reveal the full extent of his desire. He had never been so aroused. Serafina knelt up in front of him on the bed, her head at chest height to his standing form.

The Truth

"Can I touch it?" she asked.

John nodded. Serafina reached out tentatively with one hand, then gave a little squeak and pulled back.

"It moved!" she said laughing.

"I don't doubt it," said John with some amusement. "But don't laugh."

Serafina looked up at him.

"Does your little general not like being laughed at?" she asked.

Little general!

"No, he does not," said John with mock seriousness. "Neither does he like being called little."

He could see Serafina biting her bottom lip in an effort to contain her laughter.

"I'm sorry," she said, sliding a palm beneath his still swollen manhood.

He watched from above as she bent her head down and kissed him where no one had ever kissed him before. She did it so innocently, so lovingly that he began to have second thoughts about what he was about to do with her. *It was her first time. What if he hurt her? He would never be able to forgive himself. What if she didn't like it?*

Serafina turned her pale moon face up to him.

"Tell me what to do," she said.

"Serafina, you don't have to . . ."

"I want to," she said.

"It may hurt a bit the first time," said John. "But only briefly. As a rule, it should not hurt at all. Do you promise to tell me if you don't like it?"

"I promise," said Serafina reaching up to his face.

He allowed her to pull his mouth to hers. She was so hungry

A Dangerous Man to Trust?

for him. The way she kissed him made John feel as if she wanted to consume every inch of him. It was an otherworldly feeling, to be so desired. He was still having a hard time understanding how this could be. *How could she be his wife? How could she love him?*

"Lie down," he said, manoeuvring himself between her outspread legs. "And try to relax, truly relax every muscle in your body."

He kissed her throat, licked one pert nipple, then took the other in his mouth. Serafina arched her back as John placed a hand between her legs to prepare her.

"Is that all right?" he asked.

"Mm."

John removed his hand and slipped himself in slowly, partway. She was wet and ready, and he sank into her with ease.

"It feels nice," she said sliding her legs up his calves, his thighs, until her heels were at his buttocks.

She pulled him to her with her heels, forcing him in deeper. As he sank into her the rest of the way, she gave a small start.

"Are you all right?" asked John.

"Yes," she said kissing his mouth. "Don't stop."

John was slow and rhythmic and gentle, and the way Serafina moved her body in concert with his made him feel as if there was nothing so natural as the two of them in this bed joined in a truly blissful union. Serafina reached a hand up to his face.

"You can relax too, John," she said. "You won't hurt me if you let yourself go."

John was struck by the way his wife saw through to the very core of him. He had been maintaining so much control over

The Truth

his body for so long, he did not even realise it anymore. As John allowed himself to move more freely, Serafina responded in kind, and their love-making became a feverish abandon of limbs and mouths. John held out for as long as he could, and just when he thought he would lose himself completely, Serafina dug her nails into his back as she arched her torso up against him and cried out. John felt himself shatter as he erupted inside her. He collapsed beside his wife on the bed and quietly watched her breast rise and fall with her breath.

"Well," said Serafina, kissing him tenderly on the lips, "Your little general has certainly earned himself a commendation."

John met her shining eyes, and they both began to laugh as they tangled their limbs with each other's once more in an embrace.

Twenty-One

Take Flight

"We will be leaving London tomorrow," said Serafina.

She was seated with Patience in the drawing room of the Thornton house sipping tea.

"So soon!" complained Patience.

"It feels as if we've been here an age," said Serafina. "Rupert will be missing us."

"You'll be returning as Mrs. Thornton. What do you think Miss Browning will make of that?" asked Patience with a chuckle.

"I hope she'll be pleased to have a little more help running the house," said Serafina. And then to change the subject, "How did it go with the earl?" When Patience looked confused, she added, "At the ball. The ginger earl?"

"Oh, him! He was nice enough, but he passed me over for Sophia Crampton."

Take Flight

"What?"

"We had a laugh and a dance, but then his eyes caught on Sophia's enormous feathered headdress, and I seemed to lose him after that even though we were still dancing."

"How incredibly rude!"

"He's an earl, Serafina. He can have who he likes, and he likes someone taller and slimmer and perhaps less boisterous, and certainly someone wearing more feathers. It's very hard for me to put on whatever display it is gentlemen are after. I should perhaps spend more time looking at the floor and less time trying to be witty."

"Nonsense. You must be yourself, Patience, or else you will find yourself with someone who requires you to spend all your time pretending to be someone else."

"Mother told me about your public declaration of love at the ball," said Patience as she stabbed a piece of apple cake with a fork. "So you took my advice."

Patience put the forkful of cake in her mouth and managed to chew it with a smile on her face. Her iridescent violet-blue eyes were shining with satisfaction.

"Yes," said Serafina without elaborating. Patience was fairly intolerable when she was right, and Serafina did not want to 'feed the beast' as it were.

"Mother said you were effusive. Effusive! It's not a word she uses often."

"Mm."

"She said John looked quite stern and pulled you off to have a private conversation." Patience stabbed her cake once more. "How did that go?"

"Fine. It went fine," said Serafina.

"Mother said that you looked quite flushed when you

reappeared and that the two of you had your hands on each other for the rest of the evening."

"Patience, your mother does talk a lot. It seems to me you already know the answers to your questions. So why are you asking them?"

"To make you squirm," said Patience with a laugh. "And how have things been since then?"

"You were right," said Serafina, giving in and opening up, "It wasn't embarrassing at all to tell John how I felt. It brought us closer."

Patience leaned forward.

"How close?" she asked.

"Patience!"

"Serafina," said Patience, dropping her smile and radiating her most serious expression, "I need you to tell me something. It doesn't have to be now, maybe another time if you feel comfortable. Mother will never tell me, and I'm afraid I shall be woefully underprepared should I find myself in love or . . . or married one day."

"What is that?" asked Serafina, knowing full well what it was but not wanting to admit to it.

"What happens between a man and a woman . . . physically? I mean, I have some idea about kissing and touching and undressing, but the mechanics of the situation . . . I should not want to be surprised. I should like to feel somewhat in control."

Serafina knew exactly how Patience felt. She had been lucky with John. That he loved her, that he was gentle and wary and thoughtful and completely in control of himself. How would it have been with someone else? Knowledge was a kind of power, and it was so often withheld from girls, from women, out of a misplaced fear that the very knowledge itself would defile them in some way when in fact it simply made them equal partners in the metaphorical dance.

"Of course," said Serafina reaching for Patience's hand.

"Mother is adamant that I marry. And soon. Before I become a dusty book on a shelf in a library nobody visits anymore. Five-and-twenty is not exactly young."

"It's not exactly old," added Serafina.

"If I do not find a love match in the very near future, Mother and Father are likely to find a match for me. And you know how sensible Father is. The man will be a walking boredom machine . . . but likely very rich, so I suppose it won't be all bad."

"They wouldn't do that, would they?"

"Mother would give her right arm to find me a love match, but failing that, she will arrange a marriage with someone suitable, someone with whom, as she says, love may grow. Serafina, you've been so fortunate. Most of us can only dream of finding a husband as you did—on your own terms, with your own heart. It's not the rule—it's the exception."

George had insisted on venturing out with John for a walk through Hyde Park while the ladies took tea. Serafina had already taken a seat with Patience in the drawing room, but John found he could not leave without placing a hand to the back of her neck and tenderly kissing her forehead. Serafina had blushed, and John wondered if perhaps he had been a bit too forward in front of her friends. He had lingered by his wife, squeezing her hand before heading out the door with

George.

"What did I tell you?" said George as Spencer helped him on with his coat in the foyer.

"Excuse me?" said John.

They stepped out the door and down the front steps of the house under a pale afternoon sun.

"I told you she wanted you," said George matter-of-factly. "But you wouldn't believe me."

"It's a difficult thing to believe," said John.

"Actually, you're right," said George pensively. "If I were in love—truly in love—with someone, it would be beyond imaginable that she would share those same feelings. What would be the odds of that happening?"

"We could ask Molly to perform those calculations," said John with a smile.

"Astronomical. The odds would be astronomical, would they not?"

"Quite," said John striding along the pavement.

"My family is so happy for the two of you," said George without looking happy at all. "I've always felt that it was my role to protect Serafina, and I feel especially relieved to pass on that duty of protection to you."

"You have two sisters to think of," said John.

"Patience will be the death of my mother," said George. It might have been a funny statement coming from someone else, but from George, it seemed more literal than anything else. "She paints in oils," he said by way of explanation. "No delicate watercolours for her. She likes to stand out."

"Perhaps," said John in her defence, "she would like her artwork to last. Watercolours can fade so quickly. Oils have a certain weight to them—they're more permanent."

"She wants to paint like a man," said George. "It makes it difficult to find her a husband." George spoke so plainly—it was the truth without any dressing whatsoever. He was a lot like his father in that respect, and John wondered how much of this was his own natural way of being and how much might be learned. We often imitate those we admire without actually realising we are doing so. As regards George's candid comment, John did not know what to say. He understood George's concern for his sister's future, but his experience with his own sister made him feel the injustice of Patience's predicament quite keenly.

"Look at it a different way," said John. "Her strong character will make it easy to sift through all those suitors who would be, well, unsuitable. The right man will stand out."

The two of them entered the park through an enormous wrought-iron gate. The brick and stone of London gave way to green grass and shrubbery, trees and the sparkle of water in the distance. John and George walked in lockstep towards a congregation of yellow-eyed pigeons scattered across their path. As they stepped into the midst of the flock, the birds took flight as one, rising up around them in a fluttering rustle of wings and feathers. At that moment, John had the very strange impression for a few seconds of being lifted up with the birds. It was a mildly disorienting sensation and altogether unexpected and wonderful.

How strange life can be, he thought. *A man on the ground one minute, a bird in the air the next.* He immediately thought of Serafina. He wanted to share this experience with her. He wanted to take her to the park, walk her through a flock of pigeons, and show her how it feels to fly, if only for a moment.

Epilogue

Nine Months Later

It was a gorgeous sunny day at the end of July, and Serafina was sitting on the wooden bench under the willows by the lake reading her mail which had arrived that morning. She took a deep breath, fragrant with the scent of roses brought in on a gentle breeze. John had planted several large bushes nearby, and they were adorned with tiny delicate buds and blooms of peach and white. Splashing in the lake in front of her was Molly with John standing beside her as she attempted a back stroke. John was shirtless and maskless in the water. Several months ago, Serafina had persuaded him that Molly would be nothing if not impressed with his face should he show it to her, and of course, Serafina had been absolutely right. Molly loved her brother with or without his mask.

Molly stopped swimming and stood in the water which was up to her chest.

"Your lips are turning blue," said John. "I think it's time you got out and warmed up."

"All right, but can you throw me just one more time?" asked

Epilogue

Molly.

John sank down beside her, and Molly held his shoulders as she placed a foot in his interlaced hands under the water.

John counted, "One, two, three," and with a strong heave, threw his little sister in towards the deeper end of the lake. Serafina looked up as Molly hit the surface of the lake with an enormous splash. Rupert appeared out of nowhere and bounded into the water towards John as Molly swam effortlessly back to the shallows. She waded out with John, and Serafina unfolded one of several blankets on the bench beside her and wrapped it around her sister.

"You're shivering," said Serafina, rubbing Molly's shoulders vigorously through the blanket. "Go sit in the sunshine."

"I think I'll go back to the house if you don't mind," said Molly. "I have things I need to do."

"The kite?" asked Serafina.

"Yes, the kite," answered Molly. "I've almost finished the frame."

"Off you go then," said Serafina. "But make sure to dry your hair."

As Molly ran out past the willows and across the lawn chased by Rupert towards the house, John stepped up beside Serafina. He was dripping wet.

"You must be cold," said Serafina sliding a palm across his chest.

"You must be hot," said John reaching behind her and pulling her to him.

"John! You're wet!" said Serafina with a laugh.

"Come swimming with me," he said not letting her go.

"I don't have my costume."

"You don't need one."

A Dangerous Man to Trust?

Serafina hadn't planned on swimming, but now that she was at the lake, she did relish the idea of sinking herself into the cool water.

"Like old times, then," she said, stepping towards the lake fully clothed.

John reached out an arm to block her path.

"Lose the dress," he said with a mischievous twinkle in his eye.

"John!" Serafina looked towards the curtain of willows that blocked their view from the house.

"Molly won't be back. That kite is nowhere near finished, and her French tutor arrives in about half an hour. The gardener has the day off. We're all alone," said John dropping his trunks to the ground and wading back into the lake.

As her husband strode into the deeper water, Serafina drew her eyes from the muscles of his legs up over his firm buttocks and the strong line of his back. She bit her bottom lip. By the time John had sunk himself into the water and turned himself around, Serafina was standing at the edge of the lake entirely naked except for a delicate gold chain around her neck from which hung a small golden key. John had given it to her as a gift for Christmas, and she was never without it.

Serafina could feel the sun on her skin—warm and inviting. John lowered his chin to the surface of the water as he kept his eyes on her. She waded in gingerly allowing herself to savour the thrill of the cool water. When she was deep enough, she sank beneath the water and swam through the green gloaming towards John's legs, rising up to break the surface of the lake in front of him.

"You look like a water nymph," he said smiling.

"I have to tell you something," she said, placing her hands to

Epilogue

his shoulders.

"And what would that be?" asked John, stroking his fingers up her bare back. Serafina's legs floated up and around him as he stood chest deep in the water. He lowered himself, so that her entire weight was suspended in the water.

"Oh!" The cold water had done nothing to suppress John's craving for her. She could feel him beneath her thigh, smooth and hard. Serafina leaned in for a kiss which seemed so incredibly warm against the cool of the water. John's hands seemed to be everywhere at once as Serafina floated in place anchoring herself to his waist with her legs.

"John," she said pulling her face from his. "My courses have not come this month."

John looked at her, and his expression was one of sheer joy.

"Do you think you're with child?"

"Well, I'm three weeks late, so—"

John cut her off with the deepest most sumptuous kiss imaginable, and Serafina could feel the heat of that kiss sink down through her body.

"How do you think this could have happened?" asked John playfully.

"I'm sure I wouldn't know," said Serafina keeping her eyes on his while reaching beneath her. She slid her hand along his manhood, angling herself so that he could press himself up into her. She clung to him with her legs, and he held her as they moved together in a quiet and needful rhythm. Having John take her there under the blue sky in the open lake made some hidden part of Serafina come alive. There was something about the feeling of exposure, of being free of the bounds of propriety, that set Serafina aflame. She craved each increasingly strong thrust of his in a way she could not explain—her loss of control came quickly swelling up like a wave until it crashed over her with astonishing force. It took her a moment to recover herself, clinging to John's wet body as he pursued a slower and gentler rhythm.

"Are you all right?" asked John stroking a strand of wet hair from her face.

"Yes," said Serafina, "Yes, I'm more than all right."

Afterwards, they lay together under a blanket on the grass.

"I have one other thing to tell you," said Serafina stroking her husband's arm, her fingers following the rippling line of each scar. "I received a letter this morning from Jane Marcet. Did you know she writes books?"

"No, but somehow I'm not surprised."

"They aren't published under her own name, but they are very popular companions for teachers and students of chemistry."

"She is a marvellous lady," said John. "I'm so glad you and Molly were able to meet her."

"She has written to say that her publisher is looking for someone to write a series of books on mathematics and logic. Specifically for school girls. She does not have the time, and she is wondering if I would like to have the opportunity."

"That's wonderful!" said John, "Isn't it?"

"It is. I'm just not sure if I can do it all. There's Molly, and soon there will be a baby."

"Serafina," said John reaching out to hold both sides of her face. "You don't have to do it all. I'm here as well. An equal partnership, remember?"

"I don't want our baby raised entirely by a nurse," said Serafina curling into him.

"She won't be," said John. "She'll be raised by her father."

Epilogue

"She?" said Serafina raising her eyebrows.

"Or he. Either way. I'll be there for you and Molly and the baby. Trust me," said John reaching a hand up to stroke her hair.

"I trust you," said Serafina leaning in for another kiss.

Thank You!

Thank you for reading *A Dangerous Man to Trust?* I hope you enjoyed reading it as much as I enjoyed writing it!

- Receive a free subscribers-only steamy novella called *The Bull of Bow Street Meets his Match* when you sign up for my mailing list at oliviaelliottromance.com. This is Book 3.5 in *The Pemberton Series*.
- Reviews help other readers decide if a book would suit them. I appreciate all reviews, both positive and negative, so please think about leaving a star-rating or, if you have the time, a few thoughts about my book.
- *A Dangerous Man to Trust?* is the first book in *The Pemberton Series*, and you may want to follow up with the next book—*A Soldier and his Rules.* I am currently working on the fourth book in this series, so stay tuned!

Also by Olivia Elliott

You may enjoy these books in *The Pemberton Series*.

A Soldier and his Rules

He is a stern and brooding soldier who is used to giving orders. She is a passionate artist who rarely does as she's told. His haunted past and secret shame stand like a wall between them in this hot and spicy Regency romance.

A Baron's Son is Undone

He is the uptight son of a baron. She is the banished daughter of . . . a pirate? Each guards their own terrible truth that threatens the blossoming intimacy between them in this emotional—and steamy—Regency romance.

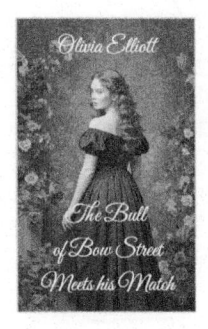

The Bull of Bow Street Meets his Match
She is a devastating beauty with a sense of social justice. He is a Bow Street runner with blood on his hands. As the first hesitant sparks kindle a blaze of fire, these two must eventually decide if love is worth the risk.

Receive a free copy of this book by joining the author's mailing list at oliviaelliottromance.com.

Printed in Dunstable, United Kingdom